TONY ABBOTT is the author of nearly a hundred books. He has worked in libraries, in bookshops and at a publishing company, and currently teaches college English. He lives in Conneticut with his wife, two daughters and two dogs.

Praise for

THE COPERNICUS LEGACY:
The Forbidden Stone

"*The Copernicus Legacy* takes you on a fantastical journey that is as eye-opening as it is page-turning. With mysteries hiding behind secrets coded in riddle, this book is like a Dan Brown thriller for young readers. The further you get, the more you must read!"
—Angie Sage, *New York Times* bestselling author of the Septimus Heap series

"Full of mystery and intrigue, this book had me completely transfixed."
—Ridley Pearson, *New York Times* bestselling author of the Kingdom Keepers series.

TONY ABBOTT

★BOOK I★

THE FORBIDDEN STONE

ILLUSTRATIONS BY BILL PERKINS

HarperCollins *Children's Books*

First published in hardback in the USA
by HarperCollins *Publishers Inc* in 2014
First published in paperback in Great Britain by HarperCollins
Children's Books in 2014
HarperCollins *Children's Books* is a division of
HarperCollins*Publishers* Ltd,
77-85 Fulham Palace Road, Hammersmith, London, W6 8JB.

Visit us on the web at
www.harpercollins.co.uk

1

978-0-00-754734-0
Printed and bound in England by Clays Ltd, St Ives plc

MIX
Paper from
responsible sources
FSC
www.fsc.org
FSC® C007454

FSC™ is a non-profit international organisation established to
promote the responsible management of the world's forests.
Products carrying the FSC label are independently certified to assure
consumers that they come from forests that are managed to meet
the social, economic and ecological needs of present and future
generations, and other controlled sources.

Find out more about HarperCollins and the environment at
www.harpercollins.co.uk/green

To my family, adventurers all

CHAPTER ONE

Austin, Texas
March 8th
11:47 p.m.

How and why—and precisely when—Wade Kaplan dreamed that his priceless star chart had burst into flame he didn't know, but the instant its swirls of silver ink and richly painted constellations caught fire, he bolted awake.

"No!"

The room was pitch-black. There was no fire.

Knowing the door between his room and his stepbrother Darrell's was open, he tilted his head toward it. Slow, rhythmic breathing. *Okay, good.* Their first official day of school vacation had hardly been restful, rushing around doing last-minute chores before his stepmom, Sara, flew off on a business trip to South America. Her flight would leave early in the morning, and despite the hectic day, he and Darrell had promised to be up at the crack of dawn to see her off.

And yet . . .

Wade pushed the sheets aside, walked to the window, and quietly raised the shade.

It was a nearly moonless night, and stars were sprinkled thickly across the velvety black. His house in the hills some miles from the Austin city lights usually meant a vivid night sky, and tonight was no exception.

Turning to his desk, he opened the top drawer and drew out a leather satchel the size of a large paperback. Not only had it not burned, but it was cool to the touch, and he realized it had been weeks since he'd last handled it. He undid its straps and removed a thick sheet of folded parchment. His skin tingled when he opened it. The map was a gift for his seventh birthday from a dear friend of his father's, a man he'd come to know as Uncle Henry. Engraved and hand-painted in the early sixteenth century, the map was a work of science, art, and history combined, and he cherished it.

Why, then, had he just dreamed of its destruction?

Wade turned the star map around until it matched the arrangement of constellations outside his window. Then, as if it had waited for him simply to look up, a meteor slid slowly across the dark, sparking as it passed. "Darrell, look!" he said instinctively, waiting for a second streak of light, knowing that one never comes when you expect it. A slow minute went by. No. That was all. He traced his finger across the map. "Right through Draco and Cygnus."

"The bad kids from *Harry Potter*?"

Wade spun around. "Darrell! Did you see it?"

His stepbrother staggered over, rubbing his eyes. "The sky? Yeah. I saw it yesterday too. What time is it? Is the world ending? Answer the second question first."

Wade laughed. "About midnight. I just saw a meteor. They're actually much more common than people think."

"And yet here we stand, staring out your window. Mom's trip comes in, like, an hour, doesn't it?"

"I know. Sorry."

Wade had known since he was a toddler that stars were energy-producing balls of fiery gas burning at incredible heat hundreds of millions of miles away. Since his very first years in school, science had been his thing, his strength. But spread out over the Texas skies—or anywhere, really—stars were also something else. Not merely randomly positioned specks blinking in the darkness.

"Darrell, look," Wade said, pointing to the chart then the sky. "That's Cepheus. See, it's a kind of box with a pointed hat on top. And there's one of Pegasus's legs. Stars are like, I don't know, messages from way out there to us down here. If only we could read the code, you know?"

Darrell squinted. "I don't really see them, but I believe you, which is part of the stepbrother code. I also believe I need to sleep or I'll die." He started back to his room.

"Uncle Henry wrote me once, 'The sky is where mathematics and magic become one.' Isn't that so cool?"

"I'm becoming one with my bed."

"Tomorrow we'll go to the campus observatory," Wade said. "You have to see it."

"It's already tomorrow, and I'm already asleep!" Darrell said. Then he turned from the doorway. "But seriously, bro. Very cool. I get it." In three strides he was on his bed, where he snorted exaggeratedly, went quiet, and was, amazingly, asleep.

Wade watched a minute longer, then drew the shade down. He folded the celestial chart and carefully returned it to his desk drawer. Where math and magic become one. Wade felt that too. He felt it like he felt his own heartbeat. Since the beginning of time, people had read whole stories in the sky, finding the past, present, and future in the seeming arrangement of star to star to star. When he thought of the kind old man who'd given him the priceless chart six years before, he smiled. "Thanks again, Uncle Henry."

Crawling back into bed, Wade felt strangely calm.

He had no idea that in the coming days he, and Darrell too, would measure their lives as happening *before* or *after* that starry night.

CHAPTER TWO

Frombork, Poland
March 8th
Eight hours earlier

The night was bitterly cold for March, and even more so near the frigid waters of the Baltic Sea.

A young woman, not twenty years old, pulled her fur coat tightly around herself. Her long dark hair waved in the constant wind off the water. Taking a deep breath to steady herself, she gazed up at the square brick tower standing tall and empty against the sky. That vague W-shaped cluster of stars flickering behind the tower was Cassiopeia, she thought. The throne of the queen.

Queen. The title meant something to her. Or might someday.

She knew she wouldn't be able to linger long. A limousine idled thirty feet away at the edge of the road near the pine trees. Four men sat quietly inside the car. A phone call was expected. The call that she had been waiting such a long time for—years, in fact. And after the call? There would be miles to travel tonight. She knew that, too.

And yet she could not move.

The longer she stared at the tower—her sharp eyes scanning the broad granite lintel over the oak door, the narrow catwalks and stairs draping the outside wall from the ground to the high peaked summit standing starkly against the sky—the more the old scene overwhelmed her.

And just like that, it was five hundred years ago, a night she had heard about so often, it seemed as real as if she had been there. Snow swirled against the walls and up to the doorstep. Normally white and clean, the drifts burned red from the flames boiling up the sides of the tower.

"Fire! Magister, awake!" A boy, sixteen years old, ran helter-skelter down the tower steps, racing to the inlet with empty buckets flying in his hands.

7

The legend has given us the boy's name: Hans Novak.

Then came the thundering of hooves, and the young woman saw horsemen, fierce-faced and monstrous under plates of angled armor. Their blades were thick with blood, their eyes wolfish with rage. The village beyond was an inferno of flame. Now they'd come in for the kill.

And there he was. The scholar. The mathematician. Magister. The man she felt she had always known. He leaped down the tower steps from its summit, his leather cloak flying behind him.

"Fiends!" he cried at the horsemen. "I know why you have come! I will not obey!" From the folds of his cloak he drew a sword—Himmelklinge, he called it: "Sky Blade." He jumped to the ground and planted his boots in the snow while the horsemen circled around, outnumbering him eight to one.

The clash of sword against sword echoed under the sparkling sky. More than a scholar, the Magister was also a swordsman, trained in the ancient arts. She smiled at that. Swordsman. He fought off one knight, then a second and third, tumbling them from their saddles. Not only Sky Blade whisked in the air, but so did his dueling dagger, its wavy blade piercing the chinks in their armor. The Magister was swift and efficient, tutored by the best swordsman in Bologna. But his ferocity couldn't last. Two horsemen roped the boy, wrestling him to the ground, his now-laden buckets spilling, cracking.

The scholar's dagger ceased flashing. Sky Blade fell silent.

"Stop!" he said, hanging his head. "Release the boy. Release him, and I will do as the Grand Master says. . . ."

The sound of the car horn broke the night air and brought the young woman back to the present. She turned, drawing a stray strand of hair behind her ear. If the men in the car had looked closely they might have seen a three-inch vertical scar on her neck below her ear. She didn't conceal it. In more ways than one, the scar was a sign of her survival.

But the men in the car dared not look. Instead, a pale runtish specimen, large-headed and bent, shivering in his thin coat, stumbled out of the backseat and scurried over.

"They have found him," the man said eagerly, drying with a finger the drool that had leaked from the edge of his mouth. "They have found the head of the five. They have found him—"

"Where?" she asked.

"Berlin! Just as you suspected!"

Her eyes lingered on the tower a moment longer.

Her eyes. One blue, one silver-gray. A condition called heterochromia iridis. A chance mutation, both a blessing and a curse. Was this what made her so mesmerizing?

Brushing a wave of hair back over her collar, she strode to the limousine, slid into the backseat, and caught a glimpse of the nameless driver in the rearview.

"Airport," she said. "We five fly to Berlin tonight."

"Yes, Miss Krause," said the driver, who had a name, though she never used it. "Right away, Miss Krause."

"Galina. My dear," said the pale man as he slipped into the seat next to her, "when we arrive in Berlin—"

"Silence," she said, and the pale man caught his breath and lowered his gaze to the ruby necklace that shone below the collar of her coat. The red stone was in the shape of a sea creature.

A kraken.

As the car roared away, Galina Krause glanced once more at the tower, standing black against the starry firmament.

In her mind, the flames—as they always did when she imagined that night so long ago—coiled higher.

"And so," she whispered to herself, "it begins."

Just before two in the morning, in the sector of the city once called East Berlin, on a street named Unter den Linden, a long black car crawled to a stop with the quiet ease of a panther.

The engine went silent.

* * *

For decades Unter den Linden—"under the linden trees"—had been cut in two by the infamous Berlin Wall. Now that the Cold War was over and the wall was down, the avenue was whole again and teeming with life. Three floors above, a dim light shone in the window of a small apartment. The haggard face of an old man blinked out over the passing cars, the raucous music clubs, the bustle of pedestrians crowding the avenue. Their night was in full swing.

All seemed normal, all seemed well.

All was not well.

Heinrich Vogel, retired professor of astronomy at Humboldt University, hobbled from the window into his study, deeply troubled.

Was the great secret unraveling at last?

And what of the future? Of humanity? Of the world itself?

He stoked the small flame in the fireplace. It blossomed. Sliding into a chair, he typed furiously on his computer keyboard, then paused. Among the seven newspapers on his desk sat the Paris daily *Le Monde*. Two hours had gone by since his dear friend, Bernard Dufort, was to have called him. He always called the instant the coded crossword appeared online. He had done so the second Monday of every month for the last seventeen years. "RIP." A morbid joke, perhaps, but one easily missed unless you knew to look for the letters near the intersection of 48 Across and Down.

Tonight, there was no call. The encoded crossword did not appear.

Vogel could only assume that the delicately constructed system of communication had been compromised. The inner circle had been breached.

As he hit Send on his computer, he wondered whether his colleague at *Le Monde* had fled his post. Or worse. That he had *not* fled his post but had perished in defense of their secret.

"In either case, I must leave Berlin," he said to himself, standing and scanning the room. "Flee now and hope my American friend will understand my message . . . and remember the old days."

He checked his watch. Two a.m., give or take. It was six hours earlier in Texas, after office hours. His friend would see the email in the morning. The clues were there. If only Roald would connect and follow them.

"I have kept you out of it until the last. Now, I have no choice. And young Wade. I dread this even more for him. The terrible responsibility . . ."

He lifted the phone from its cradle and pressed a

number into it, waited for the connection, and spoke four words.

"Carlo, expect a visit."

He set down the receiver, knowing that the number dialed and each word spoken were twisted and garbled in a way that could be unscrambled only at the receiving end. Technology had its uses, after all.

Checking his vest pocket for the fifth time in as many minutes, he fingered the train ticket. Then he placed his computer on the floor and stomped on it until its shell cracked. He removed the hard drive, bent it nearly in half, and threw it into the fire.

"What else?" He spied the starfish paperweight on his desk. It was no more than a cheap beachside souvenir. A sea star—*Asterias,* its Latin term—molded in glass.

Asterias. The name he'd called his hand-picked group of students so long ago. All that was over now. He gave the paperweight a pat, then took up a framed photograph. It was of himself two decades before, with three young men and two women standing under the blue glow of a café's sign. They were all smiling. Professor and students. Asterias.

"My friend," Vogel whispered to one of the faces. "It is all in your hands now. If only you will take the challenge—"

Something snapped sharply on the street below the apartment. Vogel's heart thumped with dread. A door creaked and footsteps thudded up the stairs. "No, no. It is too soon—"

He threw the photograph in the fire and the door burst open. Three thick men in dark suits pushed their way in. They were followed by a shrunken man with wire glasses and flat hair and a woman young enough to be a student herself.

"Who are you?" Vogel cried, dragging the glass paperweight off the desk and clutching it tightly. He knew too well who they were. The enemies of man.

The first thug knocked him down. Vogel stumbled hard to his knees, then to the floor. "Murderers! Thieves!" he screamed, while the other two men fanned out into the small apartment, turning over everything in sight. The woman stood by the door as calm and silent as a coiled snake. What was wrong with her expression? She was beautiful. Like an angel, even.

And yet . . . those eyes.

Was *she* the one?

The men tore the books from the shelves. Tables crashed to the floor. Upholstered chairs, his bed, his pillows, all sliced open. His priceless collection of musical instruments tossed aside as if they were worthless toys.

"Brutes!" the old man cried out. "There is nothing here!"

The bent man with pasty skin and spectacles perched on his nose like a second set of eyes leaned over him.

"Your associate in Paris gave you up," he snarled at Vogel. "You have the key to the relics. Give it to us."

Adrenaline spiking his old veins, Vogel gripped the starfish paperweight and slammed it hard against the temple of the pale man. "There is the key. There, on your head!"

The pale man pawed his bleeding temple. "What have you done to my face, you fool?"

"Improved it!" Vogel snapped.

One of the thick men knelt and wrapped his massive hand around the old man's neck. He grinned as he brought his fingers together.

"Breathe your last, old fool!" shrieked the pale man.

Vogel burst out with a cold laugh. "No. Not last . . ."

The woman glared at Vogel, then at the hearth. "He has told someone! There is something in the fire—get it!"

Without thinking, the pale man thrust his hand into the flames, screaming as he dragged the smoldering hard drive onto the floor. The photograph was already ash.

"Discover who he has told," the woman said coldly. "I should have known. The key was never here. Finish him. Drop his body in the streets. Leave no clues—"

Choking, Vogel flailed frantically. He knocked over a music stand, hoping to grip its shaft. Instead, all that came to his hand was a battered silver pitch pipe.

As life ebbed swiftly from the old man, Galina Krause stared at him from two different-hued eyes. One blue. One silvery gray.

"Go ahead, Vogel. Play for us. Play your swan song. . . ."

CHAPTER THREE

Austin, Texas
March 9th
8:03 a.m.

Wade and Darrell took turns yanking on the door of the observatory at the University of Texas. It wouldn't budge.

"And that's why Dad gave you the key," Wade said.

"Which I gave to you."

"No, you didn't."

"I'm pretty sure I did," said Darrell.

"When?"

"Before."

"Before *when*?"

17

"Before you lost it."

Wade grumbled. "*I* didn't lose the key. I *couldn't* lose the key. I couldn't lose it because I saw Dad give it to you. In his office. When he dropped us off to run Sara to the airport."

"Sara. You mean the lady I call Mom?"

"Sara lets me call her Sara," Wade said. "Which is beside the point. The key? Remember, Dad took it from his desk drawer? He handed it to you? Do any of these images ring a bell?"

Darrell patted his pockets. "No bells are currently ringing, and I still don't have the key."

"You must have left it on his desk." Wade shoved Darrell aside and retraced his steps down the narrow iron staircase to a small office on the third floor of Painter Hall.

Wade's father—Darrell's stepfather—was Dr. Roald Kaplan, a professor of astrophysics at the University of Texas in Austin, and Painter Hall was the home of an eighty-year-old observatory housing one of the largest telescopes that still operated by an intricate system of cranks and pulleys.

Wade sighed. "Darrell, you have to see this telescope. I can't believe that after what, three years, we haven't brought you in here. It's total steampunk, all winches and gears and levers and weights."

A flicker of interest flashed across Darrell's face. In typical fashion, he responded off center. "I do enjoy the punk which is called steamy."

It being spring break, both boys were looking ahead to a long week of no school. Which to Wade meant nine days of reading astronomy textbooks and nine nights of studying stars from the university's observatory. He was pretty sure that to Darrell vacation meant some strange combination of hibernating and nonstop eating.

Or thrashing his Stratocaster at maximum volume.

Darrell had been trying to form a band for months with no luck. Wade felt there were two reasons for that. First, Darrell wanted to call his band the Simpletones, which was supposed to be ironic but maybe wasn't. And second, he only wanted to play surf-punk, which Wade was pretty sure was not a thing.

They pulled up to their father's office. Wade grabbed the knob, tried to turn it. That door was locked, too.

"Are you kidding me?" he said. "Dad won't be back from the airport for another half hour. I have to show you this scope. I wonder where Campus Security's office is. They'll let us in—"

"Don't move. I think I grabbed a campus map," said Darrell, shoving his hands into his jeans pockets. "If

Security is even up yet. It's only . . . eight-ish. Which for some reason reminds me I'm hungry."

"You ate a muffin an hour ago."

"Exactly. One whole hour. You think Dad will let us go for an early lunch? How long do you think all this will . . . oh."

"'Oh,' *what*?"

Darrell slid a dull brass key out of his pocket. "Is this what we're looking for?"

"I knew it," Wade growled. "Come on."

"Fine, but are we still talking about nothing to eat?"

Wade laughed. "Sorry, bro."

Darrell mumbled something, then hummed a raucous guitar solo as they made their way back up to the dome. Good, thought Wade. This is what Darrell did when he was more or less happy. Obsess about food and hum riffs.

Five minutes later, the boys pushed through the door of the old observatory, and the atmosphere of the large room washed over them like a wave of the past.

Darrell whistled. "You weren't kidding, steampunk!"

Centered directly below a huge copper dome stood the famous Painter Hall telescope. A twelve-foot-long iron tube built in 1933, it was poised on a brick platform and was meticulously balanced by a giant weight, making it easily maneuverable into any position. Wade explained that the scope's lens measured a mere nine inches across—compared to, say, the McDonald Observatory's scope, whose mirror was thirty-six feet across. But this was a historical instrument, and Wade loved that. He loved the places where science and history crisscrossed. There was something exciting about lenses and gears and mechanisms that made exploration that much more, what was the word, *human*.

Wade had long had a thing for the old Painter Hall telescope, ever since his father first brought him into that round room. It was there he learned to locate the planets and constellations. It was in that observatory that he'd read the myths that lay behind their exotic names. It was there where he'd come to appreciate his own tiny place in the vast cosmos of space.

Where math and magic become one.

"Not bad, huh?"

"Not bad at all." Darrell jumped up to the platform. "Cables, cranks. Levers. A clock drive! Mechanical future stuff. I love it! What awesome stuff can it do?"

"Not much in the daytime, but we'll come back tonight for some real stargazing. Don't mess with anything until I find the operating instructions. You'll love the way it swings around with just a touch." Wade plopped down at a small desk near the door. His father was writing a history of the telescope and had set up a research station there. "Just wait. Mars will be as close as a dinner plate."

"I wish I were close to a dinner plate," said Darrell. "Do you still have nothing to eat?"

"Since the last time you asked? No. But why don't you check those pockets you never check?"

"Because I obviously don't carry food with me . . . oh." Darrell pulled a slender packet from his other pocket. "Gum is food, right?"

"It is if you swallow it," said Wade.

"I always do."

Before he'd met Darrell and his new stepmom, Sara, three years ago, Wade had hoped for the longest time that his real mother and father would get back together. He was crushed to realize they weren't going to, and he was still having trouble accepting that the past was really the past. But he saw his real mom often (she lived in California now) and was coming to understand that you move on and learn to live with lots of stuff. He also had to admit that the new families were working out really well.

"Can you believe Mom's going to be lost in the

jungles of South America for a week?" Darrell asked from the platform. "Well, not lost, but hunting down some crazy writer?"

"I know, a week with no phones, no electricity, nothing."

"Except bugs," said Darrell. "Lots of bugs. Then she flies to New York. Then London. My jet-setting mom."

"Sara's supercool," Wade said.

"Yes. *My mother* is."

Any way you looked at it, the best part of the deal was Darrell himself. From the instant the two boys were introduced, he'd become the brother Wade had always wanted. They complemented each other in just about every way, but at the same time, Wade and Darrell couldn't be more different.

Darrell had short dark hair, olive skin, and deep brown eyes that he got from his Thai father. Wade was fair-skinned, sandy-haired, and lanky. Darrell was five feet four and a guitarist of strange loud stuff that might be really excellent or might just be loud. Wade was three inches taller and owned an iPod full of Bach, because Bach was not loud, was the most mathematical of composers, and was someone his mother had taught him to love. Darrell was a junior tennis pro. Wade wore sneakers like a junior tennis pro. Darrell was comfortable with just about everyone. Wade felt more comfortable with Darrell than he did with himself. Finally, Darrell was usually smiling, even when he was sleeping, while Wade had invented neurotic worrying.

And he felt a sudden jolt of worry at exactly that moment.

While searching for the telescope's operating manual on the desk, he'd accidentally moved the mouse on his father's computer. The screen saver flickered away and an email message popped up. Without wanting to, Wade noticed the sender's name.

Heinrich Vogel.

"No kidding?" Wade whispered. "Uncle Henry?"

"No. The name is Darrell," said Darrell from the platform. "I thought being my stepbrother for three years you would know that."

"No. Dad got an email from Uncle Henry. We were just talking about him. You know he's not really my uncle, right? He was Dad's college teacher in Germany. I haven't seen him since I was seven."

Darrell hopped down the stairs and peered over Wade's shoulder. "Emails are private. Don't read it. What does it say?"

Wade tried not to read it, but his eyes strayed.

Lca guygas eamizub zb.

Bluysna luynaedab odxx sio wands.

Juilatl Ica Hyndblaub xanytq.

Rdse Ica loaxma uaxdtb.

Qiz yua Ica xybl.

Darrell frowned. "Does Dad read German? Or is that Russian?"

"Neither. It's got to be some kind of code."

"Code. Wait, is our dad a spy? He's a spy, isn't he? Of course he's a spy, he never told me he was, which is exactly what a spy would do. I knew it. It's that beard. No one really knows what he looks like under there."

"Darrell, no."

"He's probably a double agent. That's the best kind. No one's a single agent anymore. Or, no, a *triple* agent. That's even better. Wait, what is a triple agent—"

The door squeaked open. "So there you are!"

Wade shot up from the desk the moment his father entered the observatory. "Nothing!" he said.

Roald Kaplan had run track in high school, had been a champion long-distance runner in college, and still ran the occasional marathon. He was trim and tall and handsome behind sunglasses and a dark, close-cut beard. "Sara's safely off on her flight to Bolivia. Thanks for hanging out here, while we did our last-minute zipping around. What are you guys up to?"

"Well," Darrell piped in, "I found gum."

"And I . . . ," Wade said, ". . . didn't?"

Darrell cleared his throat. "Wade's odd behavior means he's worried. Which, I know, is not breaking news, but he found something bizarro on your computer . . ."

Wade pointed at the computer screen. "Dad, I'm sorry, but it was an accident that I saw the screen at all. I know I shouldn't have read the email, but I saw it, and . . . what's going on? It's from Uncle Henry, but it looks like code."

Dr. Kaplan paused for a long moment. His smile faded away. He leaned over Wade and tapped the keyboard. The email printed out on a nearby printer. Then he deleted the message and shut the computer off.

"Not here. Not now."

CHAPTER FOUR

"Can you at least tell us why Uncle Henry's writing to you in code?" Wade asked when they got into the car. "Is he in trouble? Or in danger? Dad, are *we* in danger?"

"You worry too much," said Dr. Kaplan, unconvincingly.

"Is Uncle Henry a spy?" asked Darrell. "Because if he's a spy, that's huge. A spy in the family would actually be terrific and awesomely cool. As you probably already know, I would make a perfect spy—"

"Boys, please," Dr. Kaplan said, weaving through

27

campus traffic and onto the streets. "I'm sure Uncle Henry is just fine, and I'm almost positive it's some kind of joke message. In any case, it won't make sense to you—or even to me—until we get home. There are a couple pieces of the puzzle I need to figure it out. Until then . . ."

Puzzle? Wade didn't know what to say. He sat quietly looking out the window for the next twenty minutes as they drove from campus into the hills west of Austin.

Darrell did not sit quietly. "I think I have it. Uncle Henry is a professor in Germany, but he's secretly doing spy stuff. He's a master cryptographer, and he's trying to recruit you to be a spy too. Dad, if you can't do it, I'll do it. Sure. I know professors make a good cover. They pretend to sit in their offices all sleepy over their books and stuff while secretly they're running all kinds of spy missions. But middle school kids are even better. No one would ever suspect us. Wade, you could be a spy, too. Of course, you'd do the desk stuff while I go around the world with my band as a cover. Not that the Simpletones would be a cover band. We'd play all original stuff. They call that being in the field. I'd be a field agent. *Agent* being the technical term for 'spy' . . ."

Darrell hadn't stopped talking, but as he was often forced to do when his stepbrother thrashed on guitar,

Wade had to tune him out to be able to think.

Ever since Uncle Henry had given him the antique celestial map on his seventh birthday, Wade had been a fanatic about star maps and charts and the courses and routes of celestial bodies. He'd stayed up every night for weeks studying the map by moonlight and flashlight. Of course, he learned most things from his father, a brilliant astronomer, but it was probably Uncle Henry's star map that stole his deeper imagination. The chart was old and strange and mysterious, and in his mind Wade associated all those qualities with the stars themselves. Between his father and Uncle Henry, Wade learned to love the night sky more than anything.

When they finally turned into the driveway of a sprawling home overlooking a shallow valley, Darrell practically exploded in the backseat. "Uncle Henry *is* a spy! Someone's casing our house!"

As Dr. Kaplan slowed the car, a shape darted along the side garden and disappeared under the roof that hung over the front door.

Wade stiffened. "Dad, tear out of here—"

"Yoo-hoo!"

A girl in shorts and a stylishly slashed T-shirt strolled out from under the overhang to the car, wheeling an orange suitcase behind her.

It was Lily Kaplan, Wade's first cousin, his father's niece. "Surprise, people!"

"Lily? This *is* a surprise," said Dr. Kaplan, rolling down the window.

"Like, what are you even doing here?" Darrell asked.

"Like, nice to even see you, too," Lily said, snapping a picture of Darrell on her cell phone. "Oh, I'm posting that face." Her thumbs flew over the phone while she talked.

"I'm supposed to be on vacation with my parents in Paris right now," she said. "That's in France. One of my school friends was even coming with me. We were going to shop. Well, *I* was going to shop. Big-time. But then Mom got the flu. Also big-time. Then Dad had to fly to Seattle for work. So good-bye France, and that's why he called you, Uncle Roald, and . . . wait. You *did* talk to my dad? He said he was going to call you."

Dr. Kaplan frowned. "I . . ." He fished out his cell phone and tapped it several times. "It must have run out of battery. I'm so sorry I didn't get his message."

Lily clucked her tongue. "No one should ever let his battery run down. I never let my battery run down. Your phone is like your brain. More important, even. Anyway, my dad dropped us here for the week and— ta-da!—here we are."

Something sparked in Wade's head. *"Us? We?* Here *we* are?"

Lily turned and made a little wave toward the house. "Becca came with me. Wade, you remember Becca, right?"

Of course he did.

Becca Moore.

The instant Becca walked out of the shade of the overhang, Wade stood up like a soldier at attention. He couldn't stop himself. It was instinctive and weird. He knew it was. But more than being weird, it hurt, because Wade was still in the car. You don't stand up in cars. Even convertibles, which his dad's car was not. As Wade jammed his head into the ceiling, he knew it must look epically dumb.

Guys didn't stand up for just anyone.

But then, Becca Moore was not just anyone. She was . . . interesting. His brain wouldn't let him go any further than that.

Interesting.

Becca was born in Massachusetts and had moved to Austin when she was eight. She was tall and fair and had long brown, almost black hair tied in a loose pony-tail. Wade was a little afraid of her because she was so smart, but she didn't broadcast it and was almost as quiet as he was, which was another cool thing about her. As she walked over to the car, she was wearing a faded red 2012 Austin Teen Book Festival T-shirt, slim blue jean leggings, and mouse-gray ballet flats so soft they made no more sound than if she were barefoot.

Interesting.

Dr. Kaplan got out of the car and hugged both girls. "Well, we're glad to have you visit. Come on in!"

Darrell couldn't stop laughing as Wade unfolded himself from the car and limped to the front door.

No sooner had they all piled inside than Lily spun around. "Pose!" She snapped another picture with her phone. "So awesome. Wade with his eyes closed. Darrell looking like . . . Darrell." Then she found a seat in the living room, tugged a sleek tablet computer from her bag, and instantly began to type on its touch-screen keyboard. She looked up. "I'm writing a travel blog. But you knew that, right?"

No one knew that. If Wade had realized he would end up on the internet, he might have combed his hair that morning. Or washed it.

Lily grinned as she typed. "Vacation Day One. The Big Disappointment. A week with my cousins Wade and Darrell. I can barely bring my fingers to type these words . . ."

Darrell frowned. "Ha. And also, ha."

Tearing his eyes away from Becca, who sat quietly on the couch next to Lily, Wade watched his father move distractedly around the living room. The coded email from Uncle Henry was obviously on his mind. Of course it was. Code? What did code even mean, except keeping a secret from someone? Who would Uncle Henry and his dad need to keep secrets from?

When the snappy conversation between Lily and Darrell finally paused, he spoke up. "Dad, the email?"

"I need your celestial map," his father said, as if he'd been waiting for a lull, too. "The star chart Uncle Henry gave you when you were seven."

Wade blinked. "Really? Why?"

"You'll see," his father said.

CHAPTER FIVE

In the quiet of his room, Wade slid open the top drawer of his desk. He removed the leather folder as he had the night before. The map, so precious and so rare, would now, suddenly, be the center of everyone's attention. *But why did Dad want the chart?* Puzzling over this, he brought it into the dining room, where he found them all sitting around the table.

His father pulled out a chair for him. "Wade, open the map, please . . ."

He unzipped the folder and opened it flat, revealing the thick sheet of parchment creased over itself twice.

He saw, as he hadn't in the darkness of his room the night before, faint, penciled letters on the backside, reading, *Happy Birth-day, Wade*. Carefully, he unfolded the parchment on the table and spread it out faceup.

Becca leaned over it, her eyes glowing. "Wade, this is so gorgeous. Wow . . ."

"Thanks," he said quietly.

Spread out, the map was about the size of a small poster. It had been engraved in 1515 and was exquisitely hand painted. The heavens were colored deep blue, and the original forty-eight constellations described by the ancient Greek astronomer Ptolemy were drawn and starred in silver inks. Crater, Lyra, Orion, Cassiopeia, all the others. Evenly spaced around the map's edge was a sequence of letters in gold forming an incomplete alphabet, which had always puzzled Wade and about which his father had offered no real explanation.

"Okay, so," Dr. Kaplan said, taking a deep breath. "First we have the email." He produced the printed email from his blazer pocket, then carefully traced his fingers over the letters bordering Wade's star map. "Uncle Henry gave you this chart for your birthday, knowing you would like it."

"I love it," Wade said almost reverently. "It's what really got me super-interested in the stars."

"I know," his father said. "Maybe you don't remember me telling you, but it wasn't the first time I had seen this map. Heinrich showed it to me while I was still a student, quite a few years before you were born. He had a little apartment then; he still does."

"Have you seen him since then?" Becca asked.

"Once, then letters, email once in a while," he said. "Heinrich had always been a collector of antiques. One night twenty or so years ago, in front of me and some other students, he unfolded five identical printings, all hand-colored, of the same map from the sixteenth century. This map. As we all watched, he took out a pen, dipped it in gold ink, and without a word, inked an alphabet around the edge of each one."

"But the alphabet is messed up," Lily said. "It's only got . . . seventeen letters." On her tablet she typed in the gold-inked letters framing the star map, while Darrell did the same on a yellow pad.

C D F G H I J K M O P Q V W X Y Z

"Of course." Dr. Kaplan slipped on a pair of reading glasses. "We noticed the same thing. Heinrich told us our alphabets were one part of a cipher—a code—of his own invention. He said we might have to use it someday. Before we ever needed it, he said, he would see that we each received one copy of the map. Then he put them away before we could really do any figuring. And that was that. I never thought much about the maps again until your seventh birthday, Wade, when he gave you this one. He brushed off any mention of the code then. I assumed it didn't matter anymore."

Darrell shook his head slowly. "But it does matter. And it proves I was right. He was a spy. He was pretending to be a professor, but he was a secret agent."

Dr. Kaplan cracked a smile. "I really don't think so. He's retired now, but he was one of the foremost physicists of his day. When he first showed us the maps, he swore us to secrecy. He called our little group of five students *Asterias*. That's the Latin name for the sea star. We were, Heinrich said, like the five arms of the starfish, and he was the head. It seemed a little silly at the time. A professor's whimsy. But we were graduating and going our separate ways, so we all agreed. In the last few years I lost communication with most of them, and he's never asked me to use the code. Until today."

Wade breathed in to try to calm himself. It didn't work. A hundred questions collided in his brain. "Are you saying that the cipher on the map will decode the email?"

"But not all the letters are there," said Becca. "If it's

a standard substitution code, it needs all twenty-six letters."

Everyone looked at her.

"Substitution code?" said Darrell. "Uh-huh. Putting
aside for a moment what substitution codes even are,
how do you know about them?"

Becca blushed a little. "I read. A lot. Last summer I
read all the Sherlock Holmes stories. You know what I
mean, right, Dr. Kaplan?"

He smiled. "I do. Sherlock Holmes solves substitution
codes in several of the stories. When we asked Heinrich about the missing letters, he just winked and slyly
tapped the side of his nose. We pressed him about what
he meant, and he said, 'when things are missing, you
look for them!' You're all pretty brainy, so the first step
for us is, what letters are missing?"

Lily had apparently already figured it out and told
them with a grin. "*A*, *B*, *E*, *L*, *N*, *R*, *S*, *T*, and *U*!"

"Good," Dr. Kaplan said. He wrote them on Darrell's
pad.

A B E L N R S T U

"Nine letters. The cipher begins as a fairly simple
Caesar code, a substitution code originated a couple of

38

thousand years ago by Julius Caesar for his private letters. Heinrich was a student of ciphers, and he modified this in his own way.

"So, the letters *not* on the map form a secret word or phrase. You unscramble the missing letters to find the words, then put them at the beginning of the alphabet to make the full twenty-six letters again."

"Nine letters could spell a lot of words," said Darrell.

Dr. Kaplan nodded. "But they should somehow be familiar to the person for whom the code is intended . . ." He paused, stroking his chin. "My diary. I kept a journal then, a student notebook, where I wrote down lecture notes and random things. It's in my office. Hold on." He left the room at a trot.

"We can start," said Becca. "*A*, *B*, *E*, *L*, *N*, *R*, *S*, *T*, and *U*. Let's think."

The dining room went quiet, except for Darrell's pencil scratching and occasional humming and Lily's fingers tapping on the tablet's screen. Becca frowned and looked off across the room.

Wade tried to think, but the image of Uncle Henry inking the maps in gold was mesmerizing. Was it by candlelight, their student faces glowing? Was his apartment as hushed as their dining room was right now? Why did he do it in the first place?

His father returned, leafing through a small black notebook. "Maybe the answer is somewhere in here . . ."

"I get the words *rest*, *nut*, and *eat*," Darrell said finally.

"Of course you do," said Lily. "I see *ears*."

"I get *lean burst*," said Becca with a smile. "Do I get a prize for using all the letters?"

Wade resisted jumping up and shouting, "Yes, you do!"

But the more he studied the letters, the more they began to shift places like the panels in one of those number slide puzzles. This was how his mind often solved math problems. His father said he was a natural at numbers. And now, apparently, at letters, too.

Common combinations . . . *S* . . . *T* . . . slid forward and back . . . vowels moved and moved again. Fixing his eyes on the letters, Wade went through them again, again, then *click*. Solved. Or sort of solved. He cleared his throat. "Well . . ."

Four faces looked at him.

"One thing the letters spell is *blue star* with an extra *n*," he said. "I don't know what the *n* stands for, but a blue star is a real thing. If a star appears blue, it means it's approaching Earth."

Dr. Kaplan stared at the letters on the pad, nodding. Then he turned to the last page in his notebook and smiled. "Oh, boy. Close. Very close. But look."

As they watched him, he slowly rewrote *blue star n* as *blau stern*.

"*Blau stern*?" said Becca. "That's *blue star* in German."

"Exactly," Dr. Kaplan said, showing them the words in his notebook. "*Blau Stern* was the name of the café in Berlin where we met after classes—"

"I knew it!" said Darrell. "Your spy hangout!"

CHAPTER SIX

Roald blew out a fast breath. "Hardly, Darrell. But we've done it. Good work. What we do now is take the secret phrase and add it to the beginning of the incomplete alphabet to make a full twenty-six letters."

They rewrote the alphabet.

B L A U S T E R N C D F G H I J K M O P Q V W X Y Z

"Now we arrange the normal ABC alphabet under it?" asked Lily.

"Not quite," Dr. Kaplan said. "Instead of a second

alphabet, Heinrich added an extra step. We need a number key. We have to know how many letters we count from the coded letter to find the proper letter for the substitution."

"Is there a number on the map?" asked Lily. "Maybe we already have the number key, but it's hidden on Wade's chart."

"Smart, Lil." Becca squinted over the map. Wade noticed a little thing she did when she was concentrating. A squiggle of her lips.

Dr. Kaplan stood. "Smart, yes, but there are hundreds of numbers on the map. Coordinates, degrees. I can't help but feel that Uncle Henry would point to the number directly, with a specific clue—"

"Maybe he did, with this," said Darrell. He flipped the corner of the map over. In faint script it read *Happy Birth-day, Wade*. "Mom told me that pencil marks are great on manuscripts. They last for years but they can be erased. Anyway, a birthday is a number."

"Holy cow," said Lily. "Wade, what's your birthday?"

"October sixth."

"Ten and six," said Becca. "Sixteen. So the substitution for each letter is sixteen letters away? Let's start."

They counted sixteen letters from each letter of the first two words of the coded message.

Lca guygas . . .

became

Mzo apiaoq . . .

Darrell tried to pronounce it. "May-zo app-i-ay-ock?"

Lily turned to Roald. "This isn't a language, is it?"

"No," he said. "We must have gotten the substitution wrong."

"Wait," said Becca, tapping the map. "If your uncle likes codes and puzzles, maybe he meant *everything* about the message to be a clue, right? So what about the minus sign in 'birth-day'?"

Wade leaned over the faint pencil marks. "Maybe that's just the European way of writing it. Is it, Dad?"

His father raised an eyebrow. "Or maybe Heinrich is asking us to *subtract* the day from your birthday. In other words, October sixth isn't ten *plus* six, it's ten *minus* six. Let's try four."

They did.

Lca . . .

became

The . . .

"I know that word!" Lily screamed. "That's it!"

Dr. Kaplan laughed. "So the number is four. We count off four letters from the letter in the code to give us the correct letter, like this."

He scribbled on Darrell's pad for the next few minutes, then showed them.

$B = S$

$L = T$

$A = E$

$U = R$

$S = N$

$T = C$

$E = D$

$R = F$

$N = G$

$C = H$

$D = I$

$F = J$

$G = K$

$H = M$

$I = O$

$J = P$

$K = Q$

$$M = V$$
$$O = W$$
$$P = X$$
$$Q = Y$$
$$V = Z$$
$$W = B$$
$$X = L$$
$$Y = A$$
$$Z = U$$

"If we're right about this decryption code, where the email message uses the letter B, it really represents S, and so forth down the line. So when the whole message is translated . . ." Dr. Kaplan scratched away on the pad for several minutes. He breathed in and out more excitedly until he dropped his pencil and spoke.

> "The kraken devours us.
> Strange tragedies will now begin.
> Protect the Magisters Legacy.
> Find the twelve relics.
> You are the last."

Wade felt a twinge in the center of his chest. *You are the last.* That was never a good message, especially when it was in code. But the other words? Tragedies? Legacy? Relics?

"Magister," said Darrell. "Is that like a magician?"

Dr. Kaplan shook his head. "More like a master. A title of respect. Like *professor*."

"Okay, but we're not calling you Magister, Dad."

"And kraken?" said Lily. "What's kraken?"

"Sort of a giant squid," Becca said. "A sea monster. It's in legends and stories and things."

Wade blinked. *Where does she get this stuff? Substitution codes and krakens? Is it really all that time she spends poring over books or is she an actual genius? Either way, she's kind of amazing.*

"How did your uncle know yesterday about the tragedies they're talking about this morning?" asked Lily.

"What tragedies?" Darrell asked.

"The things going on all over. It's been on the net all morning. Look." Lily linked to a news page on her tablet and scrolled down. Below the political news was a photo report of a building collapse in the center of Rio de Janeiro, in Brazil. Below that were several pieces about an oil tanker sinking in the Mediterranean. "It's pretty weird, isn't it, that they both happened at kind of the same time as his message? They're tragedies, right?" Lily looked from one to the other of them. "I think they are."

"They are, of course," Dr. Kaplan said over the tablet. "But I don't know . . ."

"Call him," said Wade. "Call Uncle Henry now and find out what he means."

"You absolutely have to, Uncle Roald," Lily added.

Dr. Kaplan glanced at his watch. "It's six hours later there. Afternoon. He should be home. All right." He found the number in his notebook. Sliding his cell phone from his jacket pocket, he realized once again that it was dead and plugged it into its charger. Then he went into the living room and keyed the number into the home phone. He put it on speaker, and set it on the coffee table.

It rang five times before a woman answered, *"Ja?"*

"Hello," said Dr. Kaplan. "I would like to speak to Herr Heinrich Vogel, please. It's urgent."

There was a pause. *"Nein.* No. No Herr Vogel. I em Frau Munch. Howze kipper." The woman had a thick accent. It took a moment for Wade to understand her.

"Housekeeper," he whispered.

"Can you please give Dr. Vogel a message?"

"No mess edge."

"It's short. Please tell him to call me. My name is—"

"Herr Vogel no call. Herr Vogel iz ded!"

CHAPTER SEVEN

Wade turned to his father. "Dad?"

Dr. Kaplan appeared to freeze for a moment. Then he slipped off his glasses and rubbed his eyes, the phone crackling on the table. "Excuse me, I don't think we heard you. Are you saying . . . Heinrich . . ."

"Ded. *Ja. Ja.*" The voice rasped from the other end. "Ze fun . . . fun . . ."

Becca silently mouthed the word, "Fun."

"Fun . . . fun . . . eral. Tomorrow mornink. *Alter St.-Matthäus-Kirchhof.* Here. Berlin. *Elfen glock.*"

"Eleven o'clock?" said Lily.

"*Ja, ja.*"

"Wait. This can't be right," said Wade. His chest was burning. "I mean how? How did he die? When?"

The voice on the other end went in and out.

"Frau Munch," his father said, leaning over the phone. "Frau—"

"Hurry. You vill mizz ze boorial!"

The line clicked. She had hung up.

The children stared at one another, listening to the dial tone until the phone blinked and the connection was severed. Lily set it back in its cradle.

Wade felt suddenly dizzy, as if freezing water streamed down his back, while the inside of his chest was on fire. "Dad?" He lowered himself onto the sofa and felt Becca's hand touch his shoulder.

Uncle Henry . . . dead?

Dr. Kaplan slumped down next to him, nearly buried by the cushions. "Wade, I'm so sorry. This is . . . unbelievable. How could Heinrich be dead?" He looked at the wall clock. "I can't go . . . not with you here and Sara flying off to South America." He seemed as deflated as the pillows around him.

Darrell picked up the translated email and read over its few words. "I mean, I didn't know Uncle Henry, but something about this isn't right. He sends you a strange email, a *coded* message, and now he's dead? This is way too suspicious."

Wade stood up from the sofa. Becca's hand slipped away. "Dad, what do you think we should do?"

His father pressed his fingers to his temples and rubbed them in slow circles. "Kids, I don't know yet. It's too sudden. But I'm fairly sure there's no time to do anything. Certainly not while your mom's away." He took in a deep breath. His face was drawn and gray.

"At least call her," said Darrell. "She needs to know."

Roald glanced again at his watch as if trying to find more information there than it could deliver. "She'll be in the air now, but I'll leave a message. Lily, could you look up the flight to La Paz, Bolivia, and see when her first layover is?"

"Sure thing." She tapped and swiped her screen.

Roald dried his eyes and dialed Sara's number. "Sara, hi. I know you're in the air now, but call me when you get to your first stop—"

"Atlanta in two hours," Lily reported. "But there's a storm."

He nodded. "Everybody's fine, but a dear old professor of mine has . . . passed away. Heinrich Vogel. You've heard me talk about him. His funeral is tomorrow. In Germany. Of course, I'm not going to leave the kids for a second. Lily and her friend Becca are here, too. I feel I should go but, well, call me from Atlanta when you land, and we'll sort this out." He hung up.

"Does anybody seriously think his death has *anything* to do with the email and the code?" Becca asked. "It's kind of too James Bond to be real."

"Bond is real," Darrell whispered.

"I wish his housekeeper had told us more," said Wade. "Why didn't she tell us?"

"And these things in the news?" Lily said. "They can't really be connected to Uncle Henry."

"I can't imagine how they could be," Roald said. "They sound like accidents, tragic, but unrelated." He flipped page after page of his notebook. "The Magister's Legacy. Magister. That sounds slightly familiar." He started pacing as he read. "Heinrich, what are you trying to tell us . . . ?"

Wade knew his father always paced when he was thinking through math problems. This was something else entirely.

"Bring us with you," Becca said suddenly.

Roald turned. "What?"

Lily jumped up. "Yes! Six of us were going to fly to France, but we got airline credit instead. I bet that's more than enough for a bunch of tickets to Germany.

We have our passports already. We should go, Uncle Roald!"

Dr. Kaplan laughed nervously. "No, no, no."

The boys looked at each other. "Dad, we all got passports for Mexico last year," said Darrell. "And you could use some backup. Europe is all about spies, isn't it?"

"Maybe not so much anymore," said Becca.

"No, there are tons of movies," Darrell said. "They call it the—"

"The Cold War," Becca said. "That's over now."

"Or maybe that's what they want you to believe—"

"Kids, really? Spies? Backup? Heinrich was an old man. It might just have been his time to go. What do you think this is all about?"

Wade didn't know what it was all about.

He didn't know anything except that Uncle Henry died right after they got a coded message, and his father wanted to go to Berlin for the funeral of his old friend. Of *their* old friend. Uncle Henry was connected from the beginning with his own deep love of astronomy.

"Maybe we *can* fly there, Dad," he said quietly. "After Atlanta, Sara's going to be unreachable for a week anyway. Uncle Henry told us to find some relics. Well, Europe has tons of relics. Dad, really. I think we should go."

"Wade . . ." His father trailed off, his eyes turning from his notebook to the email message on the table and the coded star chart spread out next to it. "Maybe I can ask my assistant, Joan, to stay for a couple of days to watch over you. You remember her. She's young and fun. Well, youngish. And she has a poodle now—"

Darrell snorted. "Dad, remember last vacation? She ran screaming out of here after only two hours with Wade and me. I think we'd better go with you."

"No one's going to Europe!" Dr. Kaplan said, wiping his eyes again. "We can't."

Lily sidled over and patted his arm with her tablet. "But we could, Uncle Roald. He was your teacher, your friend, and Wade's uncle. We can so do it. According to the airline website the next flight is completely doable. We can totally make it. I've got the credit codes for tickets right here. I just checked, my dad is fine with it. I think we should all pack our chargers and go."

"You already checked with your dad?" Roald said.

Seeing his father's expression beginning to soften, Wade wanted to hug Lily. If Becca had said what Lily just had, he wouldn't have been able to stop himself.

His father stood in the center of the room, his eyes shut, his head tilted up.

Wade knew the look. His father needed quiet while

he worked out the last few elements of a problem. He was brilliant that way. On the other hand, if his father thought like that for too long, he might anticipate the hundreds of reasons not to fly to Berlin with a bunch of kids and remember someone to stay with them while he went alone.

"Dad, I want to go," Wade said.

"Me, too," said Darrell. "I think we should. All of us. As a family."

"Boys . . ." Roald started, then wrapped his arms around them. "All right. Yes. Yes."

"I'll book the flights now and call a cab," said Lily. "Better pack. Only a little over two hours to takeoff!"

CHAPTER EIGHT

Nowotna, Poland
March 9th
10:23 p.m.

Frost was forming over the rutted fields of northern Poland.

Three giant klieg lights cast a brilliant glow on a stone-faced man in a long leather overcoat, making his trim white hair look like the peak of a snow-capped mountain. He stared down at the dirt being excavated shovelful by shovelful from a pit.

"Fifteen days and nothing," said a voice over his shoulder. "The men are exhausted. We should try another location."

The white-haired man half turned, keeping his eyes riveted on the work below. "She told Dr. von Braun the exact spot. She knows these things. Would *you* like to tell her that we gave up?"

The second man shrank back. "No. No. I'm simply saying that perhaps the coordinates are wrong and there's been a mistake."

"Fraulein Krause makes no mistakes."

"And yet fifteen days and still no—"

Clink.

The white-haired man felt his heart stop. The shovelers froze in their places, turning their eyes up to him. He clambered down into the pit, the workers helping him from ledge to ledge. He reached the bottom and shooed them away. Holding a flashlight in one hand, he took a soft brush from the pocket of his coat and cleared away centuries of dirt from the object lodged in the ground. First he revealed a corner. The object was rectangular. This quickened his heart. She had told him: *a bronze casket the size of a Gucci shoebox.* As a man of fine taste, he knew exactly the dimensions she meant. More brushing, more clawing gently at the centuries of caked dirt, and a bronze box revealed itself.

Carefully, he extracted it from the ground.

"Light! More light!"

Two work lights were refocused on the box. With the handle of the brush he cleared the dirt from the rim of the chest's lid. Setting it on level ground, he undid the clasp that held the lid to the body of the chest. He drew in a long breath to calm his thudding heart and lifted the lid for the first time in five centuries.

Inside, amid the tattered remains of its velvet lining, was a leather strap, a sort of belt, half-rotted away as if it were the skin of a corpse. On it, however, and catching the spotlights' beams as exquisitely as it would have on the day it was last seen, sat a large ruby in the shape of a sea creature with a dozen coiling arms.

A kraken.

The white-haired man turned. "You were saying?"

At the same moment a thousand miles south, the same starry sky looked down over the streets of an Italian city packing up for the night. Bologna on a warm March evening was heaven, mused a middle-aged woman at a café table. The street was deserted, save for the shopkeepers and café owners sweeping, turning their chairs over, and lowering their louvered security gates in preparation for tomorrow morning's rush. She sat on a wicker chair, sipped the last drop of espresso from her cup, then set it down in its saucer and picked up her cell phone.

"Answer this time," she said aloud. She pressed the name for the fourth time in the last ten minutes. Holding the phone to her ear, she heard the same message, brief and clipped. After the tone she said, "Call me, Henry. Please. It's about Silvio. I have discovered something about his accident last year. Something he intended me to find after all this time. I need to speak with you as soon as you get this." She ended the call.

Across the piazza, chimes sounded. She glanced up at the six-hundred-year-old tower, then at her phone. The clock, a nineteenth-century addition, wasn't more than a minute off.

Cars were fewer now. She had to get going to her office, a short stroll from the café. Her lecture on Michelangelo's poems was early the next morning, and there were final notes to assemble. Her husband, Silvio, a longtime reader of the artist's poetry, would have loved to be there to listen. Now, she realized, there was only one reason he wouldn't be.

As she reached into her bag for several coins, a black car rumbled up the cobbled street toward the café. It drove across the open square and shrieked to a halt, skidding on the stones. The rear door flew open, and a man wearing an oily black suit leaped out.

Instinctively, the woman screamed. *"Aiuto!* Help!"

From inside the café came the sound of a broom dropping, the quick scrape of chairs. *"Que?* Signora Mercanti?"

The oily man outside wrapped one arm around the woman's face, the other around her waist. She kicked furiously with her heels, knocking over the small table. The man dragged her into the backseat. The car roared away.

When the café owner rushed out three seconds later, all he saw was an overturned table and a small saucer spinning on the pavement.

CHAPTER NINE

Becca Moore nearly screamed, "I'm going to Europe!" when she caught herself and slapped her hands over her mouth. "I'm so sorry!"

"For what?" asked Wade, looking up from his backpack.

The house was in a minor uproar as Wade, Darrell, and Dr. Kaplan rushed from room to room, grabbing clothes, stuffing duffel bags.

"I almost said something dumb," she said. "Go pack."

Becca knew her face was red. She always blushed when she made social mistakes. And even when she didn't. Never mind that she had wanted to go to Europe since forever. Or that before they came to this country her grandparents were their own melting pot of French, German, Scottish, and Spanish. Or that Europe was home to all the cultures she adored. Or that it was the place they actually kept Paris and Rome and Madrid, not to mention Berlin.

She had never really believed that she would get to Europe with Lily, and when the trip was canceled she knew she had jinxed it by not believing it would happen in the first place.

Lily! She sat on the couch next to her, sorting through her own luggage. *What a kind of angel to invite me in the first place. Me! The total opposite of her cool, together, plugged-in self!*

Yet now, mere hours after that disappointment, here they were, going again! Having met Roald Kaplan through Lily's dad, her parents were fine with the change in plans. There was nothing stopping her.

But how thoughtless she nearly was!

A man had died. Dr. Kaplan's old teacher. Wade's sort-of uncle.

"It's okay," said Wade, pausing in his packing to reach his hand toward her arm—which Lily glared at— but not quite making contact. Becca had noticed that about him. He was . . . reachy. But from a distance. She smiled at him, but he'd already looked away.

I have a goofy smile anyway. Which is why I don't use it a lot.

"He's mostly okay," Lily whispered when Wade left the room. "But, you know, he's all mathy and stuff like his dad." She wiggled her fingers in the air over her head then leaned closer. "Darrell, kind of a mystery, no? Bottom line, you and me will have to stick together to stay sane."

Becca laughed. "Deal."

Dr. Kaplan came in to retrieve his notebook. When he saw the girls, he breathed out a kind of sad laugh. "Sorry, not the best reason to go to Europe. You should stuff what you need into a carry-on. We need to travel light. Two days max, and we're home."

"Already done, Uncle Roald," Lily said with a smile.

For Becca it was easy. Three tops, extra jeans, sweater, assorted junk, comb, small bag, book. While everyone ran around gathering last-minute things and setting timers and locking and relocking doors, she watched Wade carefully pack the decoded email and the star chart in the leather folder and slip it into his backpack as calmly as if he were a kind of planet and they were all moons orbiting him.

Beep!

Lily gasped. "Taxi! Here we go!"

The first flight they'd been able to book from Austin-Bergstrom International was United Airways Flight 766, leaving at 12:15 p.m. After a layover in Washington, D.C., to change planes, they were due to arrive in Berlin just before eleven o'clock the next morning, meaning they'd have to rush to be at the Alter St.-Matthäus cemetery on time.

The airport was a madhouse. Becca knew it would be and steeled herself against the noise as best she could. Anywhere crowded made her feel a little crazy and a little edgy. So many people, so many eyes. From the moment they entered the terminal, she didn't think, she didn't listen, she just followed Lily through ticketing and security.

"I've done this a few times," Lily whispered to her as they hustled along. "You see all kinds of people in airports. The best advice I can give? Don't make eye contact."

"I normally don't," Becca said. "Anywhere."

Lily laughed. "I noticed. It's fine. I'll tell you when it's okay to look up. We'll be at the gate soon. You can relax. Gawk at Wade or something."

"Gawk?"

"Kidding!" Lily laughed halfway down the next hallway.

Wade? Was it obvious? NO EYE CONTACT!

CHAPTER TEN

Minutes later they arrived at the gate. Keeping her head low, Becca sat next to Lily, immediately opened her backpack, and slipped out her book. It was a big one, guaranteed to take days. Reading, if it was possible at all, was the best for turning off the noise.

She opened to page 190. Chapter XXXII.

Already we are boldly launched upon the deep; but soon we shall be lost in its unshored, harborless immensities.

Odd line to be reading just now, she thought.

"A little light reading?" said Darrell, from the seat next to her in the waiting area. "Is that a history of the universe or something?"

"No . . ."

Wade tilted his head to read the title. "*Moby-Dick*, by Herman Melville. That's a guy's quest to find a giant whale, isn't it? But then he finds the whale, the ship sinks, and everybody dies?"

"Not everybody," said Becca. "This is my second time through."

"Actually," said Darrell, "my mom once worked with a manuscript by Herman Melville. Dickens too. Well, everybody. After Bolivia, she's flying to New York to talk to Terence Somebody about donating his stuff to the university library. She's the chief archivist in the rare books department."

Becca flicked a glance up at him and smiled. "I know. Your mom is so cool."

Darrell beamed. "I made her my mom, you know. She was just a regular person before I came along."

Wade squinted at him. "You have such a weird take on stuff."

The first boarding call was announced and Dr. Kaplan sat up. "I'm calling Sara again, just to touch base and tell her what we're up to."

It was clear that Wade's father was worried about doing such a huge thing without his wife's input. That was kind of nice. They seemed really close, and Becca figured they must talk about everything. But not this time. The call went to voice mail again. He talked for a bit, asked her at least to text, and closed the phone.

"Mrs. Kaplan will get the message before we get to Washington," she said, "and you can talk to her during the layover."

"Oh, go ahead and call her Sara," Darrell said. "Everybody but me does."

"Thanks," Dr. Kaplan said, smiling just like a dad, she thought. "Do call her Sara. And me Uncle Roald, or just plain Roald. I'll tell you, I will feel better when she knows exactly what we're doing."

Which is . . . going to Europe! she screamed inside.

"Passengers for Flight Seven Sixty-Six to Washington, D.C., and those continuing on to Berlin, we are now boarding group three."

Twenty minutes later, as the plane was taxiing into position for takeoff, Wade and Darrell leaned all over each other—and Lily—to get the best view of the city while they took off. It was the last thing Becca wanted to look at. She didn't mind riding in cars. She kind of liked buses. Trains she really loved. Giant birds made of heavy steel that somehow defied gravity? Not so much.

The engines whined impossibly loudly, and the jet started rolling fast. She gripped the seat handles.

"That's my arm, you know," said Lily.

"Sorry—"

"You get used to it. Settle in. Next stop, Washington!"

Her stomach was feeling somewhere between weightless and sinking as the jet rose. After a few minutes she realized that the noise was there to stay, making talking uncomfortable for anybody but Darrell, who seemed to be keeping Wade from paying attention to anyone else. Fine. Even Lily, who loved to chat, finally gave up and just typed her blog post.

The engines droned for the longest two hours in history before she managed to doze off.

"Finally!" Dr. Kaplan said when the jet touched down at Washington's Reagan airport, where they had to switch planes. As soon as he turned on his phone it buzzed with a missed call. He listened for a minute, pressed a button, spoke several words, then ended the call.

"Because of storms in Atlanta, Sara nearly missed her connection to Bolivia and had to run," he said.

"She's already in the air again and will probably be off the grid until the end of the week at the earliest. So it's just us. Let's use the restrooms, eat, then get some newspapers for the flight. See if we discover any more disasters. Maybe find a link."

Their layover was shortened when the Atlanta storm system threatened D.C. They hurried back to the gate from the food court, stopping quickly at a news kiosk on the way.

Because her grandparents lived in Austin and baby-sat often over the years, Becca had learned several foreign languages early. Her French wasn't great—her German and Spanish were better—but she could read it more or less without a dictionary, so when she saw a copy of *Le Monde*, she bought it. Not that she knew exactly—or even vaguely—what they were looking for. *Tragedies?* The whole world was tragic some days. And here she was going digging for more.

"Final boarding call for Flight Three-Fifty-Four to Berlin."

"We're off!" Dr. Kaplan ushered them into the Jetway. The cabin door closed soon after they took their seats, and the jet taxied out on the slick runway.

"You can hold my arm if you want to," Lily whispered to her.

She laughed. "It's okay. I'm a pro now."

Hardly. Her lungs felt squashed during the long climb to cruising altitude, and her brain pounded like hammers on an anvil.

"Breathe," Lily said. "You'll stay alive better."

"Thanks." They finally leveled out. "Maybe I'm not such a pro."

"Guys, listen to this," Darrell said, a London paper in his lap. "The oil tanker in the Mediterranean near Turkey that we heard about? They know now that it had seventeen people on board. That's pretty tragic."

Then Wade folded his newspaper over and showed it to them. "Is this anything? There was an accident between a truck and a stretch limo outside of Miami. So, the truck driver disappears from the scene but they find him wandering a hundred miles away at almost exactly the same time as the accident."

"It probably wasn't even him driving the truck," said Lily.

Wade shook his head. "There were witnesses at the accident who identified him. Plus, he had the truck keys with him."

"Okay, that's a little freaky," said Lily.

Dr. Kaplan took Wade's newspaper and read the article. "Heinrich was a dear friend, but he retired some years ago. He kept to himself. I hate to say it, but maybe his email might just have been him getting old. You know, it happens. And he passed away, and there's no link between these things at all."

Becca found herself stuck on the words "passed away." They sounded so peaceful and so unlike the coded message. *Devours. Tragedies. Protect. Find.* Besides that, they didn't really know *how* he died, did they? His housekeeper hadn't said a word about that.

She was about to close *Le Monde* when a short news item caught her eye. "It's not huge, but there was a death at the newspaper's office in Paris. A person from the night staff accidentally fell down an open elevator shaft. He was killed."

"Wade, remember this," said Darrell. "I do not want to go like that. No way."

"I'll try to make sure you don't," Wade said.

Roald turned. "One of the five in our little group from twenty years ago works at *Le Monde*. I wonder if he knew the man who died. I haven't talked to him in ages. His name was Bernard Something—"

"Bernard Dufort?" Becca asked.

"Yes! We called him Bernie. Is he quoted—"

Her blood went cold. "Bernard Dufort was the man who fell down the elevator shaft. Police are calling it an accident, but the investigation is continuing."

Something happened to Dr. Kaplan then, Becca thought, and it was different from the other weird news about truck accidents and building collapses. His face grew instantly dark and he seemed to fall inside himself. Was it because the bad news was starting to connect? *Strangely* connect? The email. The death of Heinrich Vogel. The newspaper stories. And now Bernard Dufort.

Darrell leaned to him. "Was Bernie a good friend of yours?"

Roald closed his eyes for a second. "Not really. I mean, a bit. He was just one of us in Heinrich's little Asterias group, you know?"

"Do you think that's what he was talking about?" Wade asked. *"'The kraken devours us. You are the last.'* Maybe this is what he meant. The last of Asterias. Are you in danger?"

"No, Wade, no," his father said firmly. "Of course not."

"But do you keep up with the other people in the group?" asked Darrell. "How do we find out—"

Roald raised a finger, and they all went quiet.

"These newspaper things, I can't really say. Uncle Henry and Bernard, that's a different story. Once we're on the ground there, we'll probably learn what really

73

happened. In the meantime, we'll be fine if we stay together."

"We won't be any trouble, honest," Lily said, glancing at the rest of them with a quick nod of her head.

"Heinrich was a good man," Roald said firmly. "A good human being. Let's pay our respects. And then we'll see what we see. You're right about not being any trouble, Lily. You four are not leaving my sight. Not for a second."

He breathed calmly, smiled at each of them, then slid his student journal from his jacket pocket, pulled his glasses up, and started reading.

The food carts began rattling down the aisle, and Becca leaned back to read *Moby-Dick*. She stopped pages later when the ship's crew neared the environs of the great white whale.

With greedy ears I learned the history of that murderous monster against whom I and all the others had taken our oaths of violence and revenge.

Monster. Moby Dick was a giant whale, a sea monster. As she read the words over, she wondered once again what Uncle Henry meant in his message when he said *kraken.*

CHAPTER ELEVEN

For as long as he could stand it, Ebner von Braun was immersing the thin burned fingers of his left hand in a bowl of ice water that he carried with him.

Ceramic. Venetian. Thirteenth century.

Four very odd years with Galina Krause had taught him something of the arts of ages past. "Use this," she had said, a baffling act of compassion, he'd thought, until she added, "and stop whining about your disgusting fingers."

The elevator stopped. Subbasement Three.

The door slid aside and, as usual, the dull white

ceiling lights of the laboratory made him oddly nause-
ated. The lab smelled of temperature control, clean-room
disinfectant, and fear.

Not to mention the infernal buzzing, a white noise
that Ebner wasn't certain came from the lab or from
him. His ears had begun to ring nearly four years earlier, after one of the Order's experiments. It was now
like a continuous waterfall of ball bearings from a great
height into the center of his head. The sound was always
there. An evil companion. A familiar spirit, as the old
stories of Doctor Faustus termed it.

Like seven similar installations across the globe,
this control room was large and white and completely
devoid of personality. Unless you counted the artfully
unshaven young scientist sitting at a long bank of computers.

Ebner had chosen Helmut Bern from the most brilliant of recent graduates, but while he was certain of
Bern's uncommon talent for digital surveillance and
electronic decryption, Ebner was still unsure about the
darkness of the young man's soul. He watched the slender hands move over the keyboard. Swift, yes. Accurate,
undoubtedly. But how dedicated?

"Sir?" Helmut said, twisting his chair around.

"Is the computer ready?"

"It is, sir." The young scientist tapped a slim silver briefcase on the counter next to him. "It contains everything you requested. Battery life is essentially infinite. No blind spots anywhere across the globe. I'm curious, why did you have me construct such a thing at this particular time?"

Ebner glared. "You're curious? I'm curious. Have you reconstructed Vogel's hard drive?"

Seeming disappointed, the scientist glanced at the ceramic bowl Ebner cradled in the crook of his arm. "Very soon. Sir."

On the neighboring monitor was a live-camera feed of the former Edificio Petrobras in Rio de Janeiro. Construction crews and crime scene investigators swarmed the crumbled gray stone and glass in what Ebner knew would be a futile effort to find the cause of the collapse.

"Vogel's final email?"

"Coded."

"Crack the code."

"By morning."

"Morning?"

"At the latest."

While Ebner might have adored the speed of this conversation in a film, spare questions and clipped commands were *his* thing.

Young Helmut Bern, no matter how brilliant he may have been in his own unshaven way, had no business mimicking his style. It stunk of irony. Only those in command were allowed the privilege of irony. Workers, no matter how little or how much they were paid, were still workers, unwashed masses of common folk, and their duty was to obey him with smarmy respect. Even sniveling was preferable to snarkiness.

Smiling to himself, Ebner drew his hand from the ice bowl, shook his fingers, and set the bowl on the young scientist's desk. Slowly, he took out from his breast pocket a blue leather-bound notebook, turned to the first blank page, and wrote the name "Helmut Bern." Next to it he set down the words "Iceland. Station Four." He added a question mark for good measure and closed the notebook.

"The tanker off the coast of Cypress?"

"Good news," Bern said, clacking his keyboard. The image dissolved into text, and he read from it. "Our divers have already made contact with the hull, and undersea building has begun. Habitation can occur as early as next week. Would you care to examine our current experiment?"

So many experiments. So many missions around the

world undertaken on Galina Krause's specific orders. His ears shrieked.

"The Australian Transit? Yes." Ebner stepped toward the inner laboratory. It was walled in tinted glass to shield the radioactivity of the light beams.

"Excuse me, Doctor . . . ?"

Ebner paused, half turned his head. "Yes?"

"The twelve items. I mean, why now? After all this time."

Ebner wondered if he should say anything. Would it be unguarded to speak? Silence was a kind of power, after all. Miss Krause had taught him that.

But bringing someone into your confidence, that was power, too. He decided, for the moment, to be distant. "Miss Krause recognizes an urgency. There is a singular alignment of causes."

Helmut Bern stroked his unshaven chin. "Do you mean to say there is a timetable?"

I say what I mean to say!

Ebner brushed it off. "Life is a timetable. You should concern yourself with your own." He liked the way that sounded, even if he was unsure exactly what it meant. It had its desired effect nevertheless. Helmut Bern bit his tongue, turned to the screen, and said no more.

Ebner walked through the open door of the inner lab.

The gun—if he could call it that, a ten-foot spoked wheel of platinum alloy in whose center stood a long, narrow cylinder of steel, coiled with a helix of ultrathin glass fiber—occupied one half of the room. In the other sat a cage of white mice, the most intelligent of their experimental patients. Ebner laughed to himself. *Little good will intelligence do them where they're going.*

The elevator door slid aside in the first room. The nameless driver leaned in, spotted Ebner. "Time," he said.

Ebner withdrew from the inner laboratory.

Time. It's always time.

He passed Helmut Bern's desk, dipped his hand into the bowl of lukewarm water, removed it, and shook the drops from his fingers. "I must return this priceless bowl to Miss Krause now," he said, staring down at Bern. "It must be empty."

"Sir?"

"Remove the water," Ebner said as softly as he could.

Bern pushed back his chair. "Sir?"

"Here. Now."

The young unshaven scientist, glancing from the nameless driver at the door to Ebner, lifted the bowl. He brought it to his lips and drank down the water.

"You're welcome," said Ebner.

"Uh . . ." Bern murmured. "Thank you, Dr. von Braun."

Ebner could not help his own lips. They curved into a thin smile. He now wondered whether Iceland was in fact the proper place for Helmut Bern.

Taking the empty bowl and the silver-cased computer, he joined the driver in the elevator, pressed Up, and left.

CHAPTER TWELVE

B erlin was gray. It was cold. It was raining.

When the kids pushed out of the enormous arrival terminal the next morning in search of a taxi, the air hit them heavily with diesel exhaust and cigarette smoke and the odor of strong coffee.

Becca took a shallow breath. "I read that Europe smells like this."

Roald nodded. "It takes me back. I wish we weren't here for this reason."

"One cab left," Wade called out, hurrying with

Darrell to a small car with a short man standing next to it.

No one spoke as the taxi zigzagged out of the airport complex and raced onto the highway toward the city. They passed several clusters of identical high rises surrounded by small parks of bare trees.

"Not too attractive," Lily said.

Roald explained that much of Berlin had been rebuilt after the Second World War with a sense of function rather than style. The sober buildings made Berlin seem that much more cold and sad.

The cab exited the highway and entered rain-slicked streets by the railroad and after that a series of cobblestone roads in what Becca guessed was an older part of the city.

Pulling to an abrupt stop before a tall set of iron gates, they arrived at the cemetery just before eleven thirty. They got out, hoisting their carry-on bags over their shoulders.

Inside the grounds stood a soot-stained church-like building that looked as if it had been there for centuries but which Lily's tablet said was a "mere hundred and fifty years old."

Beyond the chapel, the graves and markers stretched

away into several heavily wooded acres.

Wade pointed across the park. "People are gathering over there." His words were strangely muffled in the cold air. "There's a path."

Many of the gravestones were placed in orderly rows stretching away from the path. Others with faded words and numbers seemed to have grown right out of the ground. Some stones had rain-soaked stuffed animals placed among the wreaths.

Children's graves.

One well-worn trail slithered between the trees like a snake, ending at four tall unadorned stone blocks, two of which were inscribed with names Becca knew well: Jacob Grimm and Wilhelm Grimm, the brothers who had collected folk tales in the middle of the nineteenth century. Lily snapped a picture before hurrying on.

As they crossed the grass and threaded through a stand of tall trees, Becca breathed in a scent of pine needles and tried to steady herself. She felt almost light-headed.

What was it about graveyards?

What was it? She knew exactly what it was.

When her younger sister, Maggie, had fallen ill two years ago, Becca had been terrified of losing her. She cried herself to sleep more nights than she could remember and had begun to dream of places like this—avenues of stone, the murmuring of small voices—and didn't stop dreaming about them until her sister was fully recovered and out of danger. Some of her fear she hid from her parents, who were struggling in their own way with a possible unbearable loss. Maggie was fine now, and yet . . .

Lily touched her on the arm. "There they are."

A small group of mourners clustered under the boughs of several towering beech trees. Nearby stood a sad old mausoleum overgrown with vines. The name carved into the stone over its doors was all but unreadable. A crumbling sundial stood at an angle in front of it. Time. Death. Tombs. Loss.

Melville's words came back to her. *Already we are boldly launched upon the deep; but soon we shall be lost . . .*

Something moved. Beyond the old tomb a handful of men in overalls stood among the trees, groundskeepers, probably waiting for the service to be over. Maggie's face hovered in her mind, but Becca whooshed it away with a rapid shake of her head. *No. She's fine. This funeral is not for her. This is for Heinrich Vogel. An old man. Wade's uncle.*

"I don't recognize anyone here," Dr. Kaplan whispered. "I guess all of his old professor friends are gone now, but I expected . . ." He removed his glasses, wiped his cheeks. "I expected to see another student or two."

Becca patted his arm, remembering the email. *You are the last.*

Roald and the boys advanced. Lily hung back. "I know this isn't right," she whispered, sliding her bag off her shoulder and pulling her phone out. "I mean, I know it's a funeral, but I want to get this."

"Lily, I don't know . . ."

But she took a slow video of the mourners as the priest began.

"Guten Morgen, liebe Freunde . . ."

Becca's grandmother Heidi had taught her a good bit of German, though making out conversations was always tougher than reading. People spoke so quickly and always talked on and on, moving forward, never going back, like you could do if you were reading a book.

We are something, something *here . . . friend . . . scientist . . . teacher . . . his life of* "Gelehrsamkeit" *. . . scholarship . . .*

Becca's mind drifted. Ever since her sister's recovery, she had been drawn to cemeteries, even though they frightened her. Maybe it was a kind of gratitude that she hadn't had to visit her sister in one. But an actual service was sad and she didn't need to be more sad. She rubbed her eyes, realized once more that she hadn't slept for many hours and wondered when they would have a chance to rest.

. . . final rest . . . soul's long journey . . .

No, no. Please don't go there. Blinking her eyelashes apart she gazed beyond the tilted sundial to a tomb with a broken column sticking up from it. Next to that leaned a stone with a weeping angel sitting on top. Loss and grief no matter where she looked . . .

A man appeared at the edge of the wooded path to their left. He walked slowly toward the mourners, then stopped midway, his eyes moving over her and the Kaplans.

Becca turned to see Lily still filming. "That guy over there stopped coming when he saw your camera."

Darrell stepped back to them. "You saw that, too? Here come his friends."

Two other men joined the first. One was a heavyset man with a chiseled face, wearing a slick black suit. The other was pale, smaller, and hunched over like a bent wire. The pale man spoke to the other two, who both stepped behind a tomb at the same time, as if they were connected.

Becca watched the pale man pick his way carefully

over the wet grass to the gravesite and stand close-by. His hands were folded, his head down. During a pause in the priest's words, the man raised his eyes to Becca, then to Roald and Wade, then lowered his face. She felt a weird tingle crawl up her back, as if in that instant he had looked directly through her. His glasses were thick and his posture twisted, although he was not an old man. His left temple bore a nasty V-shaped bruise, stippled with dots. It looked recent.

"Amen . . ."

The priest dribbled holy water on the casket from a small silver vessel, murmured a final blessing, and it was over. The sky seemed to darken at the same moment. The chill rain came down harder.

The crowd dispersed quickly, some to cars, others on foot on the paths and sidewalks toward the exits. Several people hailed taxis on the street. Soon the cemetery was empty except for them, the workers, and the three men by the weeping angel, still eyeing them.

She stepped toward Wade and his father. "Uncle Roald, those guys are watching us." By the time Roald lifted his head, slid his glasses back on, and turned to look, the men had gone.

CHAPTER THIRTEEN

To get out of the rain, Darrell squirrelled himself under the broad lintel of a haunted mausoleum next to the others who, he guessed, were silent because they were wondering what to do next. He was pretty sure what they should do next.

"Ever since we had that bizarro conversation with Uncle Henry's housekeeper on the phone, I keep thinking she's got to know something."

"We'll go to the apartment," Dr. Kaplan said. "But we're checking into a hotel first. We rushed to get here on time, but we can slow down now. We'll clean up, then head over to his place."

"Which brings me to my next point. There's got to be a restaurant in this city, right?" Darrell added. "Germans make good food. Maybe they don't. It doesn't matter. I'll eat whatever. Did anyone like the food on the airplane? Let me rephrase that. Did anyone *eat* the food on the airplane—"

"Darrell, you're doing it again," said Lily.

He stopped talking, but his brain kept going. *I ate it, but it wasn't good and it wasn't enough. No one else is hungry? I'm hungry. . . .*

"Why wasn't Frau Munch here, Dad?" Wade asked. "It's strange, isn't it? She answered his phone. Maybe she even lives there, or at least in his building."

"Everything's strange," Darrell said. "It's Europe."

Roald turned to face the exit, looking as if he were holding his breath to keep himself together. "I'm sure she'll tell us something that will just put an end to the mystery. First, a hotel. Let's go."

Darrell partly agreed with his stepfather—she'll tell us something—but he wasn't sure that the mystery would end soon. It probably wouldn't. A coded email from a friend who was suddenly dead *had* to mean something in the spy capital of the world. Of course it did.

Thanks to Lily's online searching, they found an inexpensive hotel and checked into two rooms, one for Lily and Becca, one for the boys and their father. Darrell wanted to drop his junk off and get right back out on the street—*Strasse*, Becca told him—but sitting on the bed was a mistake. He could almost hear it screaming at him to lie down on it. He sank into the soft mattress, hoping it was as bug-free as it appeared. By the time his eyes opened, it was already midafternoon and everyone else was waking up too.

Lunch in the hotel dining room was something drowned in heavy sauce, but there was a lot of it, so that was good. When they stepped onto the busy *Strasse*, it was nearing dinnertime, the restaurants were lighting up, and he was feeling hungry again, though apparently no one else was.

They found a cab to Uncle Henry's, and at twenty minutes to five they pulled to a stop in front of squat, faceless building on a broad, divided avenue called Unter den Linden.

Roald glanced into his student notebook, checked the building number, and closed the book. "This is it." He paid the driver and they climbed out. A string of sirens two or three blocks away went *eee-ooo-eee-ooo*, like in the movies. Police? Fire trucks? Spies?

No, spies don't use sirens.

A woman bundled against the cold murmured something as she stole quickly around them and up the street. Was *she* a spy? Or just cold. He could see his breath and started stamping his feet.

"Heinrich lived on the third floor," Roald said, stepping up to a wide door set between a pair of waist-high planters with evergreen bushes in them. He pressed the bell. It rang faintly inside. No answer. He rang again. Again, no answer.

"Now what?" asked Lily. "Should we wait for someone to go in and tag along?"

"Or force our way in," Darrell added. "Wade, you and me—"

"You and me what?"

"Hold your horses," Roald said. He knelt down and reached behind the planter to the left of the door, slid his fingers up the side, and stopped halfway. When he drew back, he was holding a key ring with two keys.

"Cool!" said Wade. "Hidden in plain sight. How did you know?"

"Heinrich always left extra keys for late-arriving students."

"Like you?" asked Becca.

"Oh yes. We used to talk long into the night. All of us."

Using one key for the outside door, they entered a deserted lobby barely illuminated by a small ceiling fixture.

"European electricity," Darrell breathed. "From the Dark Ages."

Lily chuckled. "As long as it charges our phones."

They climbed two flights of narrow stairs. The steps creaked, and it was nearly as cold in the stairwell as it was outside, but the building was otherwise quiet. They stopped at apartment 32. Roald raised his hand to knock on the door, then murmured that the apartment was empty. He unlocked it instead, and they entered.

"Hello?" Wade said quietly. "Anyone?"

No sound. The rooms were dark and without heat. Lily found the nearest light switch, and a table lamp came on. The living room looked neat and orderly, as if it had just been cleaned, except for one extremely dusty table by the street window. Becca picked up a silver pitch pipe from it. "Was Heinrich Vogel in a barbershop quartet?"

"No. A modern music group," Dr. Kaplan said. "But then, maybe I didn't know him all that well—"

Clack. Thump. Clack. Thump.

Darrell's heart flew into his throat. "Someone's coming up the stairs!"

Before they could move, the door swung open, and an elderly woman with thin gray hair leaned into the room. She scanned the space from wall to wall as if she didn't see any of them.

"Wer ist da?"

Everyone looked at Becca. "She asked who we are."

"We're friends of Heinrich," Darrell's stepfather said, coming forward with his hand outstretched. "I was his student a long time ago, Roald Kaplan."

"Ah, ah," the woman said, not taking his hand. "I speak at you on ze telephoon. *Amerikaner.* I am Frau Munch."

She hobbled into the room and settled herself familiarly in an overstuffed chair. She raised her head and blinked for some time before speaking. "I see not well. Zis is why I no go to funeral. Zere are *sree* of you?"

Darrell held up a hand with all his fingers outstretched, which she did not look at. "Um . . . five," he said.

"Fife! Ah. Zo. You have question marks?"

"Yes," said Wade, glowering at Darrell's hand, which was still in the air. "Can you tell us how Dr. Vogel died?"

"Wade, perhaps . . . ," his father said.

"No, no. Is fine," Frau Munch said, drawing her eyebrows together in a fierce scowl. "I vas not working two night ago. He vas alone and must have gone out. Ze *Polizei* discovered him on ze *Strasse* behint ze buildink. He vas joked."

"Joked?" said Lily.

"*Ja!*" Frau Munch wrapped her hands around her neck. "Kkkk! Joked!"

"Choked," Lily said softly. Her face was white. So was Becca's.

Wade seemed to be teetering on his feet. "Do you mean he was . . ." He swung around. "Dad . . . Uncle Henry was . . . ?"

"Are you saying he was murdered?" Dr. Kaplan asked.

Darrell felt suddenly weak. He slumped into the chair by the window next to the dusty table with the pitch pipe on it.

"Ze *Polizei* are searching for his killer. Zey believe it is a rubbery gone rong and zat ze killer iz a seef."

Darrell wondered for a second if Frau Munch was using Uncle Henry's code to talk. "Excuse me? A . . . *seef*?"

"*Ja.* You know. Seef. Rubber. Burk-a-ler!"

The words stuttered in his mind, until he finally understood. "Thief, robber, burglar!" he said.

"Zat iz vut I set. Und, like I set, I klean apartment

sree times week. I vas not here two night ago ven he died."

Lily nudged Darrell and whispered in his ear. "For a lady who can't see too well, she sure keeps the place spotless."

It was true. Except for the extremely dusty table next to his chair, the place was immaculate. He peeked under the furniture to see if she vacuumed as well as she dusted.

"Is there anything more you can tell us?" asked Lily.

"No," Frau Munch said. "I em done. You go now."

Dr. Kaplan rose haltingly to his feet, though the old lady didn't. "Well, thank you. Herr Vogel was a dear old friend. I was one of the group of students he called Asterias—"

All at once, Frau Munch stiffened in her chair. "Asterias? Asterias! *Ja, ja!*"

She rose awkwardly from the chair and limped directly toward Darrell, though she didn't appear to see him. She stood squarely in front of the dusty table by his chair, raised a thin hand, and with her fingernail began to spell out words in the dust. It took minutes, as she carefully formed each letter. When she was done, she spun around, holding the pitch pipe in her hand. "Who is moosical here?"

Everyone looked at Darrell. He raised his hand.

No response. She couldn't see him.

Finally he said, "Uh . . . I'm musical. I play the guitar—"

"Zo!" Frau Munch pressed the pitch pipe into Darrell's hand, and breathed out a long breath. "Now, I hef told you vut Heinrich asked me to memorize. I leaf ze rest to you now."

She made her way to the door and down the stairs.

Clack. Thump. Clack. Thump.

They all stared at the dust marks on the table, except Darrell. Something glinted on the floor under the desk, and he got on all fours to examine it. "It looks like Frau Munch doesn't vacuum as well as she dusts. Dad, did Uncle Henry have a starfish paperweight?"

Roald nodded. "As a matter of fact, yes. He said it was what gave him the idea to call us that."

Darrell delicately tugged a V-shaped shard of glass from under the desk. "This looks like one arm of a starfish. It's sticky with something red."

Becca stared at the fragment of glass. "One of the guys at the funeral had a bruise on his forehead that kind of matches that shape. Did anybody else notice that? It was all red and swollen."

"I saw it too," said Wade, studying the piece of glass.

"It was nasty, as if he'd been bashed with something. Dad, is this . . . this isn't blood, is it?"

Dr. Kaplan examined it under the lamp. "It could be . . ."

"Oh . . ." Darrell wiped his fingers on his pants.

"Hold on, now. Blood?" Lily moved closer to Becca. "What exactly are we saying here?"

Wade took the shard back from his father. He held it gingerly between his fingers and looked at Darrell. "I guess we're saying that maybe Uncle Henry slammed that guy with this paperweight and that's how it broke."

He seemed to be searching for more words when Roald let out a long breath, shaking his head slowly.

Scanning the darkening room as if looking for another clue, he said, "If . . . *if* this paperweight has blood on it, and if the blood belongs to the man at the cemetery, it means that the police are wrong. Uncle Henry wasn't killed on the street. It may mean that the man at the cemetery killed Uncle Henry. And he may have done it right here."

CHAPTER FOURTEEN

Wade stared at the bloody glass and his head buzzed.

Murder. In this room.

"If this was not a robbery . . ."

"If this was *not* a robbery . . ." Dr. Kaplan swung around to Lily. "Bernard Dufort's fall in the elevator in Paris. Are the police still saying it's an accident? Can you look it up? Becca, can you translate?"

"Instantly," Lily said, tapping her tablet. Becca stood next to her.

Wade leaned over the dusty table at an angle. The

first line was in Greek, not a single word of which he understood, but he knew what it looked like from his astronomy books.

ἀγεωμέτρητος μηδεὶς εἰσίτω

This was followed by two lines in code.

Lca Ayulc himab ds lca Cyzb ir Gzjrauhyss
Rixxio lca nsihis, rixxio lca wxyea

He recognized the first word of the coded part as *The*. "Dad, Becca," he said, digging in his backpack for the celestial map. "Do either of you know any Greek?"

She shook her head. "Baklava and spanakopita. That's all."

Roald snapped to attention. "I only know one line of Greek. Heinrich taught it to me. To all of us in the group. It was a famous quote from . . . wait . . ."

He pulled out his student notebook and went directly to the end. He read the words on the table. "I can't believe it . . . or maybe I can. This is it. I wrote the quote in here. Heinrich began his semester lectures with it. It means, 'Let no one untrained in geometry enter here.'

But it's also . . ." He closed his eyes. "I'll remember it in a minute—"

Becca looked up from Lily's tablet, her face pale. "Paris police no longer think Bernard Dufort's death was an accident. There was a fire in his apartment in Paris, and the elevator cables at the newspaper office may have been tampered with."

Wade felt his breath leave him. Uncle Henry was murdered in this room. Maybe the man at the cemetery did it. And now, a second murder? "Dad, we should talk to the police. The paperweight is evidence they don't know about. It'll help them catch the killer—"

The traffic grew suddenly chaotic on the street below. Horns blared. There was shouting, a screech of tires. Becca went to the window. Wade peeked out through the curtains next to her. A long black limousine had stopped awkwardly in front of the building and traffic was backing up behind them. Four men emerged from the back.

"The guy with the bruise!" said Becca. "We need to get out!"

"Someone memorize the message," said Darrell.

"I have a better idea," said Lily. She stood over the table and snapped a picture with her phone. *"Now* let's go!"

"Hurry!" Dr. Kaplan tugged Lily and Darrell to the door.

Everyone dashed out of the room except Wade. He took one last look at the writing on the table, then ran his sleeve across the top. Frau Munch's coded message, whatever it meant, existed now only as a photo on Lily's cell phone.

"Get over here!" Becca hissed from the top of the stairs.

He jumped down the steps after her and found Frau Munch standing guard in the lobby and pointing to the back door as if she could see it. The front door thudded. It burst open. Wade flattened against the wall and watched several thick-necked men push across the tiny lobby and straight up the stairs.

Did they follow us from the cemetery—

Becca pulled him roughly out the back door and into the alley. The sun was setting, and the cold night air closed in. She hurried him into a long passage of black brick. He stole a look over his shoulder. No one yet. They came out a block behind Unter den Linden. Taking a quick right, Dr. Kaplan hustled them into a crowd of young people bubbling with conversation. They mingled as far as the next street, then turned at the corner of an avenue of high-end shops, Charlottenstrasse, where

Lily made a noise that sounded like a squeal.

"Are you all right?" asked Darrell.

"Just . . . the . . . shops . . ."

A sudden series of screeching tires made them jump, and they ducked under the arched opening of a restaurant. Dr. Kaplan froze when he looked inside at the tables.

"Dad, what do you see? Dad!" said Wade. "Is someone—"

"It's not that," he said. "It's just that . . ." He scanned the streets in every direction. "A lot has changed, but I think the Blue Star is not too far from here, if it still exists. I need time to sit and figure this whole thing out—"

A motorcycle raced down the street, zigzagging among the pedestrians. The kids turned their faces toward the windows.

"It's still there, I found it!" said Lily, holding up her tablet. Roald nodded at the picture. "We can walk to the Blue Star in about half an hour. Down Charlottenstrasse . . . a right, two short lefts, straight . . ."

Pulling themselves together, the kids and Dr. Kaplan made their way from street to street. It was nearing 6 p.m., and Berlin's early nightlife was already a glittering mass of crowds and smoke and music and traffic.

"Maybe we should stay off the big streets," Wade said.

"Good idea," Darrell added.

Roald quickly reworked Lily's internet directions to keep them off the main routes as long as possible, though even the narrower side streets were packed with pedestrians. They skirted across several well-lit open parks, then through a modern department store that reminded Wade of an airport mall, brimming with customers even at night.

"There's been so much building since I was here," Roald said, glancing right and left to get his bearings. "I hope the place is open when we get there . . ."

Thirty-three breathless minutes after they started, they found themselves crouching under the bare trees of Lützowstrasse, staring across the street.

Buried in the shadow of its larger neighbors, its windows steamed over and dim, stood the Blue Star, forlorn, in bad repair, possibly harboring a dangerous clientele. But an amber glow from inside signaled that it was open for business.

"Hard to believe it's still alive," Dr. Kaplan said as they made their way warily down the sidewalk. "It was gasping for life twenty years ago. We helped Herr Hempel mop the floor and stack chairs at the end of the night. Or early in the morning. We talked forever . . ."

Two motorcycles snaked by close and fast.

"Spies," Darrell grumbled, huddling into his collar. "Spies everywhere."

Wade herded them forward. "Let's get off the streets. Now."

Looking both ways, Roald pushed them straight through the heavy doors and into the depths of the tavern.

CHAPTER FIFTEEN

" *Willkommen in den Blauen Stern!*"

Wade liked the look of Christina Hempel from the instant she flashed her cheery smile and repeated her welcome in fairly articulate English.

She was a woman in late middle age with big red hair and big everything else. When Dr. Kaplan explained how as a student of Uncle Henry's he had known her father, she grew more animated, giving them a table by the window with a view of the street in both directions.

"Heinrich Vogel's favorite table. He still comes once a year to commemorate his wife's birthday," she said.

"Alas, Frieda passed away several years ago now."

Roald's expression fell. "I'm so sorry to be the one to tell you. Heinrich also passed away. Just two days ago."

Frau Hempel put her hands to her face. Tears rose instantly to her eyes. "Oh no. Father loved him so. How?"

Wade's blood ran cold when he thought of *how*. "We're still finding out," he managed to say. "But I didn't know Uncle Henry was married. Dad, did you?"

His father seemed to retreat into himself for a moment. "No. I mean, yes, but I never met her. He married later in life."

Frau Hempel wiped her cheeks. "Oh dear. This is too sad. Yes, Frieda Kupfermann was her name. She passed some years ago. And now him. So sad." She left menus on the table and disappeared behind the counter.

Wade sat quietly, looking out at the street and saying nothing, though he couldn't stop his thoughts from circling his uncle's death.

Death? It's not regular death. It's murder.

No one else said anything either until Lily opened her cell phone. "I'm emailing the photo I took of the table in the apartment to my tablet, so we can see it bigger."

Wade unfolded the celestial chart on the table. "The

first word of the dusty message is 'the,' so I'm pretty sure the code number is still four."

"Here, use this," his father said, handing him his student notebook. "I wrote down the decryption alphabet on the plane. We should be keeping all the information we find in one place."

"Good idea." Slipping a mechanical pencil from his backpack, Wade studied the computer photo, noodled around on a blank page of the notebook, and decoded the first line of Frau Munch's message.

Lca Ayulc himab ds lca Cyzb ir Gzjrauhyss

. . . became . . .

The Earth moves in the Haus of Kupfermann

"Kupfermann?" said Lily. "As in Frieda Kupfermann, Heinrich's wife? I wonder what *that* means."

"*Haus* is 'house,'" added Becca. "Could Uncle Henry want us to go to his wife's family's house?"

Wade liked how Becca called *his* uncle *her* uncle. "Maybe that's it. But 'the Earth moves'? What do you think, Dad?"

His father surfaced from his thoughts. "It might be

108

that. I'm not sure. *Haus* is a term that in German can mean any number of things."

"A shop, for instance," said Lily. "Like *Alsterhaus* and *Carsch Haus*. Those are German stores I read about."

"Or a hotel," Roald went on. "There are also twelve 'houses' in astrology. I'm sure Heinrich knew them, even though they were not by any means scientific and none of them are named Kupfermann. I'll ask Frau Hempel what she knows. Keep working." He left the table.

Wade decoded the second line more quickly.

Rixxio lca nsihis, rixxio lca wxyea

. . . became . . .

Follow the gnomon, follow the blade

"*Gnomon*?" said Darrell. "*Gnomon*'s not a word. Do it again."

Wade did. Twice. "It still spells *gnomon*." It was not a word he or anyone else knew. He wondered about the old saying that two heads are better than one to figure out a problem. Sometimes it probably worked pretty well. But four different heads all chattering about a bunch of dusty words made his own head feel like imploding.

"I can look it up," said Lily.

"No, keep the code on the screen. I'll try again." Wade started decoding again when his father returned to the table.

"Frieda Kupfermann was the last one in her family," he said. "Their real estate was sold years ago, and there's no longer any Kupfermann house in Berlin. She did say that Heinrich always joked that Frieda's name amused him. *Frieda*? I don't get it. I suppose we could try decoding it, but our hostess didn't know any more than that."

"It still says, 'Follow the gnomon,'" said Wade.

"Gnomon?" said Dr. Kaplan, pushing his glasses up and leaning over Wade's translation. "It says 'gnomon'?"

"I told him he did it wrong," Darrell said.

"Is it a real thing?" asked Lily.

"Absolutely. The gnomon is what you call the blade of a sundial. It's what casts the shadow that points to the time—"

"Sundial?" Becca practically exploded. "Are you kidding me? There was a sundial at the cemetery! Didn't you all see it? At that old tomb near the service. It had vines all over it and there was a sundial in front—Lily, you must have gotten it on your video."

Lily sent the video from her phone to her tablet. When it came up on the screen, she froze the image of the tomb.

The crumbling sundial stood leaning in front of the old mausoleum, and because of its sunken angle, its blade pointed directly into it. Over the heavy-looking iron doors on the face of the tomb was its occupant's name, carved in elaborate old Gothic letters. Several of the letters were in shadow, and some had worn away. It took them a long moment to decipher the carving, until Lily enlarged the image and they all realized at once.

K . . . u . . . p . . .

The name on the tomb was Kupfermann.

Wade blew out a cold breath. "The house of Kupfermann is his wife's tomb. Is that it? He wants us to go back there? He wants us to follow the way the blade of the sundial is pointing? Why? What's in there?"

All eyes turned to Dr. Kaplan. He stared at the translated message, then stood up. He walked across the room, walked partway back, then turned again.

"Dad?" Darrell said.

His stepfather flicked his finger up as if to say, "Hush!" and closed his eyes. A full minute went by before he released a long, slow breath. Then he sat and flipped over several pages in his notebook, searching. He stopped. "My German isn't as good as yours, Becca. I know *Mann* means 'man.' What does *Kupfer* mean?"

Becca stared blankly at him. "Um . . ."

"Copper," said Lily. When everyone turned to her, she said, "What? There's a translation site."

"Copper man?" Darrell said. "Is that more code?"

Looking from the star chart to Wade's decoded message to the lights of cars zipping past outside the restaurant, Roald flipped three more pages in the notebook, stopped, stood up, and began rocking on his feet.

"Kupfermann. Copper Man. That was the joke of Frieda's name."

Wade could practically hear the gears meshing one after the other until his father finally spoke. He said one word.

"Copernicus."

Darrell frowned. "Uh . . ."

"It's where the Greek quote comes from," Roald said, looking at a page in his notebook. "Heinrich wanted us to remember it because the quote also appears at the beginning of *On the Revolutions of Heavenly Spheres*, the treatise by Nicolaus Copernicus that describes how *the earth moves* around the sun.

"In the first message, Uncle Henry says 'the Magister's

112

Legacy.' Copernicus's students called him Magister. Heinrich is saying that Copernicus's legacy—whatever it is—needs protecting. I have no idea what it could be, but the gnomon of the sundial at his wife's tomb is pointing toward it—"

The bell rang over the doorway, and two stone-faced men entered. They didn't look like students. They wore dark suits and had obvious bulges near their armpits. They sat down on the other side of the doorway with a clear view of the darkening street.

One of the men started pawing his cell phone while the other glanced at a menu.

Or pretended to.

CHAPTER SIXTEEN

Darrell's heart thumped like a Fender bass laying down a funk riff. If they were right, Heinrich Vogel had been murdered by the goons from the cemetery. By natural extension, if the two guys at the other table had managed to tail them from Vogel's apartment, they must be killers too.

He knew all too well from movies how things went from here.

The men would follow them into the street. They'd corner them in a filthy alleyway. They'd wait until no one was watching, pull out automatic weapons with silencers, utter a couple of German words, and—*thit-thit!*—end of story.

"Those guys are killers," he whispered. "We need to pay our bill and get out of here. Far out of here. Like home. Or Hawaii. I vote for Hawaii." Both stone men were staring at him now. "Oh man . . ."

"What are we going to do?" Becca asked, her head bent low.

A young man carrying a tray with four giant water jugs on it suddenly appeared at their table with Frau Hempel, who whispered cheerily at the kids, "Gather your things. I think you had better come with me."

"Is there a back way?" asked Lily. "The last place we escaped from had a back way."

"There's a way," said Frau Hempel, "but it's not in the back."

The moment they threw their bags over their shoulders and got up from the table, the two men pushed their chairs back and stood. In a move that baffled Darrell even as he saw it happen, the waiter with the water jugs jerked awkwardly between the tables. Then his feet twisted, the tray tipped, and the four glass jugs crashed onto the men's table and exploded.

One of the men screamed like a lady, while the other tried to follow the kids but slipped in the water and fell. Then the waiter flailed and slipped, dragging the screamer into the pile. Frau Hempel tugged the Kaplans into the room behind the counter and shut the door firmly.

"Kurt is training to be a clown," she said. "He thanks you for the opportunity to try his act. This way."

They dashed through another door and down a narrow set of steps into the cellar of the cafe. It was ancient, half carved out of rough stone, half finished off in diamond-shaped oak shelves holding hundreds of wine bottles.

"Quickly now, and hush," she whispered, putting her finger to her lips. They followed her to the end of the wine shelves and turned a corner into a small alcove. Tugging a lever on the topmost shelf, she stood back as the shelving sprang out about twelve inches.

She clicked a light switch, revealing a passageway leading steeply under the tavern. Strung along the ceiling of the passage was an electrical cord, dipping every few feet to a bare lightbulb. The bulbs cast only enough light to see that the passage went on and on.

"These tunnels were built by East Berliners trying to escape under the Wall to the West," Frau Hempel said. "They are cold and wet and nasty. But they are seldom traveled now. That's why there are so many rats. They have made their own metropolis under Berlin. A rat city."

Wade shivered. "An underground city of rats. Wonderful."

She laughed. "But these tunnels will get you out of here faster than any other way." From upstairs there came the sound of shouting and wood cracking.

"Thank Kurt for us," said Wade, moving into the passage.

"We owe him," Becca added. "And you."

Frau Hempel smiled. "Kurt's also a wrestler, so he'll be fine. Now, take the passages, making right turns when you have the opportunity, and you will come up near . . . well, you'll see. You will be miles from here and safe. Good luck. Be careful. Now go!"

Dr. Kaplan hugged her. "You've saved us."

As they followed the dim light, hurrying down the tight passage into the first turn, Darrell really hoped that they wouldn't lose themselves, wandering forever and ever in the unending darkness . . . of an underground city . . . of rats.

BEWARE
OF
MONKEYS

CHAPTER SEVENTEEN

An underground city of rats.

As Lily hustled forward in the dark with no clear view of the way ahead because they were all taller than her, she knew—she *knew*—that those creepy little fur balls were just waiting to sink their needle teeth into her slim pink ankles.

Rats were all she could think about. They took over her mind like spies had taken over Darrell's. Rats and spies. And murder. Murdering rat spies. Why not? This was hardly Texas.

The tunnel got narrower still. And smellier. She

growled so softly she was sure no one heard her.

Why isn't anyone talking? Hello! Aren't you as scared as I am? Actually, I doubt that. I can do scared like nobody else.

"We're going back to the cemetery now, right?" she mumbled. "After we get out of here? We're going to find a cab or something and go back to the tomb?"

"Right," Darrell said over his shoulder. "The blade of the sundial points to something inside."

"Maybe the Magister's Legacy," Wade said. "Or the relics. It all goes back to Copernicus and how the earth moves."

Everyone is so smart. Like they have libraries for brains. Get me aboveground where I can get some Wi-Fi, and I'll show you smart.

"Let's get there ASAP. Even a cemetery in the rain is better than being underground with an army of giant rats . . ."

"Who said anything about *giant* rats?" Wade said.

"Any rat is a giant rat, as far as I'm concerned—"

"Kids . . ." Roald huffed, slowing his steps. "The lightbulbs end up ahead. We'll have to hold hands to not get lost."

"Or maybe Lily could just hum," Darrell said. "Since she's at the back, we'll always know we're together—"

"Hey," Lily snapped. "I could lead, you know."

"I'm just saying I'm not real sure about the holding hands thing," Darrell said. "So many questions. Whose hand will I hold? Which hand? How tight? Plus holding hands makes me think of skeleton bones. I don't want to touch bones . . ."

"You," said Lily, "are weird—"

"I hear something," said Wade. "Listen . . ."

There was the noise of traffic above them. Cars, the rumbling of streetcars and trucks, the zipping of motor scooters. Then a sound from far behind. Footsteps?

"Keep going," said Becca. "Lil, take my hand."

They hurried on as best they could. Every so often, the ceiling soared and they saw levels of girders beneath the streets, the half-finished excavation of subway tunnels, maybe, and odd circles of light that Lily couldn't keep from saying looked like solar eclipses, which she thought sounded smart, until Wade explained they were merely rings of street light around manhole covers. Fine. Manholes. Tunnels. Cemeteries. Rats. Murder. Whatever.

If I survive tonight, this is all going into my blog.

Roald slowed and faced them. "A stairway," he whispered as he pointed to a narrow set of iron steps, nearly as steep as a ladder, clinging to the wall. "It must go up to street level."

"The street is good. That's where they keep the air," Lily said, aware how lame the joke was but not caring. *Just get me out of here!*

Becca nudged her. "I'm so going to gulp it in."

"I'll check it out," said Dr. Kaplan.

"Me, too." Darrell grinned at Wade. "You stay."

"Why me?" Wade asked.

"I'll wait," said Becca, breathing shallowly.

"I will, too," said Wade.

"I'm not staying down here a minute more than I have to," Lily said. "Sorry, Bec. I'm going up."

Darrell and his stepfather took the stairs up slowly in single file, and she followed, stepping as softly as she could. She couldn't look down. At the top stood the doorway of a small room built of cement blocks. A plank door stood at the end of it, ringed with faint light.

Roald knocked on the door. Nothing. Then he turned the knob. "Locked solid." He glanced back down the steps. "There might be another exit later on down the tunnel."

"No," said Lily. "Please, we're not going back down here. Isn't there something—"

Darrell suddenly kicked the door hard with his foot. The knob fell to the floor with a clank, and the frame cracked. "Like that?"

"Darrell," Roald groaned. "My gosh, your foot!"

"It's fine," Darrell said, pretending to limp across the small room but grinning all the same.

Lily grinned back, pushing lightly against the door. It opened a sliver. A heavy, warm farmyard stink rushed through. She peeked around the door. "Oh . . ."

"Oh?" said Darrell.

She nodded. "Oh, as in, 'Oh, we're at the zoo.'"

"No way." Darrell pushed the door wide. Before them stood a long, wide corridor, dimly lit and lined with vertical bars on both sides. Cages. There was little movement from inside the cages. At the opposite end of the corridor stood another door. A chatter of voices was coming from behind it, mixed with the occasional sound of a car or scooter motor.

"This could be our way to freedom," Darrell whispered. "As long as we don't wake up the animals—"

The steps creaked as Becca and Wade crept to the top.

"More footsteps in the tunnel," Becca said. "I guess Kurt couldn't hold those guys off forever. We need to get out. Now."

Without a choice, they entered the caged corridor as quietly as they could. Wade tried to close the door firmly behind them, but thanks to Darrell, the knob was gone.

It took a single step for them to realize that they were in some species of ape house. There were enormous hairy gorillas curled in lumps and sleeping under pale pink light, while smaller chimps and spider monkeys scurried up and down fake trees or lolled on mounds of artificial grass.

Dr. Kaplan raised a finger to his lips and eased forward to the far door. Darrell crouched behind him, followed by Lily, with Becca and Wade behind her. For once, thought Lily, she wasn't the last one.

Halfway to the door and breathing through her mouth, she remembered why she hadn't been in a zoo for years and realized she didn't miss it.

Just then, a motor scooter zipped by outside, beeping. A monkey shrieked in response, jumping up and down. Before they could get all the way down the corridor, the hall erupted with screeching, and things were suddenly flying through the air.

"They're throwing poops!" Lily shrieked. "Get out of here!"

They plowed full speed into the far door and burst through it, butting their way through a squad of zoo guards who had converged on the ape house.

"Hey!" the guards yelled. *"Halten Sie! Es ist verboten!"*

"We're sorry!" Dr. Kaplan called out as they ran.

"No need for a refund—thanks!" Wade added.

A guard blew a shrill whistle and alarms went off in three locations as they raced down the paved paths to the nearest exit. Just as the perimeter lights began flashing, Roald helped them over the fence and dragged them down the sidewalk. He whistled at the first cab that came down the street. It shrieked to a stop. "Get in! Hurry!" he cried.

"St. Matthew's cemetery," Becca said as they jumped in.

"Alter St.-Matthäus-Kirchhof!" Lily added in what she felt was a pretty decent accent, until the driver replied, "Certainly, Miss."

The cab took off as a half dozen zoo security carts jerked to a stop on the sidewalk and more alarms rang. Guards swung their fists and shouted after them, but they were already spinning around the corner.

They had made it.

CHAPTER EIGHTEEN

Sitting on the padded seat in a warm cab was heaven after what Lily was already calling "the rat and monkey–poop adventure." She wanted to enjoy the warmth, but as usual, the others were brainily rushing ahead of her, connecting dots, making guesses, whatever.

"So, Dad. Copernicus," said Wade. "Sixteenth century. Tell us everything you know about him."

"Yeah, and don't skimp on the legacy and the twelve relics part," Darrell added, nudging Roald while nodding at the taxi driver. "And you should probably whisper."

"Is the Copernicus Legacy even a historical thing?" asked Becca. "I mean, I know we're being followed, so there has to be something, but now that we know it's Copernicus, does the first message mean more? The kraken and the relics?"

"Hold on," Roald said, obviously trying to pull himself together. He slipped his notebook from his pocket and held it up to the passing street lights. "Good thing I kept this. Heinrich's course in the history of astronomy was my first of many with him. He covered it all. Here it is. Copernicus," he breathed. "Copernicus . . ."

For the next seven minutes, as the cab roared from street to street in the dead of night, they listened to what he knew.

"He was a mathematician, born in 1473, in Toruń, Poland. There are blanks in what we know about him, what kind of person he was. Mostly we have public documents. He did most of his calculations on the movement of the stars and planets based on his knowledge of mathematics, and on unaided observation. The telescope hadn't been invented yet."

"That was Galileo, right?"

"Good memory, Wade. Yes. Sixty or so years after Copernicus. There were instruments, of course. Astrolabes and sextants and compasses used by sailors to plot the movement of stars, and Copernicus knew all about those, I'm sure.

"The key thing he discovered was that Earth moves around the sun. Before he figured that out, everyone believed that Earth was the center of the universe, and that all the planets, the sun, the stars, everything, revolved around it. Copernicus proved, through math and simple observation, that it couldn't be so."

"The Earth moves in the Haus of Kupfermann," Becca said.

"Exactly." Roald flipped over a page, then another. "Earth really *had* to orbit the sun for any of the numbers to make sense. It was the only way to explain the movement of the stars and other planets."

Lily's heart was still *ka-thump*ing too hard from their ape encounter to make complete sense of it all. She knew about Copernicus. That was basic astronomy. Before Copernicus, astronomy was a kind of cult science, right? Astrology. Alchemy. Almost a kind of magic. She'd heard of all that in school. Copernicus was a big deal because he finally said that we weren't the center of the universe. Which must have bothered a lot of people.

"Copernicus was one of the truly modern thinkers," Roald was saying. "His students called him Magister—

Master—and we call him a revolutionary for a good reason. Nothing was quite the same after people really understood what he had discovered. That Earth is just one of many planets. Not that special."

Becca had been looking out at the wet streets when she turned to them. "Didn't he only publish his discovery just before he died? Isn't that part of his story? That he was worried what people would say?"

That sounded really familiar. Lily turned on her tablet.

"That's true," Roald said as the taxi entered a patch of slow traffic. "He was troubled about the effect on society of his revolutionary discovery. The Catholic Church was very powerful, and he was a canon, a kind of church teacher. He was finally convinced on his deathbed by a young astronomer to publish his work. I forget his name—"

"Rheticus," said Lily, holding up her tablet so that everyone could see. "He showed up near the end of Copernicus's life and—" Without a warning, the screen went black. "Hey!"

The cab driver braked the car abruptly, nearly sending Wade into Becca's lap, as a large silver SUV roared past them at high speed.

"My apollo cheese!" the driver said. "Some pipples is

128

rude and do not sink of uzzer pipples!" After the silver SUV sped by, a second black one, then a third, shot after it as if they were part of a caravan. They tore around the corner and disappeared.

Lily stared aghast at her blank computer screen. "Please don't die on me now." She swiped her fingers across the glass.

Just as the driver pulled back onto the street, the screen blinked twice and glowed as before.

"And we're back!"

CHAPTER NINETEEN

Nestled in the plush backseat of her powerful silver SUV, Galina Krause fixed her eyes on the computer image of a man in a canoe on a river in the jungles of Brazil.

The canoe was in one piece. The man was not.

"Fool!" The driver with no name screamed to the taxicab he had just forced off the street. "Idiot—"

"Silence," she said. "Continue to Unter den Linden."

Ebner von Braun glanced at Galina as she studied the computer screen with her gray and blue eyes. He wondered what his illustrious grand-uncle would have thought about him. A theoretical physicist of such brilliance having gone over to—what did they call it?—the dark side?

He probably would have scolded me, Ebner thought, *and rapped his gold-tipped baton across my knuckles. At which point, I imagine, his eyes would have twinkled as he offered me a glass of cognac.*

"To power!" he would have toasted.

Perhaps, someday, we shall toast together . . .

Pushing back the dark hair from her cheek, Galina cooed into her cell phone. "You have been careless, Mr. Cassa. I will give you twelve hours to settle your affairs in Rio and bid farewell to your family. By"—she paused to check the computer time—"six a.m. your time you will be dead." She ended the call smoothly, turned to Ebner, and said, "Make it so."

He bowed his head, and his words—"Of course, Miss Krause"—sent a wave of nausea into his throat. Ebner had something to tell her that she would not enjoy hearing. It wasn't good news, and he was hesitant even to bring it up. Yet when she found out later on her own—and she always found out—he would be in more than one piece himself. He was suddenly aware that her eyes were no longer on the computer screen. They were on him.

"Well," she said, "spit it out."

Ebner cleared his throat. "The elevator incident in Paris was a necessity, I'm afraid. The victim, a minor sort of man, was not merely a writer at the newspaper, but an inseparable part of the secret organization Vogel had built. *Le Monde* had hired the man seventeen years ago. His name was Bernard—"

"Spare me his name," Galina snapped. "How did their system work? Was there a failsafe? A backup?"

Ebner went on. "We believe that the simplicity of their method was responsible for its success. There was a system of rotating keepers of the secret. One led to another and another and another and finally to the Frenchman. A brief message was sent from Vogel on the evening of the second Monday of every month. Ber . . . this man in Paris published each coded message in print and online in *Le Monde* editions throughout the world. This was how the various members of the organization were notified."

"The message?" she asked.

"Simple. The letters RIP. In English, Rest in Peace," Ebner said. "The letters would be positioned in the puzzle according to a series of ever-changing number tricks based on the number twelve."

She breathed in sharply. "Twelve. Of course. Vogel

was informing the others that the legacy *rests in piece*. Because we must assume that his death launched the Protocol, this is now no longer true."

Ebner shuddered slightly. The word *Protocol* was a terrifying piece of terminology. As he understood it, it meant that the twelve relics, no matter where they were across the globe, were destined for their final, irreversible journey.

"No other communication seems to have been made among the participants. To increase security, most members are unaware of one another. Only Vogel, as their communications chief, knew all of the . . . the Guardians."

"The Guardians," Galina repeated softly. "And the man in Paris gave resistance?"

"Naturally, at first," said Ebner. "We had to convince him to speak. He told us about Vogel not on the threat of his own death, but on that of his family. He said it was a miracle we found him. It was. But miracles end like everything else. He told us what we needed to know. Then he died. Tragically."

"And the Paris police? The newspaper?"

This was it. The big messy problem. Two of their agents in Paris had been slipshod. Because it was a death of a journalist, one of Dufort's colleagues was

133

now burrowing deep into the tragedy. So far, he had discovered only a small fragment of evidence, but it was enough. "A cover-up will be possible, of course, but it will cost money," he said. "I have wired the Banque Nationale—"

Galina moved her head slightly. Her eyes bore into him. "I will go to the top, the director-general of the *sûreté*. In the meantime, discipline the Paris agents. Permanently."

"As you wish, Miss Krause."

"You hesitate?"

Ebner sucked in a cold breath. "It is only that too many bodies are not invisible. Neither are collapsed buildings or sinking ships."

"Time is against us."

"Which is why we are working already on several fronts to achieve the Order's ultimate goal. The experiments, the laboratories, as well as this search for the twelve—"

"You are not saying the challenge is too great for you, Ebner von Braun?"

"Galina, please. Not at all. Only that we are doing everything we can while maintaining secrecy. We must remain an Order of ghosts, after all." He was suddenly aware that his choice of words could have unfortunate connotations. "An invisible presence, I mean."

She lowered her magnificent eyes to his chest. "Discretion, then," she said. Then she turned her face to the window. The rain had changed over to thick wet snow somewhere on their drive. "This family who visited the tomb? Who are they? What do they know? Could Vogel have shared the secret with them?"

"A man and his brood of children? I doubt it," Ebner said. "But we are running their identities through our databases even now." Ebner flexed his bandaged fingers. "If anything turns up on Vogel's hard drive, we shall know by morning."

"By . . . *morning*?"

"Before morning," Ebner said. "Much sooner than morning." *Note*, he thought, *Helmut Bern at Station Two must quicken his reconstruction of the hard drive.*

"And the old man's apartment was cleared of evidence?"

"Every stitch," said Ebner. "We left it exactly as his housekeeper normally does." *Or had they?* He had not been there to supervise the work personally, always a risk. That was ever the problem faced by a global organization with—what had he called it?—a singular alignment of causes.

Galina narrowed her gaze at Ebner. He glanced away,

couldn't look directly into those eyes. They were stronger than a death ray. And he should know about death rays. Those experiments had been completed at Station Three in Mumbai just last month.

"And if you are wrong . . ." she started.

"I know," said Ebner, swallowing hard. "My own elevator accident."

CHAPTER TWENTY

As Wade stepped to the cemetery gates a hand touched his arm.

"Wait here," his father whispered. "I'll find a way inside."

Yeah, inside the park of death!

He watched his father trot down the sidewalk. He knew his dad had run track in college, and he admired all the trophies in his study at home, but now he wished the man weren't so quick. In seconds he was around the corner and gone, and Wade felt strangely abandoned. It being the dark of night, frigid, and now snowing didn't help either.

It also occurred to him that his father, being an adult, was taking a far bigger risk than he and Darrell and the others. Running from men in cars, rushing through foreign streets, fleeing in underground passages! The kids might be thought of as just fooling around, being carefree tourists. But not his dad. What did it mean that he was doing this?

That this is life-and-death stuff.

The gates appeared so much taller at night than they had that morning. And the gnarly spikes at the top seemed left over from a medieval weapon factory.

Maybe because they were far from home, it was night, the snow was wet, or the lights from passing cars floated like ghosts through the trees, but the dark graveyard seemed suddenly haunted.

"Someone's probably following us right now."

"Darrell, come on," Wade said.

"I can feel it," he said, twitching as he looked in every direction. "I've always been able to feel those things. I'm sensitive to changes in the air or something. I was that way even when I was small. Things like movement in the dark. Footsteps. Whispers. Eyes staring at you from behind stuff. It all goes in my brain and creates a total sense of doom. It's happening right now. And it's getting worse."

"*You're* getting worse," said Wade. "And I mean that in the politest way possible. You're freaking everyone out."

"It's not *me* freaking everyone out," Darrell said, shifting from foot to foot like a tennis player waiting for a serve. "It's that we're breaking into a cemetery at night. A *cemetery*. At *night*!"

"Okay, already!" said Lily. "Becca's scared enough."

"We're *all* scared enough." Becca shivered as she huddled under the arch. "Plus this suddenly seems extra insane, to be out here like this. I feel sick to my stomach. Not to mention exhausted. Maybe we should just go back home. All the way home. To Texas."

Wade wondered if he agreed with that, when his father appeared at the same corner he had vanished around, waving them over.

"It's basically like Fort Knox here," he said, "but I found an opening in a hedge along the side wall. There's a gate, but it's only a little over waist high. We can climb over it."

Ten minutes later, after a lot of back-and-forth checking from Darrell and waiting until there were no passing cars, they had vaulted over the low gate onto a pathway. *In the park of death.*

"Keep close to the wall," said Darrell, crouching like

a secret agent on a mission. "And whisper."

They crept along the inside of the wall until Lily, enlarging a map of the cemetery on her tablet, located the path they had taken earlier in the day, and they hurried through the trees to it. The snow had turned back to rain by the time they arrived at the Kupfermann tomb.

At night the tomb looked even sadder than it had that morning. A small peaked house of black stone, it was crowded over by vines, its door columns were cracked, and its walls were hairy with moss.

Rain pooled on the dimpled, weathered face of the sundial and the angled blade bisecting it.

"'Follow the gnomon, follow the blade,'" Darrell said. "It looks like the blade of the sundial is pointing right *inside* the tomb."

Lily took a step back. "I just thought of something. If this is Uncle Henry's wife's tomb, then is he . . . in there now?"

Roald turned away for a moment, then back. "I guess he is. They must have laid him to rest inside after everyone left the service."

"Then we really shouldn't do this, should we?" she asked.

Dr. Kaplan ran his fingers through his hair, plainly

not liking the idea. He cleared his throat. "No, we shouldn't, and wouldn't. Except that Heinrich was telling us to. I have to think that his wish is more important than respecting the sanctity of a tomb."

"Maybe it *is* respecting him," Becca said quietly. "He kind of led us here, all the way from Texas."

Wade looked up to see her blushing.

"Okay, then," Lily said. "Following the clue is like his final wish."

Wade choked up a little, crouched, and stared both ways along the angle of the gnomon like a gunsight. "Looking up, there's nothing but sky. But if you stretch a line down from the high point of the blade, it looks like it would hit the ground somewhere on the back right side of the tomb floor."

"Boys," Roald said. They stepped up to the threshold.

The wide door was made of mottled bronze. It was as heavy as a vault door and large, but it must have been hinged with great care and oiled regularly, because when the three of them tugged on the handle, the door opened silently and with ease.

The inside of the tomb was a black room.

Lily tapped the flashlight app on her phone, and the room lit up with frail gray light. In the center were two raised stone coffins, one older than the other, both recently cleaned. On the top of each lay the carved effigy of a figure in a shroud.

"Uncle Henry and his wife are together now," Becca whispered. "I'm so sorry, Dr. Kaplan and Wade."

"Thank you," they said together.

Darrell squinted into the dark. "The gnomon points to the rear corner. Lily . . ." The phone light washed over dull slabs of concrete fitted into one another. There was nothing particular in the back corner of the room.

"Shine it there," said Dr. Kaplan, and Lily trained the light over the rear wall. "Keep going . . . stop."

Roughly in the center of the wall was an old-style representation of the solar system, carved in deep relief. Seven perfectly round rings surrounded the sun, the inner six of which had a small raised half sphere on them.

"The Copernican solar system of six planets and the sphere of the fixed stars," Dr. Kaplan said, counting from the sun outward. "Mercury, Venus, Earth, Mars, Jupiter, and Saturn. Only with the telescope would they discover Neptune and Uranus."

"The message said the Earth moves," said Becca. "Maybe it does. Lil, could I see the light?" She took the phone and moved up to the rear wall. The planets were half spheres of varying sizes protruding from the surface of the wall. "Earth is the third planet?"

"Third rock from the sun," Darrell said.

Becca reached up and touched it. Nothing happened. She pressed it in. Nothing. She grabbed it tightly under her palm and turned. The brief sound of grinding stone came from the rear corner of the tomb. Shining the light there, they saw one stone slab tilted ever so slightly up from the floor as if it were hinged.

"Holy cow!" Wade knelt to it. On the edge of the thick slab was an indentation, inside of which sat a rusty iron ring about the size of a bracelet. "Darrell, help me—"

Together the two boys took hold of the ring and pulled up with all their strength. The stone slab lifted away from the floor.

CHAPTER TWENTY-ONE

"To the cemetery!" Galina Krause snapped from the backseat.

The SUVs tore away from Vogel's apartment so closely that they practically touched bumpers. A caravan of evil.

"But why there?" Ebner asked before he could stop himself. *Fool!* he thought. *Why say it out loud?* He lowered his head and tapped furiously into the computer on his lap.

Galina turned to him slowly. *She is giving me the death stare again,* he thought. *What if I don't look up? Should I say what I was thinking—that the housekeeper told us nothing of use?*

"You are thinking that the housekeeper knew nothing."

How does she do that? How does she know what everyone's thinking? It isn't very . . . human. But then, when you are as beautiful as an angel you don't have to be all that human.

Luckily her tone was not angry but amused. He was safe for now.

"As a matter of fact," he managed to say, "I *was* thinking that."

Galina stared out the side window at the passing cars. "On the contrary. Frau Munch may be a blind old crone, but she knew one thing."

"Kupfermann Haus?" Ebner said, clacking into his silver computer. "But even on threat of death, she could have made it up. We should have followed through. In any case, the closest Kupfermann Haus I can find is an inn in Bavaria. We are certainly not going to Bavaria—"

"You are not a student of the dead, are you, Ebner?" Galina asked, running her forefinger along the bruise on his temple. It stung when she did that, but how could he tell her to stop? "I knew instantly what Vogel meant when he chose that name. The tomb of his wife's family. The key to the location of the first Copernicus relic is hidden in the tomb. Do you know their names yet?"

Ebner waited until she drew her finger away. "Shortly, I will. But they seem a common tourist and his children."

Galina turned her icy eyes on him again. "The man apparently knew Vogel and may not be as common as we would like him to be. Have the Crows meet us at the cemetery. As for the children, have you forgotten how children have changed the history of the world? Must I remind you of the story of . . . Hans Novak?"

Ebner hung his head and clacked away on his keyboard. She had mentioned the name. No one mentions the name. "No, Miss Krause. No. Of course not."

She turned to the window and whispered into her cell phone. Ebner hated it when she whispered in front of him.

The SUVs sped faster toward the cemetery.

CHAPTER TWENTY-TWO

The stone steps leading down beneath the upper tomb were narrow and shrouded in darkness.

"Follow the gnomon," Darrell whispered in Wade's ear. "Sure. Into the tomb. Then down into some kind of prehistoric crypt. Then where? Because if there's one thing I know it's that where there's a crypt, there's a crypt keeper. Remember that."

"Got it." Wade crouched and eased his way down one step at a time. His legs were quivering. He paused and looked up. "Dad, you're coming down with us, aren't you?"

A siren screamed on the streets outside the cemetery. Everyone froze. It got louder and louder, then its tones modulated, and it faded in the streets.

The Doppler effect, Wade thought, to steady himself. The decreasing pitch of an object retreating from you. *Science. You can count on science. It's rational. Logical. There are no crypt keepers. No ghosts. Rats? Well, maybe.*

"I think I'd better keep watch up here," Dr. Kaplan said. "Just in case."

"In case . . . of what?" asked Lily.

"I don't even know," he said frankly, "but I'm sure people would be angry if they saw us doing this. I'd rather they deal with me. Wade, take my notebook. Write down any words if you see any. Then let's get out of there. Go back home. Case closed."

Wade gulped in a breath of the somewhat fresher air of the tomb and continued his descent to the floor below. Lily, who had the phone again, and Becca followed him. Darrell finally put his foot onto the first step, saying, "If we find skeletons of the last kids who did this, I'm going to be very upset."

The walls on either side of the stairs were black with age and slimy with lichen.

"This is like . . . ," Lily started, then stopped when she flashed her light on the walls below. "Uh-oh . . ."

Niches cut into the walls were crammed with dozens of skulls and stacks of detached bones.

Darrell lowered his head. "I knew it. We're going to die. I'm officially upset."

"It's a catacomb," Becca whispered. "With, it looks like, hundreds of skeletons."

Wade nearly fell on an iron grate that had long ago fallen out of the wall, littering the steps with shards of cracked bone. He lifted the grate out of the way. "Are these Frieda Kupfermann's ancestors? There are so many."

"Not all of them," said Lily. She shone her light over several niches, all bearing the identical date from 1794. "Maybe there was a plague. Or a war?"

"Let's either get back up or keep going," said Darrell. "I can't stay here anymore."

Passing the bones as quickly as they could, they discovered a sunken floor with an opening in the same right-hand corner as the tomb above.

Because no one else seemed eager, Wade crawled slowly down four steps into a lower compartment, and they followed.

The floor dimensions of the subcrypt were the same as the main tomb above, but its ceiling was so low that the kids had to move forward on their hands and knees.

Underwater. That's what it feels like. Being underwater.

Darrell was snorting over and over, noisily trying to expel the musty air. Becca was quiet. Thinking, probably. *She's always thinking.*

"Huh," said Lily. "Look at this."

In the dim phone light, they saw walls covered with graffiti, but not the spray-painted sort you see on city streets. These were notes, numbers, initials, and pictures scratched into the stones like ancient hieroglyphs. Some were very old.

"Here are initials from 1607," whispered Becca. "People have been coming here for a long time."

"And it looks like they all died here, too," Darrell said. "Keep moving."

Secured to the front wall of the tomb was a plate made of the same mottled bronze as the tomb door above them. Wade knelt in front of it and Becca inched up beside him. "It's too small to be a burial vault," she said. "It looks more like the door of a safe."

Stamped on the plate was a small, shield-like crest with a flourish of three capital letters entwined so intricately it took them several minutes to make them out.

"G . . . A . . . C," Lily said finally.

There was also a quote inscribed above the door. It was in English.

THE FIRST WILL CIRCLE TO THE LAST.

"I'm writing it down." Wade flipped the notebook to the end. Beneath the translation of Uncle Henry's email and the words Frau Munch had written, he added these new words.

Other than the crest there were no marks anywhere on the vault except a tiny round spot about the size of a dime in one corner. Shining her cell phone light on it, Lily ran her fingers over it.

"It's not a button, is it?" Becca asked.

"I'll tell you what it looks like," said Lily. "It looks like the grill of a microphone. The kind on computers and phones. Look." She tugged out her tablet and, sure enough, there was the very same kind of circle in the corner, although the tablet's was much smaller.

"Voice recognition maybe?" said Darrell. "A security thing?"

"Kids," Dr. Kaplan called from above. "Did you find anything? What's down there? We can't linger." His words were clipped, worried.

"A safe or something," Lily said.

"Can you get it open?"

"We'll try," Wade replied.

Darrell shook his head. "Okay. So, even if this is a

safe and there's no way to open it but a microphone on the door for security, what are we supposed to say into it? We have no clue."

Becca shook her head. "Except we probably *do* have a clue. We've gotten this far on clues Uncle Henry gave us. He supplied us with a bunch of them. All the quotes. Wade's star chart. The sundial. The name of this tomb. There have been clues every inch of the way here. Maybe there's something in what we already know."

"So for the safe to open, we say some words into the microphone?" asked Wade, reading the notebook. "Which words? What if it's keyed to a certain voice?"

"But Uncle Henry told us to come here," said Lily. "Why did he do that if we can't open it?"

Darrell made a sudden jerky movement. "Hold on." He dug his fingers into his pocket and pulled out the pitch pipe Frau Munch had shoved in his hand. "Maybe the secret thing isn't a voice at all. What if it's music? I mean, the *howze kipper* gave us this as part of Uncle Henry's last clue. Maybe because someone would need it to crack the safe."

"Which makes sense," said Lily. "If this safe is part of the secret, it probably wouldn't be only one person's voice, right? If something happened to that person, the safe could never be opened—"

"Someone's coming, a car," Dr. Kaplan hissed from the top of the stairs. "You need to get up here." There came the distant sound of vehicles approaching.

"Keep going," said Becca. "How many notes are there on the pitch pipe?"

"A complete octave, including sharps and flats," said Darrell.

"Play all the notes into the microphone," Becca said.

Darrell leaned close to the tiny grill on the bronze plate. With each note he played, Wade hoped the safe would pop open and they could get out of there. But nothing happened. The vault didn't budge.

"Kids, what's happening down there?"

"Do it again," said Lily. "I heard something when you played certain notes. Do it slowly."

Darrell played the notes again from lowest to highest.

A . . . *click* . . . B-flat . . . B . . . C . . . *click* . . . D-flat . . . D . . . E-flat . . . E . . . F . . . F-sharp . . . G . . . *click* . . . A-flat . . . A . . . *click.*

A tiny noise sounded behind the safe after three notes. A, C, and G.

Becca closed her eyes tight, then opened them. "That's another clue. A, C, and G are the letters on the crest. Play them in the right order. G, A, C."

Darrell played the three notes. The safe clicked three times, but did not open. Then he played the notes in every combination of the three. The safe still didn't open.

"Maybe play them all at once," said Lily. "Not separately, but altogether. They call it a chord."

"I know what a chord is," Darrell said, giving her a look. "But the three notes are all around the pitch pipe. I know I talk a lot, but I don't have three mouths—"

Lily laughed. "But we do! I mean, what if no single person can get in there, but you need several people. That's kind of a security thing, right? Three of us can play all three notes at the same time—"

"Get up here now!" hissed Dr. Kaplan. "More cars are coming. The police must know we've broken in. We're going to be arrested!"

Becca shook her head. "We only need two people. If we stop the A-flat with a finger, G and A are close enough for one person to play them at the same time. That leaves one person to play C. Who's going to do this with me?"

"I'll take G and A," Wade blurted out despite himself.

"Get up here!" Dr. Kaplan shouted. "I mean it!"

"Do it," Lily urged. "Hurry up."

Wade found himself cheek to cheek with Becca, her hair against his face, their breaths practically mingling.

She nodded, and they blew out the three notes at the same time. G, A, C.

Click-click-click. Tumblers shifted behind the bronze door, there was a sudden whisper of release, and the safe in the lower chamber of the Kupfermann tomb at St. Matthew's cemetery in Berlin swung open.

"Miss Krause, the gate is locked—"

"Drive through it!" Galina shouted from the back-seat. The silver SUV bounded over the sidewalk, burst through the gate, and roared down the main road of the cemetery.

It lay on a velvet cloth inside the compartment as if it had been there for centuries.

A slender dagger.

Its blade, narrowing from an inch wide at the hilt to a point as sharp as a needle, was formed of burnished iron, and its razor-like edges undulated like a silver wave.

Carved into its contoured ivory handle, twined in the same manner as the letters in the tomb's crest, were two initials.

AM

Wade reached in and took up the dagger, and the moment he touched it his ears began to buzz and his heart pounded. "Oh man, it's heavy. And feels really old. This is so . . ."

"Kids! It sounds like a military invasion up here!" Dr. Kaplan whisper-yelled. "We—need—to—leave!"

Wade just had time to grab the velvet cloth and shut the safe door before Becca yanked him by the collar toward the stairs.

CHAPTER TWENTY-THREE

The three SUVs swerved into the lead of a second group of vehicles racing in from another entrance.

Galina's black hair flew back into Ebner's face as she lowered the window. "Cut the lights. Stop here."

The nameless driver did as he was commanded, and Galina slid from the vehicle as silent as a snake. The other vehicles parked nearby. A large dull-gray van pulled up last.

Frail light flickered behind the open door of an old tomb with a Gothic name on it. *I was right. Again.* Herr Vogel was a man of humor, after all. Even in death, he revealed a joke. Kupfermann. Copper man. Copernicus.

"Galina." Ebner tilted his computer. "The recipient of Vogel's email." The screen displayed the photo of a tall man with a close-cut beard, standing in a lecture hall.

"A teacher?"

"Astronomer."

"Of course." Thrusting her hand inside her coat, Galina removed a silver pistol. "Send in the Crows."

Seven men in ski masks emerged from the back of the gray van and converged on the tomb like ghosts, slipping past the bronze door without a sound. Galina tilted her face up and scanned the open sky. It had cleared, and there were stars everywhere, so much more visible over an old graveyard than from the living streets.

Stars and the dead and the past.

Her heart pounding, Galina again saw the snowy Frombork tower in flames. And—as if the two things were connected by more than memory—the scar on her neck began to sting. It burned as it had when she received it, four years ago, a gift of three brilliant doctors in a distant Russian clinic.

Three brilliant doctors who were, alas, now dead. There had been flames in the snow there, too, a tragic fire that destroyed that clinic. Fire was an efficient way to unmake so many things.

"Miss Krause . . ."

She refocused on the heavily armed man trotting toward her.

"The tomb is empty," he said, pulling off his mask. "There is a crypt beneath the floor and a hidden safe."

"And?" she said.

"Also empty."

Galina Krause gripped the slim handle of her pistol, rage trembling through her arm, her hand and fingers. "No," she said quietly.

"Miss—"

"No. No. No!" And she fired into the trees. One, two, three, four, five times.

CHAPTER TWENTY-FOUR

Wade froze as the quiet night exploded in gunfire. Five shots. Then silence. He spun around
and stared into the dark.

"Somebody fired at some trees," Becca whispered,
sidling up next to him behind a nameless tomb.

"Kids, wait." Roald held up his hand and gazed at
the Kupfermann mausoleum. Lily and Darrell crouched
at the corner of the tomb and peered around. "Is that
the man there, the one with the bruise on his face?"
Without waiting for an answer, he added, "They killed
Heinrich."

Wade felt dizzy for a second and leaned back on the cold stone. His body was frozen, hollowed out. The echo of gunfire still rang in his ears. And now there was no doubt. Even his father accepted it.

Secret codes. Bizarre clues. An old dagger. Murder.

Protect the Magister's Legacy.

It was real.

They stood breathless at the edge of the woods and watched a small army of men in dark camouflage uniforms and ski masks pour silently over the ground around the mausoleum. In the midst of them stood the hunched man with the bruise on his head. There was also a beautiful lady with a silver handgun. Younger than a lady. Only a few years older than they were.

"Who *are* those people?" Lily whispered.

"Cemetery security? To keep body snatchers away?" whispered Darrell. "Who would steal bodies anyway?"

"I've seen that big silver SUV before," said Lily. "I think it was the one that drove our cab off the road."

"Maybe it's the German FBI," said Darrell.

Dr. Kaplan shook his head. "Ski masks? I don't think so."

"If they're after us, we are so outnumbered," Becca added.

"They were either looking for us or for this," Wade

said, holding up the strange dagger.

"I'll take that," his father said, studying the dagger briefly before wrapping it in the velvet fabric and slipping it inside his jacket pocket.

A spray of flashlights poured into the tomb, and the young woman with the gun joined the pale man at the door.

Wade's head swam. Everything collided with everything else. He ran over the weird sequence of events that had brought them from the Painter Hall observatory to the shelter of these trees in a German cemetery. What was Uncle Henry trying to tell them? What led to his murder?

Find the Twelve Relics.

Well, is the dagger one of the relics?

If not, what is the Copernicus Legacy?

"I agree with Wade," said Lily. "If people are after the dagger, and they . . . you know . . . offed Uncle Henry, we could be next. We should definitely go to the police. What do you think, Dr. K?"

He was about to speak when there was a sudden whoop of sirens at the cemetery gates, followed by the roar of black-and-white sedans. Two police cars tore into the grounds.

Darrell pumped his fist. "Yes, bust them good!"

The first sedan stopped near the silver SUV. All four doors opened and three uniformed policemen emerged, along with a short man in a tuxedo who looked like he was on his way to a party. Instead of any confrontation, however, there was a round of quiet talking. Then the policemen bowed to the woman and shook hands with the pale man in spectacles.

"What was *that*?" said Darrell. "The police *bowed* to her."

Tuxedo Man motioned to another policeman, who retrieved something from the car's trunk. Wade watched as two cops draped yellow caution tape across the door of the Kupfermann tomb. More talking. A light laugh broke the night air. Was that *her* laugh? Another round of bowing. A few minutes later the policemen returned to their cars and drove back through the battered front gate, pausing to beep twice before entering traffic.

"So maybe we shouldn't call the police," said Becca. "If they're in this together, this is so over our heads."

Dr. Kaplan tugged Wade and the others through the trees and deeper into the wooded area that led to the road. "We'll get a cab out of here."

"To where?" Wade asked. "Dad, what are we going to do? Go back to the hotel? And what are we going to do with the dagger?"

Roald scanned the rain-slicked street in both directions. "I don't know. I'm still thinking. But . . . come here, all of you." And he hugged them all tight. Wade felt his father's chest heave as he spoke.

"This is real, and it's dangerous. And we absolutely need to do the right thing. But before I even know what that is, we need to stay together. Do you hear me?"

"Yes," they all said.

He released them. "Okay. First things first. We get as far away from this cemetery as possible."

Keeping to the shadows, they worked their way from street to street until they spotted an electric tram rumbling toward them.

"We can think while we ride," said Lily. "Come on."

They climbed onto the tram, Lily, Darrell, and Dr. Kaplan first, then Wade. He reached out to grab Becca's hand as the tram started up again. She took it and stepped onto the car.

"Thanks," she said quietly, her eyes fixed on the street receding behind them. "Wade, I'm scared."

Wade felt that when Becca pulled her hand away from his, it was the barest instant later than she could have. "Me, too."

CHAPTER TWENTY-FIVE

Schwarzsee, Germany
March 10th
11:43 p.m.

It was not supposed to be this way, Galina fumed as she strode up the marble steps of her lakeside estate northeast of Berlin.

Her recent unexpected trip to Katha, in north-central Myanmar, had forced her to leave Ebner in charge. Under his bloodless, often sniveling facade, he was a brilliant physicist at the uppermost tier of his profession, a man capable of the most inhuman and ruthless acts. He knew much, perhaps more than anyone alive, about temporal physics, but she alone understood the vastness and daring of the grand plan, and its critical, momentous timing.

Never mind that she had worked her way swiftly, unprecedentedly, through the ranks of the ancient Order—her progress was still not fast enough. Time was running out.

Time.

Running out.

In her mind stood the image of an hourglass, its sand pouring through the glass's tiny waist, collecting in a mound in the bottom, increasing the time gone by, diminishing the time left. She would no longer be able to turn it over. Not anymore.

This was it. One hundred and ninety-seven days left. Barely more than six months.

She paused. "Tell me their names now."

"Their names," Ebner murmured from his position five dutiful steps behind her, "are Dr. Roald Kaplan; his son, Wade; his stepson, Darrell Evans; a niece, Lily Kaplan; and her friend, Rebecca Moore. All from Texas."

She pushed in the front door of the mansion. "Kaplan is, of course, a former student of Vogel's?"

"Humboldt University class of 1994, Vogel's last year. Perhaps the least likely member of Asterias. Until now. An astrophysicist and mathematician. His son, Wade, is following that path, has a talent for mathematics. Vogel sent the boy birthday gifts."

"Gifts? Yes, of course. Wade Kaplan. Their phones and computers?"

"Being tracked, Miss Krause, as of one hour ago."

Galina stopped but did not turn. "Is there a Mrs. Kaplan?"

"On business in South America. An archivist."

She nodded slowly. "And the vault?"

"Our forensic team has collected samples from every inch of the tomb. We will know within the hour exactly what the crypt contained. That is where we must focus our energies if we are to stay on schedule. What would you like me to do right now?"

"See that the jet is fueled and on the runway. We will leave the moment we know where the object leads. If my suspicions are correct, it will be somewhere in Italy. In the meantime, track their every move, and rescind the death order on Bartolo Cassa. Put him on standby. Leave now."

She heard the physicist's steps halt abruptly and retreat down the hall behind her as she swung through a set of ornate doors to an inner chamber. She pushed back on the doors and listened to the lock click shut. She bit her lip to keep from screaming. The pain in her neck came and faded and came again, as if someone were plunging an icy blade into her throat. She had not felt such pain since Russia four years before. Her body stiffened to stone. Her veins hardened to ice.

The pain eased finally. Her muscles relaxed. Calming herself, she licked her lips. Blood. It all came down to blood. So, the pain was coming with more frequency. Fine.

One hundred and ninety-seven days.

She strode haltingly across the marble floor, breathing slowly, slowly, until her body moved as before. She loved these cold rooms. Her estate. Her sanctuary. A domain of silence within the silence of stone.

How she missed the long days without sound, absent of voices, devoid of the roar of engines, the chatter of insignificant people. Perhaps that was why the image of the deep night sky drew her as the moon draws the tides. The heavens rolled out above the earth like an inexhaustible sea of sable dusted with silver starlight. Cold sky. Cold earth. Cold stone. Cold silence.

She touched the scar on her neck as if it were the key to what she would need to do next. She stepped across the chamber and through a second set of double doors into a taller, broader hallway.

Down the corridor and to the left, at the bottom of a

set of narrow stairs, lay a passage beneath the ballroom to the rear of the building. Along the way, she slowed to take in the images on the oak-paneled walls, then stopped, smiling at the prizes of her collection: seven unknown portraits of the artist Paul Gauguin painted in seven moods, at seven different times of day, by Van Gogh in 1888 in Arles, and an eighth, "Gauguin as Saint John," rendered by the artist from memory on his deathbed in Auvers-sur-Oise. They were worth, what? Hundreds of millions of dollars? A billion?

And the next sequence—thirteen charcoal sketches on vellum, known among historians as the long-lost winged horses of Michelangelo—what would the art world say if they knew the sketches had survived?

Or the instrument on display at the end of the corridor, a walking staff whose tip concealed a spring-action blade. The so-called rapier-staff crafted by da Vinci himself. Its worth? Too great to conceive.

And yet all these masterworks were nothing next to what she truly wanted. All twelve relics of the Copernicus Legacy.

Galina continued around the corner, down the stairs through two small libraries, across a gallery, and into the innermost room of the house.

Standing in the exact center of the marble floor, she

glanced down at the complex mosaic beneath her feet. A legendary sea animal. Even as she pressed her heel into the center stone, she formed the animal's name on her lips. "Kraken."

The floor lowered silently beneath her—one, two, three levels—before it came to a hushed stop in a large subbasement.

The armory.

The temperature of the circular room was cool, its atmosphere electronically controlled to preserve the unique and fragile weapons arrayed on its walls. Galina stepped off the platform and it rose back up and fit into the ceiling, a ceiling slightly arched and painted with the night sky fully constellated. The ceiling was designed and painted by the Italian master Raphael in 1512 by order of the last and greatest of the Teutonic Order's Grand Masters, Albrecht of Hohenzollern—Albrecht the Great.

It was to the wall portraits that Galina went first, her heels clicking slowly across the marble floor.

Albrecht's massive portrait glared over the room. Galina knew the man's face as if it breathed, so long had she ruminated over the image, painted in 1516. His long, bulbous nose, the firm jaw, the dashing sideburns, his eyes like fiery coals lodged deep in the twin caves beneath his fierce brow. She could hear his voice as if he spoke then and there and to her alone.

Find the relics!

It is the highest duty of the Order!

It is my command!

Side by side with his portrait hung that of young woman, younger than Galina herself, ill and dying and already Albrecht's wife. But young women were different in the early sixteenth century. They had to be; life was bitter and short.

Despite her well-documented illness, the girl was exquisite, pale as alabaster, her golden brown hair worn in the fanciful braids so newly exported from the Italian courts, her face sought after by artists across the continent.

Galina gazed at the two portraits, the two souls long separated by death. The Teutonic Order was in her blood as it was in theirs. She had grown up knowing the power of the Knights and her own family's long and twisted involvement with them. Her great-grandfather's sacrifice. Her father's horrifying death. Hundreds of years of violent history that had brought her to this time and place. And of the Magister, too. The astronomer and scholar. The swordsman. Nicolaus Copernicus. His role in her family's history was no less vital.

Galina's struggle to concentrate the great power of the modern-day Order was fraught with difficulty, lies, secret pacts, treachery, murder. But the stakes were so very high. As brilliant in her own way as Albrecht's dying wife was beautiful, she had proved her value to the aging autocrats and listless minions of the Order. For four years, she had built from its decayed remnants a modern global corporation as vast and varied and powerful as it was hidden from view.

Now, having ascended the ranks of the Order nearly to the summit of power, only one thing remained. Her obtaining the twelve relics. The first was nearer than ever before. The first would lead to the second, the second to the third. She knew the verse. *The first will circle to the last.* Soon she would have all twelve. Breaking the organization of protectors and finding Heinrich Vogel was key. But it had taken so long. Four years. And now, a scant six months remained, with the real work just beginning. Already there were new players. These new Guardians. These children.

Galina knew never to underestimate children.

She had been one herself so recently.

On the wall hung the first pistol ever invented, a large wood and iron "hand cannon," or *pistala*, from twelfth-century Bohemia.

"Lovely, but unreliable. This one instead."

Still consumed with the beauty of the portraits, a tear formed in her single blue eye, a tear she let trail its way down her cheek as she unbolted from the wall a gas-operated, laser-sighted titanium crossbow.

CHAPTER TWENTY-SIX

"You're sitting on my foot," said Lily.

"Why is your foot on the seat?" Darrell snapped.

"Because that's the way I sit!"

"It's wrong—"

"*You're* wrong!"

"*Bitte! Ruhe, bitte!*" said the streetcar conductor, scowling back at them, as he slowed to a stop, which he seemed to do at every single street corner in Berlin.

"Which means 'please calm down, please,'" whispered Becca.

Lily growled to herself. The streetcar was crowded

with late-night passengers and, as usual in these sorts of situations, because they were trying to stick close together and she was the smallest and everybody thought she was sassy and could take it, she got stuck getting crushed between big people with big elbows. *Me. The technician who needs the most room of all to manage my equipment.*

She poked her own elbows out as she turned on her tablet.

Darrell groaned and shifted his weight onto Wade, while Wade, she noticed, seemed to do everything he could not to lean on Becca.

Roald stood by the tram's stairs, running his finger along a map of the streetcar's route. "A bit of a ride left," he said. "Nine stops and we get off. Our hotel is a couple of short blocks from there."

"I hope they're short," said Darrell. "We can all use some sleep."

Becca stared out the tram windows at the slick streets. "Sleep. I think I've heard of that. I just want to wrap myself up in blankets and never come out."

As the screen flickered to life, Lily realized that Becca was just as distracted, confused, and worried as the rest of them, and needed to "please calm down, please" herself. It didn't matter that Becca never really seemed to break out and have any crazy fun. Becca was Becca. Quiet and thoughtful. Lily couldn't imagine being with anyone else on this whatever-it-was. Darrell, on the other hand . . .

"Please give me room, please," she said, nudging him sharply with her elbow.

"Oww!" he grumbled. "Do *you* have the dagger now?" he whispered.

"No. But that's exactly what I'm looking up," she whispered. "For which, by the way, you're welcome."

She scrolled down images of short swords and vintage daggers until she came upon a print of a dueling weapon that looked sort of similar to the one Uncle Roald had slipped inside his jacket.

"It could be a dueling dagger," she said. "You know the way in movies sword-fighting guys have a sword and a dagger? And they use the dagger to block the other guy's sword? Ours looks like that kind."

"I hope it doesn't mean that we're supposed to fight someone," Wade said, keeping his voice low.

"No one's going to use this thing," his father said.

"But why did Uncle Henry hide it in a secret crypt under his tomb?" whispered Darrell. "And what does it have to do with Copernicus? He was an astronomer. A mathematics guy. Stars and numbers. He wasn't a fighter."

Becca leaned over her. "Lily, see if there's more info on where that kind of dagger comes from. Or the initials on it. *AM.*"

Lily leaned back. "Yes, ma'am."

"Dad, do you think this might have belonged to Copernicus?" Wade asked. "Maybe it's valuable."

His father stroked his beard. "We don't know enough to make any guesses."

Which sounded to Lily like something a science teacher would say. The tram made another s-l-o-w stop. Three passengers got off. Probably going to sleep. *How much longer . . . ?*

"I'm thinking that some clues might just lead to other clues," Becca was whispering, "and that the real secret—whatever it is—isn't the dagger at all. It makes sense, right? I mean, Uncle Henry didn't make it easy to get this far. The email, the birthday clue on the star chart—which he wrote six-and-a-half years ago!—Frau Munch's message in the dust, the tomb, the gnomon. It's all codes and half clues, places, word games, quotations, number tricks. If the codes and tricks are clever enough, you shouldn't be able to figure it out. Unless you have the key. Maybe the dagger isn't the final secret but a key to the next thing. Maybe the real secret is pretty far down the line from the dagger."

Lily stopped swiping the screen and turned to her. "Becca Moore. Those are more words than I've ever heard you say at one time."

Becca blushed. "I just get the feeling that we're at the beginning here."

Which may be true, but Lily didn't like the sound of it. Searching for clues and never getting to the end seemed like it might get boring really fast. Then again, she'd have a chance to shine. She knew better than anyone where to find stuff online, and that would totally speed up the solving of clues.

"You might be right, Becca," Roald said. "If Heinrich's secret was big, he'd have layers of clues to hide it. He loved word clues. Maybe the dagger is even a word clue. What they call a *rebus*."

Darrell twitched so much then, Lily could practically see the goofy gears in his brain grinding to come up with some joke involving the word *rebus* and school bus or something. He finally shook his head slightly, which meant that his brain had failed him.

"What's a rebus?" he asked.

"An object or a picture that doesn't mean what it usually means," Roald explained, "but is referring to its name or the sound of its name or something else about it."

Wade frowned. "You mean like a picture of an eye might mean 'I,' as in 'me, myself, and I'?"

"Exactly," Roald said. "So, because a dagger has a point, maybe the clue is that it's pointing to something. Or its letters spell out a clue. Or maybe it's a key."

"Maybe it's all of those things," said Becca. "In books where there are footnotes on the page"—she rustled in her backpack and took out her book—"sometimes they mark footnotes not with numbers, but with symbols. Little ornaments. There are asterisks—stars. There are little paragraph symbols. See. Here are some."

She held up a page where there were symbols in the text corresponding to the same symbols at the bottom of the page.

* ¶ §

"There are also tiny little daggers, like this."

†

Wade leaned over Becca's book. "So the symbols in the text point to the footnote at the bottom of the page. Then maybe the dagger really *is* pointing to something. Or somewhere."

And links do the same thing. Lily followed one to another until she discovered a photograph of a short weapon that had the very same manner of wavy blade as theirs. "Are you ready?" she whispered. "This exact kind of dagger is called a pug . . . pugnale . . . *pugnale Bolognese*—"

"A baloney slicer?" That was Darrell again, hoping everyone would laugh. They didn't. They were more interested in what Lily and her computer had to say.

So there.

"A fighting dagger from Bologna, Italy," she said.

"Interesting," Roald said, looking past them through the tram windows. "I actually know someone in Bologna."

"The article says that this kind of dagger is associated with a special way of dueling that began in Bologna, in places called *sale d'armi*. Salons of fighting. Fighting schools. Some are still around. One of the most famous teachers was—aha!—a guy named Achille Marozzo—"

Becca clapped. "The *A* and the *M* on the handle part!"

"Hilt, Becca," said Darrell. "It's called a hilt. Have you never read *The Hobbit*?"

"Those nasty little guys with hairy feet?" said Lily.

"Wait," said Darrell, *"you've* read *The Hobbit*?"

"By accident!" said Lily. *Score!* "Anyway, AM was a fencing master who lived from 1484 to 1553."

"So he was around at the same time as Copernicus," said Becca. "Maybe they met. Copernicus went to Italy."

"Everybody knew everybody back then," Darrell said, hovering over Lily's shoulder. "The whole population of the world was only a couple of thousand people."

Lily laughed. "The fencing school seems to be still there—"

Wade stood up. "That's why he said it twice!"

"Who said what twice?" Roald asked. "Uncle Henry?"

Wade was practically bouncing now. "Yes! It bothered me that he would say 'follow the gnomon, follow the blade,' because why would he say follow the same thing twice? It's because he didn't. He was telling us to follow the gnomon inside the tomb, then to *follow the blade* that we found in the vault. He meant that we should follow it to Bologna, where it's from. I bet the fencing school is the next clue!"

That's good, thought Lily. *Really good. Smart Wade.*

Roald's slow nod meant he liked it, too. Then his expression changed. "Except we're not the ones to continue this." He paused to glance around at the other tram passengers. When he spoke, his voice was low and firm. "Heinrich was killed because he was hiding this. Maybe he wanted me to somehow take up the task—I'm not sure—but I *am* sure he didn't want my family put in danger. This weapon should really go to the police, but after tonight we can't be certain about them. So I'll take it to the US embassy in the morning and tell them everything."

Wade frowned up his face, then nodded slowly. "I guess."

"Or maybe just tell the embassy we have it," said Darrell. "They could be part of the conspiracy."

Roald smiled and patted Darrell on the arm. "I doubt it, but maybe." Lily realized it wasn't easy for him to know what to do. When something bad happens, you go to the police. But they couldn't. Plus Sara was out of the picture for the next few days, so he couldn't consult with her.

"Let's sleep on it," he said finally, patting the dagger inside his coat. "Things will be clearer in the morning."

She hoped so. The tram was finally nearing their hotel, and the rain was turning to wet snow again.

Noon was heavy and gray when she woke with a splitting headache. It took her a long minute to realize where she was before the combined smell of diesel exhaust, mildew, and burned coffee reminded her that she was in a cheesy hotel in Berlin.

They had returned so late the night before, and after running all around town, they had decided to leave everything until morning—the murder, the dagger, the men pursuing them, everything—and get some sleep.

Which she would have done except for Becca's snoring. Her roommate looked like a ghost, pale and drawn, and coiled in a dingy bedsheet. Becca was so smart and everything, but she so wasn't the type of person to go running from bad guys. Lily was pretty sure Becca did her best work in a library. Still, their little group hadn't done so badly. Evil gunmen might have chased them all over a big cold city, but they were all still alive. Plus, they had discovered a major thing. An ancient baloney slicer.

"Keep sleeping," Lily whispered. She unplugged her tablet from the wall and woke it up.

"Lily's Travel Blog. March 11. Day Three. Or is it two? Or four? Whatever. You won't believe it. We're being chased by goons in black suits—"

Knock.

Her heart stopped. "Yes . . . ?"

"It's Wade. You guys should get up. Dad's decided we're ending this now. We're going to the embassy, then flying home this afternoon."

Lily felt something crash inside her as she turned off the tablet. "Okay. Sure. It's too bad, though. Wade?" He had already gone back to his room. "Becca, wake up. We're going home—"

She bolted upright. "I'm awake!"

For the next ten minutes, they ran around getting themselves together, stuffing their clothes back into their bags.

"By the way, you were awesome last night," Becca said, brushing her hair over the sink in their tiny bathroom.

Lily looked up from her bag. "Are you talking to yourself in the mirror?"

Becca laughed and leaned around the door. "No! You! All that information so fast. It's too bad it's ending, though. It was kind of fun, actually. Some of it. Anyway, we wouldn't be anywhere without you."

Lily didn't know whether to scoff or hug her. "It's all on the internet."

"But you know how to get it *off* the internet and into the rest of us," Becca said, lobbing her hairbrush into her bag.

Darrell tapped on the hallway door. "Five minutes, ladies."

Lily unplugged her charger and crammed the last of her things in her bag. "Look," she said, wondering if she should go anywhere near completing the sentence she was thinking of, then plunging ahead. "I know I can be prickly."

"What?"

"My mom says I'm like her. She says it's hard for her to get close to people. She says she's a cactus mom. I know I'm a cactus, too."

"You are not." Becca's eyes were suddenly moist, and she buried her face in her bag, pretending to look for something at the bottom of it. "You are . . ." She paused. "If it wasn't for you, I'd be sitting at a sticky desk in a tiny study carrel on the third floor of the Faulk Library! This was the best—"

The door thundered. "Now," boomed Dr. Kaplan.

Two minutes later they were rushing into the lobby, where Wade and Darrell were huddled around their father, who was on his phone.

"Uh-huh. Really? Was anything . . . I can't right now, we're in . . . we're out of town. Yes. Yes. Please. As soon as I can. Thank you." He closed his phone.

"Dad? What is it?" asked Wade.

"Is it about Mom?" Darrell asked.

Uncle Roald shook his head. "No, no. She's fine. I mean, that wasn't her. It was the police back in Austin. Our house was . . . broken into last night."

"Oh no," said Becca.

"What's gone?" said Darrell. "Not my Strat!"

"The police aren't sure anything was taken," Roald

said. "That's what worries me. A rear door was forced open, but the house was in good shape. Except . . ." He turned to Wade.

"Dad? Except what?" asked Wade.

Dr. Kaplan looked at him for what seemed like forever before he said, "Your room was really torn apart. It looks like the thieves went straight to your room and ransacked everything, top to bottom." He patted Wade's arm. "I'm sorry. This is terrible. The police are investigating . . ."

"They won't find anything," said Darrell. "These guys are too good. Not to mention international. They have to be the same bunch."

Wade's face went pale. Then he unzipped his backpack and slid out the leather folder. "This. They were after my star map. Dad, they know who we are. But how?"

"Wade, I can't tell you," his father said. "This is so far beyond what I've—"

Beep!

The woman behind the desk waved over to them. "Cab is here for Keplens. Embassy and airport. Heppy travels!"

"Are we still going home?" Wade asked. "Will it be safe?"

Roald looked around the small lobby. Besides them and the staff, there were three other people. Then he glanced down at the bag at his feet. Lily knew the dagger was in there. Suddenly, he picked up the bag and nodded them all out of the lobby onto the busy sidewalk.

He looked both ways. "You know what? No. We're not going home. Not yet." He moved them past the waiting taxi and down the street from the hotel, where he hailed a second cab.

"No! No!" The first driver yelled loudly, storming into the hotel.

A second taxi pulled over. "Everyone in," Roald said.

They got in. "To the embassy then?" said Wade. "Where after that?"

"Drive down the street," Roald said as the cab pulled away from the curb. "I'll call the embassy. We need to get out of the city as quickly as we can. I don't like it here for us."

"Where will we go?" asked Becca.

"Italy," Roald said.

Darrell nearly jumped. "Dad, are you kidding?"

"My friend will help us. I don't . . . I don't like it here and I don't trust anyone. Call it irrational. I hope it *is* irrational. But there are two mur . . ." He glanced at

187

the driver and whispered. "Two incidents so far. Going home is not exactly safe right now. I believe we should keep on the move until things settle. Lily, trains might be the best way—"

"Already on it," she said, reading from the tablet. "There's an overnight train to Verona in forty-five minutes with a connection to . . . our destination."

"Bahnhof, bitte?" said Becca.

The driver nodded. "I get you zere plenty time!" He roared through the next intersection as if he were on a mission, making green lights from *Strasse* to *Strasse* in a kind of blur. Between being crushed by Darrell on one side and Becca on the other, Lily kept her eyes peeled for any silver SUVs.

Luckily, the journey didn't last long. Spinning almost completely around on the street—which pushed Wade and Becca pitch-pipe close—the taxi screeched to an impossible stop directly in front of a giant complex of white and glass.

The driver boomed, "Tren station!"

CHAPTER TWENTY-SEVEN

Wade was still trying to process the scary news that their home had been burglarized when they entered the expansive central Berlin train station. It was a madhouse, a vast modernist structure of glass and steel, roaring with voices and constant movement. The floor rumbled nonstop as heavy trains arrived and departed on dozens of tracks leading off the main concourse.

Darrell nudged him. "Dude," he whispered. "Our home."

"I know. Who *are* they?"

His father herded them toward the ticket counter, then stopped. "Listen. To understand what Uncle Henry wanted us to find, we have to stay ahead of these people, whoever they are. I told you I have a friend in Bologna. Isabella Mercanti. She was married to Silvio Mercanti, one of the Asterias students. He died in a skiing accident last year, but Isabella and I have kept in touch off and on."

"An accident, Uncle Roald?" said Becca.

His father's face darkened momentarily. "I don't think there's any doubt about that, but maybe . . . Anyway, she teaches art and literature at the University of Bologna. We'll find her. She can locate this fencing school for us. She's a good person. She'll help us."

Urging them to the ticket counter across the chaotic room, his father seemed to shift himself into gear, which was more comforting to Wade than he realized. But Becca had asked it, and it suddenly seemed possible that nothing was an accident anymore. From ships sinking to skiing accidents.

What in the world was the Copernicus Legacy, and who were these killers who wanted it?

They stood quietly in the shortest line together, their documents ready. Within minutes his father distributed tickets for five seats in a sleeper cabin to Verona and secondary tickets for the ninety-minute connection to Bologna.

"For twenty minutes, we lay low," his father said, pulling them under an awning as he searched for their platform. Wade unzipped his backpack and peeked inside. The celestial chart was safe. Of course it was, but how safe was *he*? How safe were *any* of them?

"Did everyone see the silver gun that woman had?" Lily asked

"Of course we saw it. And her," Darrell said. "How could we not see her? How could we look away?"

"Isn't the most bizarre part of the whole thing that there was this young woman in the middle of a nasty group of killers?" said Becca. "I mean, what?"

"No, no, no," his father suddenly said, tugging on the end of his beard. "I shouldn't have done that."

Wade turned. "Done what?"

"The credit card," Roald said. "I bought our tickets with the card."

"What's wrong with that?" asked Lily.

But Wade got it instantly. "Because they'll know. They can track credit cards. If they have friends in the police, it means they can do all that kind of stuff. They'll know we're here right now."

"Stay here five minutes, then go to the platform," his

father said. "I'm going to get some cash. We can stay off the grid after that. There's an ATM by the book stall."

Off the grid.

"I'll meet you on Platform Nineteen in a few minutes. It's just over there. In the meantime, take what I have, a hundred euros—that's a hundred and thirty dollars, give or take."

"Shouldn't we all go with you, Roald?" Lily asked, though Wade wasn't sure if she was afraid for his father or for them.

"No," he said. "I don't want us all to go across the big room again. We might be spotted."

"Spotted?" said Lily.

"Do as I say!" Roald snapped. "Sorry. Wait five minutes, then go to the platform and wait for me there. Take these things." He slid the dagger and his student notebook directly into Wade's backpack.

Wade pocketed the euros. "Dad, are you sure?"

His father studied the big room. His face was drawn and tense. "Just until we're safe on the train. If anything happens, we trust no one until we find Isabella Mercanti. After this, we do not separate, you hear me?"

"We hear you, Dad," Darrell said. "Hurry up, though, okay?"

He was already gone.

CHAPTER TWENTY-EIGHT

His father was too fast.

Roald Kaplan had disappeared into the throng in seconds. Wade sensed that his father was trying hard to keep his emotions under control, trying to be the same old dad for him and Darrell and the girls, but he'd never seen his father so anxious and abrupt.

We trust no one.

Was there something about Uncle Henry's message that Dad wasn't telling them? What had Asterias really been about? If Uncle Henry was dead, if Bernard Dufort and Silvio Mercanti were both dead, his dad must be in danger, too. Maybe they were all in danger because they were here together?

He didn't know.

What he *did* know, or was beginning to know, was one thing: that if his father was pressing ahead despite the danger, he himself needed to step up. Sons did that, and he needed to be at the top of his game.

The clock on the wall said 14:24. European time for 2:24 p.m. The train would leave in just over fifteen minutes. Becca, Lily, and Darrell were huddled together, facing one another and invisible from most of the people running around. *That's smart. Darrell's right to think about spies. Maybe that's who these bad guys really are.*

He glanced into his backpack at the map, and now the notebook and the dagger. He patted the money in his pocket.

"Five minutes are over," he said, his throat tightening. "Let's find our train. And be cool about it. The goons could be here already."

Darrell made a face. "Not to mention the lady with the silver gun."

"Not to mention that you *always* mention the lady with the silver gun," Lily snapped.

Platform 19 was as crowded as everywhere else. They immediately took up position behind a fat column when the platform thrummed and a giant red train rolled down the tracks into the station. As soon as it stopped, the platform became a sea of passengers descending from its doors—businessmen swinging briefcases, families dragging suitcases, carrying bundles, and pushing strollers through the crowds waiting to get on. The train idled while crews of sanitation workers poured onto it and jumped from car to car with plastic trash bags.

"I wouldn't want that job," said Darrell.

Wade watched the clock. 14:28. 14:31.

Where are you, Dad?

"Has anyone ever been on a sleeper car?" Becca asked. "I haven't."

"Once," Wade said. "I took the Texas Eagle from Austin to Los Angeles to visit my mom. If German trains are the same, there should be a corridor inside the car. The cabins are marked."

"We're in cabin seven," Lily said, trying to see inside the car, but the windows were too high. "How do you sleep?"

"Sleeping is crummy," he said. "There are benches and upper beds that fold out into a kind of bunk bed thing."

"I'm on top!" said Darrell. "The cabin is probably tiny, right?"

"But it's ours," Wade said. "There won't be strangers in there."

"Uh, yeah, there won't be," said Lily.

14:33.

His chest went icy. A thousand things could be happening while they waited like idiots there. *Dad, come on!*

At a sign from a uniformed conductor, passengers began mounting the steps on either end of their car, showing their tickets to the conductors positioned near the train. The crowding on the platform eased.

Dad . . .

"Should we wait until he gets here? Or get on now?" said Darrell, pacing the length of the train car.

"Of course we'll wait," said Lily. "We have our own cabin. The seats are ours, so no one else can take them. We're fine—"

"Uh . . . no." Becca nodded toward an escalator across the concourse. Going up to the next level of the station, their heads swiveling like owls, were four thick men dressed in black. "Are they from the cemetery?"

Wade couldn't believe how fast things were happening. "They traced the credit card when Dad bought our tickets. He was right."

"They must have a computer surveillance system," said Darrell.

"And troops everywhere," said Lily.

"Please don't call them troops," Becca said, hiding behind the column, then peering out. "I don't see the woman. But I saw one of those guys at the funeral."

The men fanned out on the level above them and scanned the platforms below. "They know we're in the station, but not which train we're taking," Wade said, turning his face away. "So they don't know where we're going. Not yet, anyway. Which means if it *was* Dad's credit card, it was just the amount, not the destination. That's good."

"Not seeing them at all would be so much better," said Darrell. "I knew this would happen. In spy movies, it always happens this way. Everywhere you look, there they are. They know things they couldn't possibly know but they still know them and that's how they know."

Wade wanted Darrell to put a sock in it, but he was right. No sooner had the first four men taken positions overhead than a second group of similar goons appeared at the end of their own platform.

Becca lowered her face. "Why is your dad taking so long?"

The large round clock on the platform column read 14:35. Less than five minutes to departure. *Dad, please!* Had something happened? Or was he just picking up snacks for the long train ride?

Lily's phone rang suddenly. "Hello?" Her eyes grew wide, and she thrust the phone at Wade.

"Hello?" he said, taking it. "Hello? Dad! What? Where are you?" Wade swung around. His father was walking quickly across the concourse toward their platform. "Dad says everybody on the train. Now!"

The kids flashed their tickets and jumped onto the train car. An announcement in German boomed over the station address system. Wade leaned out over the stairs and saw his father sprinting full speed toward Platform 25. *No, Dad. It's this one!*

Behind his father were three men from the cemetery, walking quickly but not running. Someone in the crowd shouted. Then a shrill whistle blasted. At the same instant, his father leaned forward and twisted his feet oddly. *What? Why?* Roald stumbled right in front of the men. He crashed to the floor, taking two goons down with him. Someone shouted again. Another whistle. The train squealed. The car jerked once on the track.

"Dad!" Wade yelled from the open doorway. "Da—"

Becca put her hand over his mouth. "Shh!"

A crowd of passengers jammed up against the huddle of men, apparently unsure of what it was all about.

They tried to help Dr. Kaplan to his feet. A uniformed policeman appeared, his hand on a holster at his waist, but he was blocked by the crowd around his father and the fallen men. A second policeman was joined now by several other men in suits, all hovering around his father. The train squealed again, and it started to move.

Darrell banged his fist on the door. "Dad! Dad!"

The train gasped once more and pulled away from the platform. The short policeman from the cemetery appeared now, gesticulating frantically to his men, one of whom shouted into a cell phone. Others butted their way through the crowd toward the end of their platform, but the head car was already out of the station. The train was gaining speed.

"Oh my gosh," said Lily, staring out the window as the station receded. "What . . . what . . . what are we going to do?"

"The police have Dad!" Darrell shrieked, grabbing Wade by the shoulders and shaking him. "He saved us from being caught!"

Wade couldn't breathe. "The last thing he said on the phone was about Isabella Mercanti. The lady in Bologna. He wants us to find her. He said we should try to not to get caught. And she'd help us."

"Don't get caught?" Lily frowned. "Ohhhh, man . . ."

"I have to call Mom right now," said Darrell. "I don't care where she is!"

Wade handed him Lily's phone. He tapped in Sara's cell number, as the train sped through the train yard. Everyone watched his face. "Mom!" he said, then paused and breathed out. "Voice mail. Of course. She's in Bolivia already. Mom? Hey, it's me. Look, we're on a train in Berlin and Dad just got—"

"Wait!" Wade put his hand over the phone. "They already broke into our house. They don't need to know about Sara. Plus she's off the grid. Which is what we should be. Close it."

"But I have to tell her!"

"She can't come here!" Wade insisted. "These guys may know we're going to Verona, but maybe not to Bologna. Don't give it away. End the call."

Darrell gave him a dark look, pulled away, and said, "Call you later," and hung up. "What a fail," he groaned.

"You did the right thing," said Lily.

"Nobody calls anywhere," Wade said, trying to sound calm, although he really felt like screaming and punching something over and over. Then he felt a touch on his arm. It was Becca.

"Look, your dad is . . . going to be okay. There were hundreds of witnesses back there. And we have passports and tickets," she said. "Plus a little bit of cash. The best thing to do is get off at the next stop, wherever that is. Go to the American embassy, or call it first, or whatever, and do our best to explain what's been happening. We can try to get in touch with Isabella Mercanti from there. If she's your father's friend, she'll help us."

Wade looked at her. Suddenly, he could breathe again. "Yeah, you're right. That's amazing that you could figure all that out. Under pressure and everything."

Becca sighed. "I have some practice, but never mind that. Are we all agreed?"

Everyone nodded. They found cabin seven, a small room with two facing bench seats with a narrow bed folded up overhead above each one. They sat down, trying to catch their breath as the train picked up more speed. Outside the windows the downtown was diminishing rapidly into suburbs and wooded areas broken by highways. It was a gray day like the day before. Germany was a gray place.

Lily pulled her tablet from her bag and swiped at the screen.

"The next town with an American embassy is a place called Magdeburg. It's a pretty big city—"

The compartment door jostled suddenly and squeaked open.

"Sorry, zis cabin-zee is taken-zee," said Darrell.

The door swung wide to reveal two men with flat expressionless faces blocking the way like a pair of oak trees.

"Whoa, what the—" Wade stood.

A third man with a plump red face and badly dyed black hair squeezed between the man-trees. He had a cell phone at his ear.

"Ya," he said into it. Then he lowered it. "You, show me ticket, now!"

Without thinking, Wade showed him his ticket.

The man barked into the phone. "Bologna."

At the sound of the word, Wade's stomach twisted. Why had he simply obeyed the man?

Redface turned the phone around and snapped a picture of them. *Bwip!* A moment later, he said, "Ya!" into the phone again and hung up.

In an accent as thick as peanut butter, the red-faced man with the black helmet hair said, "If you vant to zee your vater Dr. Keplen alife again . . . you vill come viss us. Now."

CHAPTER TWENTY-NINE

D arrell had expected this from the beginning.

Ugly guys with ugly guns and thick accents. "Come viss us." It was playing out like the bad screenplay of a cheesy foreign spy movie. He knew it would be this way. He was only surprised it hadn't happened sooner. This was Germany, after all. The capital of spies and murder and death and foreign movies and spies.

The tree-size men pushed them into an empty corridor. Naturally, it was empty; all the other passengers had already found their cabins and were making themselves comfortable eating warm snacks. If people had been moving in the corridor, the kids could have made a scene and the bad guys might have been arrested. Or, wait. Not arrested. The bad guys were working with the police. Or fake police. Whatever. They were all spies, and spies with accents were always bad news.

"Zis vay," the red-faced spy said. His hair shone like a jet-black bowling ball. It was probably crusty and sticky.

Never mind his hair, plan our escape!

The men marched the kids roughly down the narrow corridor, through the heavy connecting door and onto the platform between the cars. The wind was strong and nearly blew them off the train.

No escape plans came to him there.

The city had long disappeared behind them, and they were speeding through the last stretch of suburbs dotted with trees and houses, until finally there were no houses and just forest.

A good place to dump our bodies.

"Into ze next car!"

Darrell wished he had the sort of brain that would look at their situation and come up with an instant foolproof plan for escape. A movie once showed into the mind of the hero, and it buzzed like a computer, an electronic head. That would be so cool right now.

"Hurry alonk," Redface said. "Ze next car."

The train began to slow. The next station appeared in the distance. Two black SUVs were idling on the street outside the station. Not good. Sliding their guns into their pockets, the two giants nudged the children toward the end of the next car to the stairs that lowered to the platform, while their boss got on his phone again.

Checking with Mommy?

Then he had a thought. It was a small thought, but he'd seen enough movies about trains to know what happens when a train pulls into a station. He poked his fingers into Lily's and Wade's backs and whispered, "Get ready to run."

"They have guns!" Lily whispered.

"Silence!" Redface spat. "Keep movink to ze door."

Darrell took a chance, and purposely stumbled to the floor.

"Get up—"

It was a short delay, but what he expected to happen, happened. Even before the train stopped, several compartment doors swung wide and passengers plowed into the corridor.

"Run!" said Darrell. He lurched to his feet and pushed his friends forward into a tangle of passengers.

"Hey!" *"Ach du lieber!"* the passengers yelled, but the kids rammed their way through them, past the connecting door and into the next car, bounding down that corridor to the end. The train jerked once. Becca stopped short and pointed out the window. "Look!"

Two more extra-large men in suits quickly climbed aboard.

"Now there are five of them!" Lily said.

"Keep moving!" said Wade, pushing them farther away from the men. Darrell realized soon enough that they were going to run out of train, and they did. The door to the final car was locked.

"It's the baggage car," said Becca.

Lily pounded on the door with her fists. "Let us in!"

"*Eine* minute!" shouted a voice behind the door. Two bolts were shoved back. The door opened a crack. "*Was ist das?*"

As the train picked up speed, Darrell heard the thugs crashing into the car toward them. "We need to—"

Becca rattled off a couple of sentences that sounded like she was coughing. But apparently that's what German sounded like, because the mustached man behind the door let them into the baggage car, then bolted the door behind them.

"I told him I needed medication from my suitcase—"

The door shook. "*Lassen Sie Uns rein!*" grunted a voice. "*Die Kinder sind Ausreisser!* Runavays!"

The security guard growled. "Vhat now?"

"They're lying!" said Lily.

They jumped over bags and suitcases to the door at the far end of the car. Pushing it open, they found themselves staring at the receding tracks. The train was racing quickly over the miles now, approaching top speed.

Unlocking the far door, the baggage guard reluctantly let the four thick men and Redface into the car. They pushed him aside, but he snagged one of the goons and started arguing his head off. Redface and his thugs simply pushed through to the rear and trapped the kids on the outside platform.

"No more runnink!" Redface grunted. "Giff us ze key."

The wind tore icily around them. The guard inside was ranting in a high-pitched voice now.

Darrell's brain scanned their options when he suddenly came up with a second amazing idea. He dug into his backpack, pulled out the pitch pipe, and held it out over the tracks. "You want the key? Here's the key. It belonged to Vogel. One more inch, I toss it overboard."

The men froze. "No, do not," said one of them.

"Zey know nussing!" said Redface.

"Oh yeah?" Darrell snarled. "Well, this is what was

207

in the safe at the tomb. The secret you've all been looking for. That pretty lady told you to get it, didn't she?"
Nice detail, he thought, and it seemed to work. The men
mumbled at one another. As quickly as the train had
gained speed, it slowed again. They were approaching a
bridge. The lead car clattered onto it, slower still.

"Zey know nussing!" Redface repeated, his face get-
ting redder and puffier. "Get it before ze next station!"
The thugs lunged forward like the front line of the Texas
Longhorns, pinning all of them to the back rail.

The space was too cramped to hold them. Lily kicked
out, while Wade squirmed in front of Becca. Darrell
managed to wrestle his arm free and fling the pitch
pipe. One of the men shouted as it sailed through the
air, and clattered onto the tracks. Redface responded by
shoving the shouter right off the platform. "Find it! Get
it!"

That left Redface and three goons. His thoughts pop-
ping one after another, Darrell pushed forward, and
Redface fell back through the door into the baggage car,
where the guard was yelling on the phone.

Wade moved to whip the dagger from his pack but
settled for kicking one guy sideways in the knee. He
fell headfirst on the platform. Becca and Lily took turns
slapping another on the ears, while he cursed at them.

Darrell jumped at the remaining guy, pushing him off balance on his way past, and the kids found themselves back in the baggage compartment.

Redface fumbled in his coat for something, but Wade and Darrell together pushed him back outside, where he fell over the others on the platform floor. Together, Lily and Becca slammed and barricaded the door.

The guard hustled over, his mustache flapping in anger. "I hev called ze conductor!"

Wade pushed his hand into his pocket and pulled out the wad of bills his father had given him. "Help us. I'll give you euros. Just go away and leave us the key."

The men battered on the door. "Open or ve'll shoot!"

Leaning hard against the door, Wade peeled off a couple of bills, but the guard snatched the whole wad of cash. "Sank you!" He locked the platform door, then rushed away, tossing the key to Wade as he slipped into the forward car.

"Hide behind the bags!" said Becca.

Wade quickly opened the far door halfway, then joined the others behind a wall of baggage just as the three gunmen and Redface broke down the rear door and burst into the car. Seeing the far door open, they raced through it without looking. After the men had gone through, Darrell rushed over and double bolted the door behind them.

"I can't believe we're still alive," Becca breathed.

Lily burst out with something between a laugh and a scream.

"Just wait!"

CHAPTER THIRTY

Wade knew they had only moments before the creeps battered their way back in. "We need another plan."

"Don't ask me," said Darrell. "I'm all planned out."

"Plus you just threw away one of our clues," Lily grumbled. "What if we need a pitch pipe again?"

"We won't," said Darrell. "I have perfect pitch."

She narrowed her eyes at him. "I don't know exactly what that is, but you'd better have it!"

"Guys, we need to get off the train before it stops at another station," Wade said. "Or worse, a border checkpoint. How soon will we reach Austria? Anybody?"

"I'm looking," Lily said, tapping her tablet.

The train rolled through forests and valleys surrounded by mountains dotted with the occasional castle, mile-wide rivers, and twisting highways.

"Probably less than an hour," Lily said.

Wade paced the length of the car. "We can't depend on being lucky again. We'll wait for the train to slow down and since we're at the end of the train, we can just jump off and hide before anyone sees us."

Darrell tilted his head at Wade skeptically. "That's your plan? Jump off the train?"

He knew he could try to bluff it, but after crossing that bridge, the train hadn't reached top speed again, which probably meant a station was not far, so he just said, "Yep. That's it."

He opened the rear door and stepped onto the platform. As slowly as the train was going compared to the distant trees, it was speeding swiftly relative to the ground. He was pretty sure Einstein had a name for that phenomenon, but he didn't have time to search his memory for it. "Who's first?"

"You're first," Lily said instantly. "If you don't die, we'll send Darrell. If *he* doesn't die, Becca and I will go. Right, Bec?"

"Yeah, sister," she said.

Wade grumbled. "Fair enough."

The train slowed more as he lowered himself to the bottom stair. The ground on the left side of the tracks was a ridge of tufted grass. Gripping his backpack strap with one hand, he jumped, slamming hard on the ground, then rolling over twice. He looked back. The train slowed even more. *Hurry!* Becca wrapped her arms around her bag and dropped off the platform. A little gawkily, but she rolled smartly. Lily and Darrell went at the same time. Darrell landed nearly on his feet, while she rolled on the ground and came to a stop in a heap.

Pushing himself to his feet, Wade's forearm ached sharply, but not as badly as when he'd fractured it playing baseball. He turned it gently and it felt better, so he ignored it. "Everyone okay?"

They all mumbled something and wobbled toward him, which was good enough. The train rolled for a half mile or so down the rails before it disappeared behind the trees around a curve in the tracks. It whistled twice, and the brakes squealed.

"As soon as they discover we're not on the train, they'll comb the area," Becca said. "We need to be long gone."

"Comb the area," Darrell said with a smile. "Official spy talk."

"Shh." Wade listened for the sound of the train leaving the station. It didn't come. "Stops are usually shorter than this. I think the train is still there. We should see what's going on."

Lily gave him a look. "That seems risky."

"It is, but right now they don't know where we are," he said. "The more we find out the better off we'll be."

"You're saying we should spy on the spies?" said Darrell.

"Yes." Without waiting for them to argue, Wade darted off through the tall grass, hoping his friends would follow him. He'd feel pretty stupid if they didn't. Thankfully, they did.

Staying close to the shelter of the trees, they made their way stealthily around the bend in the track toward the station. A black SUV and two police cars were parked and idling next to the platform. Three thugs and Redface had exited the train and were standing near. The man who had jumped after the pitch pipe hobbled out of one of the police cars. He pointed both up and down the tracks with his one good arm, which also glinted with the silver pitch pipe. The others seemed to agree with whatever he told them. Finally one of the tree-size men reentered the train while the others drove away. The train started up again.

"So," said Lily, "what did we learn, Professor Wade?"

He released his breath. "That by keeping a guy on the train, they're not sure we're not still hiding on it. This is good. They know we're heading to Bologna because I stupidly told them—"

"We all would have done the same thing," Becca said.

Wade half smiled. "Thanks. But as long as they don't know that we found a dagger in the crypt, they don't know about Achille Marozzo or any fencing school. If we're smart, we can get there without them finding out. Plus we have Dad's friend to help us get him back."

"Fine, we learned a lot," said Lily. "Good work."

"But no way are we done with them," Darrell said.

Becca nodded. "So what's next. How do we get to Italy?"

"For starters, we'll have to find a ride that keeps us off the grid," said Lily. "Darrell, come with me. You two stay here. Two kids aren't as suspicious as four."

"Good," Wade said. As he watched the two of them head into town, he was pretty sure he heard Darrell humming. Even better.

Becca stared down the tracks long after the train had vanished. "Wade, did we do the right thing? Leaving without your dad? I mean, I know we didn't have a choice then, but we do now. Part of me thinks we should go back and just tell everyone what we know. Go to our embassy or the newspapers, and ask for help. I don't know. It's kind of crazy to be going farther away." Her eyes were dark with worry, as Wade imagined his own were.

"Yeah, I don't know, either," he said. "Except that Dad said not to trust anybody. He'd want us to stay free." He drew out the dagger. It glinted in the waning sunlight. "This is some part of the Legacy and the reason at least two people are dead. Those creeps wanted it. I think keeping the dagger safe and away from them is the only leverage we have right now." It was quite a speech, and he wondered if it even made sense.

Becca searched his face. She was quiet for a long minute, then said, "All right. We'll try to get to Bologna and Isabella Mercanti. But at the first sign of a black suit, we're heading for the embassy."

Wade laughed. "Black suit? We're going to Italy, don't forget."

"You know what I mean," she said, cracking a dimply smile.

Wade wanted to keep talking like this to her. It was surprisingly comfortable and comforting, and it kept him from thinking too deeply about what his father was going through in Berlin. He really hoped the men on the train were bluffing when they said, "If you ever want to see your father alive again . . ."

In fact, he *needed* to believe it was an empty threat. Or else he wouldn't be able to go on another minute.

There was a sudden pop from the end of the street as a truck rumbled toward them, snorting and coughing up a cloud of blue smoke. It gained speed, then suddenly slowed down and swerved to the roadside.

Instinctively, he took Becca's arm. "Into the trees—"

"Wade!" Darrell poked his head out of the truck cab. "Wade! Here's our ride. A supermarket truck!"

The driver howled with laughter as he pulled up and hopped down from the cab with Darrell and Lily.

"He said we have kind faces," Lily said. "Which, of course, we do."

"I go Bologna," the driver said. "Two times week. Come."

Becca wrinkled her nose at Wade. "What about 'don't trust anyone'? Do you think—"

"Come, come!" The driver opened the back flap for Darrell to climb in, thrashing the canvas when the others hesitated. "I no bad. I hev family. Chiddren. Two. Come. Is good truck!"

When neither he nor Becca moved, Lily marched

over to them. "He has a nice face, don't you think?"

"I know, but . . ." Wade started.

"You can tell a lot about a person from his face. And his Facebook. He's posted the cutest pictures of his kids. Look." Lily showed them her tablet. A boy was giving a girl for a ride on his shoulders. He wore a fake mustache. "I know it's crazy, but he looked okay. He had a truck, he sounded Italian, so Darrell and I made a leap. Plus he has *chiddren*. Two. And now we have our ride. Come on, guys. Darrell's already made himself at home in the back."

The driver did have a pretty good face, after all. Mostly one big smile. Not all that different from Uncle Henry's. "Okay," he said. "Thanks a lot, sir."

"Ticky tocky!" the driver replied, laughing and flapping the canvas for them to hurry. "You hide. You sleep. We be Bologna for lunch!"

CHAPTER THIRTY-ONE

The truck was jammed with crates of what Darrell told them turned out to be a chief German export to Italy: soft drinks and mineral water.

"People," he said, "we are now officially German cargo!"

"Hiding in a soda truck," said Lily, grinning as the driver secured the flap and started up again. "This is so going into my blog."

For the next three hours, the truck wove slowly down through the hills to the Austrian border checkpoint, where the driver was a twice-weekly visitor.

When the guards lifted the flaps, they saw only crates of bottles and cans and quickly waved him on.

After that the truck made stops at markets and stores along the way. The final border crossing into Italy was swift and the route more or less direct to small shops and village markets until there were only a few crates left.

Judging by a dream about his ransacked room in Austin—from which he woke in a sweat—Wade realized he must have slept through at least part of the bumpy overnight ride. Sitting up, he found that his arm throbbed from the elbow down, but not into the wrist, which moved more or less easily. That meant a muscle injury and not any kind of bone fracture. Darrell was sound asleep, his mouth open. Becca was awake, her arms wrapped around her knees with Lily leaning on her shoulder. She didn't look like she wanted to talk.

By late morning the truck was all but empty and parked at a depot with lots of other trucks. They thanked the driver again, he wished them luck, and they were soon out on the streets of Bologna.

As their first attempt to contact Isabella Mercanti, Lily dialed the University of Bologna, then handed the phone to Becca, who stuttered some halting Italian into it. She was put on hold several times, and finally connected to someone.

Becca asked for Dr. Mercanti, then listened, frowning, for several minutes, saying, "Ciao?" a few times, before shutting her eyes, saying, "Grazie," and hanging up. She moved the phone from her ear and looked at it. "It was all crackly for a few minutes—Lily, I think your battery is going—but I got most of it."

"What did they say? More bad news?" said Darrell.

"This is, what, Wednesday?" said Becca. "Isabella Mercanti missed her lecture two days ago. And the university hasn't been able to get in touch with her since then."

"Two days ago we were in Berlin," said Wade.

Lily folded her arms around herself. "This can only mean one thing, right? We're all thinking it. They kidnapped her. Or killed her—"

"No," Becca said. "Not that."

"Well, her husband was in Asterias, and he didn't die in any accident. He was killed. And now they took care of her."

Wade's legs felt suddenly as weak as his forearm. He slumped down to the curb, stared at the cobblestones, then looked up at the others. "So we're alone. We have no idea what's going on with Dad, we're alone, and we have no cash or friends. We have to do something."

Becca held out the phone to Darrell. "Start by calling your mom again. Leave a message. Tell her we need help. But that's all. She'll call back when she can."

Darrell took it and tapped in the number. He tapped it in a second time. "Uh . . . this isn't working."

Lily pulled it back. "Uh-oh. Becca, you were right. My battery's dying. That's what all that crackly business was."

"Send Sara an email," Wade said. "You can do that on a tablet, right?"

Lily threw her phone into the bottom of her bag. "She won't get it until she's out of the jungle, but yeah."

Darrell tapped in a quick message and hit Send. "Let's find what we came here for," he said.

"The Sala d'Arme," Becca said. "The fencing school."

Swiping her tablet, Lily said, "Achille Marozzo's school is on Via Cà Selvatica," pronouncing the street name slowly and still apparently managing to mangle it enough to make Becca laugh.

"It's their own fault for having so many letters in a word," Lily said. "What's wrong with 'Main Street'? Anyway, according to Google maps, we can walk to it. Follow the guide . . ."

The route was not straight, but Wade couldn't imagine that any route in what was essentially a medieval

Italian city would be. After making their way along a couple of broad avenues, they entered an older, narrower series of streets that wandered and crossed and looped and sometimes ended in blind alleys.

An hour later, they were deep among ancient ways bordered by low stone buildings, all topped with red tile roofs. And there it was, the Via Cà Selvatica, a narrow flat street at the end of which stood a motley collection of school-like buildings clustered behind a high roughstone wall. It took them a few minutes to find a door in the wall. It was locked.

"Over the wall. Come on," said Darrell. He and Wade hoisted the girls up and followed them inside the wall to a large paved courtyard. Among more modern school buildings, and not visible from the street, stood an old church-like structure with a set of wide stairs leading up to its main doors.

"The Sala d'Arme is still a fencing school," Lily said, half looking at the building, half at her tablet. "It teaches the same technique that Achille Marozzo originated in the sixteenth century and that he probably taught Copernicus when he studied in Bologna in the early fifteen hundreds. Pretty cool, huh?"

"Pretty cool," said Becca, starting up the stairs with her.

The windows were dark. And they heard nothing. Neither the clash of blades nor the yelling, shouting, and taunting that might be expected from a school of swordsmanship.

Together Wade and Darrell pulled on the bronze handles on the doors. They wouldn't budge.

"They're closed," Lily said. "We've had this problem before."

On the wall next to the doors was a sleek alphanumeric keypad with a slot for a security card under it. Clearly it would take only the right combination of digits, and they had no card.

In addition to the keypad, there was on the right-hand door a small bronze plate with the entwined letters *AM* in the center.

Between the two letters was a keyhole, though it was unlike any keyhole they had seen before. The hole was not round but slot-like, narrow at either end and wider in the middle, with little dimples on each side.

Darrell pounded on the doors. They listened and waited. Becca stood away from the doors. "Hey! Anyone! *Apra la porta?*"

No response.

"Now what?" said Lily.

Wade couldn't take his eyes from the keyhole on the

door. He bent down to examine it more closely. There were no scratch marks directly around the keyhole, which he thought was odd for what looked like a very old lock. Instead, there was a perfect circle scratched into the plate at a radius of about two inches from the center of the lock, as if the key had something attached to it that scratched the plate when it was turned in the lock.

Lily pounded on the doors to no result. "Open up, AM! We hid in a soda truck to get here—"

"Hold on." Wade unzipped his backpack and unwrapped the dagger from its velvet cover.

"You're kidding, right?" said Darrell. "You're going to stab your way in?"

"Not really," Wade said. He studied the keyhole again to see if it was big enough, then he carefully slid the dagger's blade into it.

"Okay, careful . . . ," Lily said.

With each wave of the blade, the dagger shifted up and down. It stopped when the handle guard was up against the groove scratched into the plate. Once the dagger was all the way in, he turned it gently clockwise. It wouldn't move. When he turned it the other way—counterclockwise—the lock mechanism clicked and shifted.

"Of course," he whispered. "All the planets in our solar system revolve counterclockwise. Copernicus again." He turned the dagger one complete revolution. A second. A third revolution started a soft pinging sound that lasted about ten seconds before there was a deep thunk, then silence.

"Whoa," said Darrell.

"My thoughts exactly," Becca added.

Wade knew he had a dumb grin on his face, but it was only partly because the dagger worked. He realized all at once in a strange, exhilarating rush that they had solved several codes, retrieved an ancient dagger from a crypt, eluded an army of killers, crossed half of Europe, found an old door to an old school, and were now unlocking it.

And this was just the beginning.

If Becca was right, there was more after this, and more and more—

"Are we ever going in, Smiley?" Darrell asked.

"Sorry, yeah." He removed the dagger and pushed the door inward. As heavy as the old door was, it slid open soundlessly and with ease, like the door of the Kupfermann tomb. The air inside the building was cool. It smelled of old stone. They tiptoed into a long high-ceilinged hallway of arches and columns and stood silently, looking ahead into the dim empty distance, when a bright silver sword flashed down in front of them and a voice hissed from the shadows.

"Don't move a centimeter!"

CHAPTER THIRTY-TWO

"Who invades our sacred precincts? Tell me instantly or die!"

The words had been said—in a kind of lilting English that somehow made Lily think of blue water and warm sand—by a young man in a tight-fitting white tunic and leggings. His face was chiseled and angular, and his brown hair, as wavy as the dagger's blade, cascaded to his shoulders.

"Uh . . ." Darrell mumbled. "We're . . . tourists?"

"This is an extremely *private* private school," the young man said, not dropping his sword or his Rs. "And very securely locked."

Lily felt Becca's eyes on her. *Why? Why is she looking at me when this guy's face is standing in front of us?* Then she realized that her mouth was hanging open. She closed it quietly, but not before she found herself saying, "Your accent . . ."

The young man seemed about to speak when he glanced down at Wade's hand. That old dagger was still out. The young man immediately dropped his sword to his side and bent slightly at the waist. "My deepest apologies," he said. "That is . . . a rare dagger. Very rare." His brow furrowed. "You found it in . . . Berlin?"

They shared a look. "How did you know that?" Becca asked.

The young man looked at her for a second, then back at the dagger. "There were very few ever made, nearly all of them accounted for. Early sixteenth century. But you no doubt know this already." He bowed again. "My sincere apologies. I was expecting . . . not you. May I examine it?"

"Yes," Lily replied, as if he was speaking directly to her.

Wade held out the dagger and the young man took it carefully. "Yes. This is one of Achille's blades. Excuse me, Achille Marozzo, the sword master who started our school. He founded it in this very building and had many illustrious students. But, again, you must already know this, or you would not be here. Like others who have found their way to us from time to time, you have come to visit our library, the earliest room of our school, yes?"

Books? Really? Are the relics just books?

Without waiting for them to respond, the man said "Yes, of course you have." His expression changed as he handed the dagger back. "You were not directly followed?"

"Followed?" said Becca, her first word for some time. "How did you . . . I mean, why did you think that?"

The young man narrowed his eyes. "Your visit . . . but there will be time later. Come. Quickly. As you might guess, we are in lockdown."

Why would we guess that? Who does he think we are?

He spun on his heels—quite elegantly, Lily thought—and pressed a button on the wall next to the door.

There followed the sound of bolts shifting and moving that ended with a sharp echo. "Secure once more." Then he stared at their faces as if taking notes for a portrait and swung his sword in a wide arc in front of him.

"My name is Carlo Nuovenuto. I shall escort you to the library myself. Follow me. Hurry."

And hurriedly they went, as Carlo led them down the corridor, their footsteps reverberating against the bare stone.

"Why is the school in lockdown?" asked Wade.

"I'll explain later." Without another word, he turned left into a high-walled room whose ceiling was painted with fat naked babies and clouds. From there they passed through a vaulted archway into a long red-windowed hallway. One room after another, passage by passage, Carlo Nuovenuto led them deeper and deeper to what appeared to be the very rear of the old building.

"Carlo," said Lily, smiling. "You must be Italian, right?"

"*Sì*. Half," he said. "The other half . . . many things."

Darrell made a barely audible sound in his throat. She turned to see him share a look with Wade, who rolled his eyes.

Uh-huh. You wish you looked like this guy, she thought. She was sure Darrell and Wade wondered whether Carlo could even be trusted and were hanging back, ready to leap into action if he tried anything. *Guys*, she wanted to say, *Carlo sword fights for a living!*

"By the way," he said as he paused at a small closet stuffed with fencing stuff. He reached into it. "Here's a carrier for the dagger . . . eh . . . your names?"

231

"Oh, right," said Wade. "I'm Wade Kaplan. This is my stepbrother, Darrell, our friend, Becca, and—"

"Lily!" she said.

Carlo nodded to each of them. "You'll want to protect the edges of the dagger, Wade. You may need it later. This sheath is made of a synthetic material that will keep the blade sharp, and, not incidentally, hide it from scanners and other detection equipment."

"Really?" said Darrell. "You mean at airports and stuff?"

"Just so. The sheath's strap hangs over the shoulder and conceals the weapon under your shirt."

Wade took the lightweight scabbard. "Thanks."

"This way." Carlo led them into a room that was completely unfurnished. There was a single narrow door in one wall. He approached the door. There was a sudden humming, and he stopped, producing a phone from his tunic pocket.

"*Sì?*" he answered. A voice chirped excitedly on the other end. "*Sì. Pronto.*" He closed the phone. "You must excuse me. You will be safe in the library."

"Safe?" said Becca. "It's a library . . ."

Carlo turned his eyes on Wade. "Hold tightly on to that," he said, pointing to the dagger. With a twirl of his heels and hair, he was gone.

"He's telling us we'll be safe?" whispered Darrell. "Lockdown? Did those creeps track us here? How did they find the fencing school so fast? *How are they doing that?*"

"I don't know, but we'd better hurry," said Lily. "The door looks similar to the one on the front of the building. Dagger time."

Wade inserted the blade as before, turned it counterclockwise three times, and the door opened. In semidarkness beyond the door stood a narrow corridor barely two feet wide from wall to wall. It looked ancient, but the air was dry, and there was a faint hum coming from somewhere high in the ceiling.

Air-conditioning? Lily wondered. A security camera was positioned at the end of the corridor by the other door. The red light pulsing next to the lens told them it was filming.

"Someone's watching us," Darrell whispered.

"Carlo, probably, but he seems okay," said Lily, though *okay* wasn't the word in her head. "And it sounds like he knows what he's doing. Anyway, it's too late to turn back now."

Wade slowed in the passage. "All right, but look. Carlo knows the dagger is valuable. And it's like a sign that we're good. We can be trusted. He didn't ask a lot of questions, just brought us here, so he must know what we're looking for. Why the library? Maybe the relics are books."

"Please keep moving," said Becca. "I really can't stand the dark."

By the end of the passage, they were in almost total darkness. Lily vainly tried to remember the sequence of rooms and how far from the street entrance they might be, when Wade unlocked a third door with the dagger. They descended a set of stairs into a chamber more opulent than any she had ever seen. Gold threaded tapestries of mythological scenes hung heavily from three walls. On its ceiling was a painting of the sun in brilliant yellow and crimson, with gold rays splaying out from the center to each corner.

Antique bladed weapons were arranged elaborately on the fourth wall. None were identical to their dagger, though some looked pretty close. Others were even more fanciful, including some swords that looked like desert weapons, with long curved blades and a vaguely Arabic feel to them. Lily was going to say they looked like movie props when she realized that the props were likely made to look like them.

"So Achille Marozzo made all these things?" she asked.

The room was airy despite its being underground, and there was something vaguely futuristic about it, as if the past and the future came together there.

"Probably," said Darrell. "Man, I wish we could borrow some of them. We should all have weapons. Swords would be so cool."

"And impossible to hide," said Becca. "A dagger is dangerous enough to be carrying around."

"There's only one book in the 'library'?" said Wade.

In the center of the room was a long, wide table made from a single, thick slab of oak. It was surrounded by a half dozen oak chairs.

There were two antique oil lamps at the head of the table and between them a small stand on which sat a compact, leather-bound book. It was deep red with faded brass guards to protect each corner and a pair of similarly faded clasps to keep it closed.

The brass guards were engraved with daggers like the one Wade set on the table in front of him.

Imprinted in gold across a flat panel on the cover was a title in what Lily knew now were Gothic German letters similar to those on the Kupfermann tomb. She watched Becca's face as she read the title. She seemed to stop breathing.

"Bec, are you okay—"

"What is it? What does it say?" asked Wade.

Becca slumped into the nearest chair, ran her fingers lightly over the gold letters, then translated them aloud.

✝✝✝

THE DAY BOOK OF

NICOLAUS COPERNICUS

HIS SECRET VOYAGES IN EARTH AND HEAVEN

FAITHFULLY RECORDED

BY HIS ASSISTANT

HANS NOVAK

BEGUN A.D. 1514

✝✝✝

CHAPTER THIRTY-THREE

"The Day Book of Nicolaus Copernicus?" Darrell said. "His diary? Do you think it's real? How did it end up here . . . ?"

As Becca stared at the leather cover imprinted with gold, the sound of Darrell's voice faded until the chamber became so hushed that she heard nothing save her own excited breathing.

Finally Lily tapped her on the shoulder. "Becca, can you read it? I think this is why Carlo brought us here."

Light from the lamps flickered across the gold print on the cover, as if the words themselves were on fire.

"Yes, I think so." Adjusting herself in the chair, Becca shifted the lamps on either side of the book so there was no glare, and slowly, carefully, as if she were handling something alive, she loosened the clasps and lifted the cover.

Though obviously centuries old, and solidly bound in boards and leather, its front hinge opened easily, and the cover lay flat against the surface of the raised stand.

"Um . . . everybody sit," she said. "This probably won't be fast."

Wade turned his face up to the door, listening. "It's quiet up there. I guess we're okay."

The thing Becca noticed right away when she opened to the first page was the handwriting. It was plain and legible. Copernicus's assistant, Hans Novak, whoever he was, had good penmanship.

Darrell peeked over her shoulder. "Most pen and ink manuscripts fade after a while," he said. "This is in really good condition. It's been taken care of for the last five hundred years. The air in the room is cooled to the right temperature. The light is veiled. They know what they're doing. Mom shows me lots of this kind of stuff."

For a moment, the four shared a look as if they were all thinking the same thing. Sara Kaplan. Roald Kaplan. Both were far away from them. People were missing.

Some were dead. And here they were, moments away from discovering why it was all happening.

The Copernicus Legacy. The twelve relics.

Is the secret hidden in these pages?

Becca turned one page, then another and another. "It looks to be mostly in German, but I see some Italian and Latin in here, too, so it may be a hodgepodge of different languages. I'm not as good in some as in others."

"Better than the rest of us," said Darrell, and Lily nodded.

"And there are pictures," she said, finding pencil sketches of tiny devices, motors, and mechanisms, then a series of abstract diagrams, boxes, and triangles, as well as what could only be described as great airy masses, clouds maybe, or oceans, mostly done in pencil, some in black or brown ink and washed with color.

Then a word popped out at her. A single word. *Stern.* German for *star* and one of the words that started this whole adventure. From then on, she couldn't draw her mind away from the text. Turning back to the first page, she began to translate, haltingly at first, then with more vigor as she grew accustomed to the old script.

†

I, Hans Novak, aged thirteen years, four months, eight

days, here set down these words as Magister Nicolaus Copernicus has told them to me and as I myself have lived them.

The words swept over her, drawing her back to a time and place far away from their own.

To begin, I must record what happened before my humble appearance in the Magister's story.

Nicolaus Copernicus was born in 1473 in the town of Toruń, Poland, under stars that proclaimed him a visionary and a rebel.

How true were those stars!

†

At the age of eighteen, already on the path that would later crown him with glory, Nicolaus attended the great University in Krakow.

He studied hard. I know that, of course, as everyone must have, from his brilliance. He became a canon in law at Bologna. There he met the sword master, Achille Marozzo. At Via Cà Selvatica, he learned the art of the blade—

"I knew it!" Darrell slapped his hand on the table. "He was right here! In this place. Man. Go on, Becca. Sorry."

Before he returned home to Poland, Nicolaus was given a gift from Achille. He related it to me thus:

"What is this?" Nicolaus said.

Achille laughed. "A master sword for a master swordsman! It is unlike any that I have forged so far. First you must name it."

Nicolaus drew out a magnificent broadsword. "Himmelklinge," he said. "Sky Blade."

Achille approved, handing him a second gift. "To go with it, a dueling dagger, a prototype of my own design."

"Its blade undulates like the Baltic Sea," Nicolaus said.

Achille smiled. "May they both serve you well and protect you."

"He's talking about this dagger," said Wade, holding it under the lamplight. "This actually belonged to Copernicus. Keep going."

"Uh . . ." she flipped a page. "There are several pages in, I don't know, maybe Polish? I'll have to skip them for now. Here."

I enter the story in Frauenberg, called Frombork, on the shores of the Baltic. It is the thirteenth night of the second month of the year 1514. Because I can wield a pen, I am sent by the Bishop to assist the Magister with his work.

I arrive after dusk.

The night is cold, clear. The moon is a silver sphere rising aloft over the fir trees. The sky is sapphire black.

"And I'm totally there," Lily whispered, closing her eyes.

"Do you love the stars?" the Magister asks as we stand atop his tower.

"I do," I tell him. "Though I know so little about them."

Copernicus shakes his head. "I look to the heavens, Hans, I work its numbers incessantly, but the teachings are . . . incorrect. The sun and stars, the planets, do not move as we were taught. I must know more!"

Becca paused. Were there noises from the fencing school? Faint sounds? She listened. No, she thought. It's nothing. Keep going.

†

Then comes the fateful day when a knock comes on the door. Nicolaus leaps down the stairs. "It has arrived!"

It is a ratty old scroll, said to be the secret writing of the great second-century astronomer Ptolemy, author of the infamous Almagest.

"I know about him," Wade said. "Ptolemy was the first to catalog the constellations in any kind of reasonable order. He found forty-eight of them. Dad taught them to me. They're on my star map."

"Ptolemy," Nicolaus says, "was as clever as you and I put together, Hans. This scroll describes astounding astronomical events visible only from the south. Hans, we must go!"

And so, under cover of night and deception, we lock up the Frombork tower and ride the high road south.

Becca paused to breathe slowly. "A journey south from Poland. But for what?"

"Keep reading," said Lily. "Please."

March 17, 1514. Following Ptolemy's scroll, Nicolaus and I undertake a nearly fatal voyage to . . .

"It gets all garbled here with some kind of code we haven't seen yet," Becca said. "It'll take work to figure it out. I'll skip it for now."

. . . where he uses mathematical calculations and the positions of the stars to locate an ancient device first

built by Ptolemy himself.

"It is for this," he says, "that we have risked our lives."

"Device? What kind of ancient device?" asked Lily. "Really, that's all it says? This is so not helpful."

Becca was stumbling over words she didn't know the meaning of, but they weren't the only problem. There were obvious astronomical calculations, passages that looked like primitive algebraic equations, more strange drawings.

"Does anybody else hear sounds from upstairs?" said Darrell.

They listened. Something fell, clattered to the floor. Then quiet.

"Keep going," Lily said.

Becca flipped over another three pages of coded script. "So that's followed by another screwy part."

For days Nicolaus studies the device. "Ptolemy had a vision, but his device was doomed to fail. Ours shall not."

On the island, Nicolaus builds, he steals from this and that. What he cannot find, he forges with his own hands. He invents and reinvents.

Then one evening, "Ptolemy's dream is now complete!"

Soon, the long-promised celestial event occurs . . .

"Something about an explosion of light," Becca said.

Nicolaus positions himself in the center of the device and I behind him . . . there is a hole in the sky, and the voyage begins . . .

"A *hole* in the sky?" Wade jotted it down in his father's journal. "What is he talking about? There's no such thing as . . ."

Becca kept turning pages. "This diary is coded for whole stretches of pages. It's got numbers, letters, and there's the letter V a bunch of times."

Wade turned to her, a frown creasing his forehead. What was going through his mind, she couldn't imagine, but he must have pushed his worry about his father to the side, because then he bit his lip, and his fingers drummed on the table, which she'd seen him do when he was deep in thought. "I wish I had my books. . . ."

She flipped through another several pages, then stopped at a page folded over itself. Delicately, she unfolded it, then gasped.

"What?" said Lily.

And there it was, in a sketch that reminded Becca of the famous drawings by Leonardo da Vinci. Though exactly *what* it was, she couldn't say.

"*That's* the device? What in the world is it?" said Darrell. "It looks like a globe or something . . . or . . . is that a chair?"

But she couldn't stop reading, the words coming ever more quickly.

†

Having laboriously brought the device back to _____ , *Nicolaus suddenly fears the vast power of the Knights of*

*the Teutonic Order of Ancient Prussia, their murderous
Grand Master, Albrecht, and the evil they will do if they
possess the device. "It cannot fall into the hands of these
men!"*

"You don't think . . . I mean . . . is the Teutonic Order
still around?" asked Lily. "If Copernicus was afraid of
them finding the relics then, could they be the same
bunch of people chasing us now? Are the Knights still,
you know, a thing?"

Nicolaus makes a decision.
*From the machine's giant frame, its grand armature,
he will withdraw its twelve constellated parts—without
which the device is inoperable.*
"I will entrust them to twelve . . . relic keepers . . ."
"Guardians!" I say.
*". . . who will vow to hide the device through all
time!"*

Darrell nodded over and over. "The twelve relics are
the twelve parts of the device Copernicus discovered.
Plus you know what else? I bet *GAC* means the Guardians of Something of Copernicus. All we have to figure

247

out is what the thing is that begins with *A*."

Becca's stomach twisted. "Listen to this."

The relics will be hidden far from one another and all across the world, known and unknown.

"The first relic will be presented to a man above all men who will raise it as if it were his own child," Nicolaus says.

"The relics will be bound, one to another. The first will lead to the last, so that—God forbid it should ever be necessary—the great machine might one day be reassembled.

"This, Hans, this machine, will be my true legacy."

Wade stood and started pacing around the table, murmuring. "And there it is, the relics. The secret society of Guardians to protect them around the world. The first will circle to the last. The machine, whatever it is. The Copernicus Legacy—"

The door suddenly swung wide at the top of the stairs above them. It was Carlo, with a young girl their age, who was dressed and armed for fencing.

"We're being attacked," Carlo said. "The Order has found you again. Take the book. It must be spirited away from here, kept on the move. You cannot escape up these stairs, there is another way—"

"The Order!" Becca said. "So that's who they are?"

"The Teutonic Order killed Bernard Dufort and your friend."

"You know about Heinrich?" said Wade.

Carlo pressed a stone on the wall. A hidden door sprang open. "It was Heinrich who told me to expect a visit to the school. His death caused the lockdown and invoked the Frombork Protocol. This way!"

They hurried into a corridor that inclined downward.

"What's the Frombork—" Darrell started.

"Faster!"

The passage stopped at yet another door. It swung open to reveal an even narrower set of stairs leading down into darkness.

"Do you know anything about my father, Roald Kaplan?" Wade asked. "He was arrested in Berlin by the Order and the police—"

"*Arrested* is not the word," said Carlo. "And those policemen have other masters. I know little just yet, but I will find out. You must protect yourselves and the book now. Come, hurry!" He hustled them into the next chamber and a passage that sloped upward in a curve.

"You don't really want us to keep Copernicus's diary," said Becca, holding it carefully. "It's priceless."

"The dagger was his, too," said Lily. "I guess you know that."

"Left," said Carlo, drawing them quickly into a further narrow passage. "As valuable as both are, the Guardians have taken an oath far more important. An oath to protect their children and their children's children from the Order's murderous greed and evil. It has been so for centuries."

"Are you a Guardian?" Lily asked.

Carlo bowed his head. "I am one of the many who seek to honor Copernicus's legacy and protect the relics. The road of a Guardian is often one of hiding and sacrifice, and not for everyone. But now, because the Protocol demands the relics be reunited and destroyed, we are all at risk. You included. This way—"

Carlo arrived at a steel door. He paused. "Since 1543 the Frombork Protocol, devised by the Magister himself on his deathbed, has never been invoked. The Order had fallen apart over the centuries after Albrecht's death, and the relics were safe. Then, four years ago, Heinrich Vogel detected strange new patterns of activity. A new master had emerged. With Vogel's death, the inner circle of Guardians has been breached. The Frombork Protocol has begun."

"What can we do now?" Wade asked.

"Go to Rome immediately," Carlo said. "You will find what you need at *Five, Via Rasagnole*. Remember it. *Five, Via Rasagnole*. Repeat the name."

The kids did, one by one.

"*Five, Via Rasagnole*," Carlo said one last time, and then spelled it out, letter by letter, using the Roman numeral *V* to describe the number, which Becca found odd but helpful.

"Remember this, too. You may not always find the help you seek. Some Guardians will protect their identities to the death. Others do not know their role until events discover it for them. We shall do what we can to hinder the Teutonic Order, and free your father, but your only hope is to stay ahead of them every step of the way."

"Every step of the way to what?" asked Darrell.

"The end of the journey," Carlo said. "The one that began five centuries ago—and started again in Berlin with you!"

More cries came from above. An alarm jangled, then there was the smell of smoke.

"Are those guys seriously the Knights of the Teutonic Order of Ancient Prussia?" asked Lily.

Carlo snorted. "Obviously. Now come on!"

CHAPTER THIRTY-FOUR

They flew through the door and under an arch, and plunged upward into a maze of intricate passages, a stampede of feet closing in behind.

Carlo swung around. "I'll discover what I can about your father, rescue him if necessary. Through the red door!"

They burst into a long room that smelled of gasoline and car wax. It might have once been the stables of the school, but it now seemed to be where they stored a collection of rare and antique cars.

Standing calmly in front of them was a large woman

with a wispy tangle of white hair. She barely looked up as she tugged on a pair of leather racing gloves. Carlo whipped off some words in Italian and handed her a thick brown envelope. The woman nodded slightly. Becca translated. "He told her we need a ride out of here. Fast."

Wade thought, *Is there anything Becca can't understand?*

The woman unhooked a set of keys from a collection hanging on the wall and, despite her bulk, slipped gingerly into the driver's seat of a sleek gold coupe.

Darrell gasped. "Holy cow! It's a mint 1976 Maserati. I love those!"

"Keep the diary safe," Carlo said, looking directly at Becca. "It must be taken from here now, but I will come for it later. The Order will stop at nothing."

"How do they always know where we are?" asked Lily.

"Give me your computer and your phone," Carlo said. "The Order has military-grade tracking technology. Take this instead." He slipped his hand into a pocket and removed a brand-new smartphone. "It's encrypted so they won't be able to track you at first. For emergencies only, understand? All calls under two minutes. Also . . . keep it charged. Here." He passed Lily a charger.

"Thank you!" said Becca, helping pry Lily's fingers off her tablet.

With a horrible thump, the red door buckled. One hinge popped off.

"The Order's here," said the girl. "Time for our friends to leave. *Studenti, vieni!*"

All at once, a side passage filled with the sound of thundering feet, and a stream of fifty or more fencing students poured into the garage.

"Ready?" Carlo called to them.

"Ready!" they sang in unison.

"Take positions," said the girl. The students flattened themselves against the walls on either side of the iron door, weapons raised.

"Go!" Carlo yelled to the driver. "*Buona fortuna*, kids. You will see me again!"

They dived into the car just when the door broke open. At least a dozen men in ski masks bounded in, wielding pistols with silencers.

As if they had been waiting their whole lives for this, the armed students descended on the thugs from behind, catching them off guard. The room exploded in a clash of blades and muffled gunfire.

"*Cinture di sicurezza!*" the driver shouted.

Wade didn't need a translator to tell him to strap on

his seatbelt. The Maserati roared to life, drowning for an instant the mayhem in the room. While the students lunged furiously across the floor, keeping the thugs from appraching the car, a wide garage door flipped up into the ceiling. Daylight poured in from the top of a long ramp.

With its driver laughing at the top of her lungs, the vintage Maserati fishtailed up the ramp and bounced wildly onto the busy streets of Bologna.

They had escaped.

CHAPTER THIRTY-FIVE

Paris, France
March 12th
6:12 p.m.

THWACK-K-K!

The noise-canceling headphones flattened Galina's hair, so she rarely used them. Today, however, it was necessary.

THWACK-K-K!

At 440 feet per second, the sound of a titanium arrow striking its target made the walls of the basement gallery shudder. Removing the headphones, she stared through the crosshairs at the tiny dot of red light centered on the target, flipped the lever alongside the barrel to Silent, and fired a third round.

Fhooo-wit! A bare whisper with only a slight decrease in speed—427 feet per second—and again the arrow pierced the target dead center. Yes. This was the setting she would use.

As usual Ebner was lurking around somewhere. He was rarely far away unless she sent him to fetch something. She heard his shoes scuff the floor behind her.

"The standard handgun bullet travels at eight hundred seventy feet per second," Ebner said. "Which translates to some six hundred sixty miles per hour. These arrows move at, say, half that speed—"

"The crossbow has a long and illustrious history as a hunting weapon," Galina said. "These shafts are lightweight, hollow."

Ebner glanced at the target. Three arrows dead center, stunningly accurate, a tiny teardrop of liquid sliding from each hole. He had heard about the shooting range under the streets of her French office complex, though he had never been allowed inside. She had so many estates and offices and rooms here and there and everywhere, it was a wonder she could keep them straight. But then, Galina was remarkable for that, as in so many other things.

"We are in the city. What can you hunt here?" he asked.

She turned and glared at him, imagining his head balancing an apple on it. "People. What else? The reporter digging into the *Le Monde* murder arrives home every evening after a stroll by the river. Tonight, he will not arrive home."

She took aim for a fourth time when a phone rang in the vicinity of Ebner's sunken chest. She glowered at the interruption as he fumbled to answer it.

"Ya?" he said. "No . . . no, no! You incompetent fools!"

Galina lowered the crossbow without removing the arrow. "What is it now?"

"The computer signal has been lost. The school was on alert. We have casualties. The children have escaped Bologna."

Galina whipped the crossbow up to her shoulder and fired the final arrow downrange without taking aim. It struck the target as the others had, exactly in the center. "Prepare the yacht and my jet. I must be ready to move at any moment."

"Of course, Miss Krause. My apologies. The next time—"

"There will be no next time for you, Ebner von Braun. Stop the children immediately, or I shall stop you."

With three swift gestures, she collapsed the crossbow into a fraction of its size and set it in a small case lined with fin-tipped titanium arrows. Slinging it over her shoulder, she stepped into an elevator, saying, "Street level." Ebner hurried in behind her before the doors closed.

"The Australian Transit is a success," he said. "Our office in Sydney has received the mice. One day early."

"Only one day?" she said, a taste of bitterness on her lips.

"Yes, Miss Krause. Baby steps," he said. "Shall I instruct the laboratory to proceed with the Spanish Experiment?"

She was silent as the elevator rose. One-hundred-and-ninety-seven days away was now one hundred and ninety-five. The doors slid open on a wide hallway filled with mirrors and elaborate Rococo paintings of hunting scenes framed in gold. She strode toward a set of glass doors at the far end of the hall. Ebner followed like a good puppy.

"They promise greater success this time," he added. "They are much closer to cracking the equations."

"Tell them to proceed. Inform me when you have results."

But until then, she thought, the fool children were

misplaced in Italy, and she would have to go there, after all. Her mind agonized over the loss of the children, but her bigger concerns were the Order's forces. They made mistakes. Back in the sixteenth century, Grand Master Albrecht von Hohenzollern would have been appalled at their incompetence and would have dealt with them harshly.

Failure meant beheading.

This was a different era, of course. She would have to make do. Money helped, and she had nearly unlimited funds. What she really needed was time. But sand falls only one way in an hourglass.

She knew a sole genius of particular talents to complement her own, one to help her plan move more swiftly, but, sadly, he was unavailable. Ebner was as close as she had gotten. And she had to put up with his lurking and leering.

Galina opened the glass doors and stepped outside onto a flight of stairs leading down to a grand public square. *Sunset in one hour.*

Towering over Paris's Place de la Concorde was the great Luxor Obelisk. Erected on the spot where the guillotine once enacted its vengeance, this priceless gift from Egypt was now a smog-enveloped inconvenience for motorbikes and cars to whiz around like so many toys. It was a shame that beheadings were no longer popular.

"I will wander by the Louvre before I stroll the riverbank," Galina said. "I must think."

Ebner followed her down two steps, a third.

She stopped and turned. "And by that, I mean *alone*."

CHAPTER THIRTY-SIX

The Maserati sliced its way through the Italian hills like a sharp knife through oversteamed broccoli.

Unable to avert his eyes from the road, Wade's heart thumped so wildly it pushed his lungs up into his throat, where he was pretty sure they stopped working.

"Wade, you all right up there?" asked Lily.

"Uh . . ."

The driver laughed and nodded to the back. *"C'è un cesto. Mangiate!"*

"A basket?" said Becca.

Darrell tugged at something behind his seat. "Right here. A picnic basket full of stuff. Bread, cheese, salami. Even Cokes!" He dove into it, passed it around, and the kids stuffed themselves for the first time in hours. Despite the driver sending the car squealing around a hairpin and onto a straightaway at a speed of what had to be well over a hundred miles an hour, Wade managed to wash down a hearty cheese and salami sandwich with strawberry-flavored mineral water.

"Better. Much better," he said. He turned to see Becca shaking her head at the diary. "What did you find?"

"Something unhelpful," she said. "Listen. This is from before the whole Teutonic Order thing."

As we leave the island, our precious cargo lashed to the deck of the ship, Nicolaus passes me a small scrap of paper. "To add to the diary."

"What is it?" I ask.

"The man we met . . . he shared these numbers to explain how the device made the impossible possible. Hans, what do you think?"

The winches and pulleys of my brain twist and stall as the ship sails west. Finally, I begin to see the significance of the numbers.

Becca held out the diary to Wade. Her hands were trembling. "I don't know who 'the man we met' is, but can you make sense of *this*?"

The car was cruising quite calmly—for the moment—as Wade studied the yellow, weathered page and saw the following:

$$ds^2 = -c^2dt^2 + dl^2 + (k^2 + l^2) (d\theta^2 + sin^2\ \theta d\phi^2)$$

"Algebra . . ." He puzzled over the sequence of letters and numbers, wondering at first if algebraic symbols were even around when Copernicus lived and wishing he knew more about the history of mathematics.

Dad would know.

Wade did his best to prod the winches and pulleys of his own brain and think like his father, but it wasn't working. Worry over the man's fate and the possibility of their own imminent death in Italian traffic made it impossible to focus.

He tugged out his father's student notebook. "This formula is way beyond me. In fact, I think it's actually called a metric. Maybe Dad wrote about something in his classes with Uncle Henry . . ."

The car accelerated swiftly now on a multilane high-way. On their right, the sun had begun to set behind the hills. The Mediterranean lay beyond them.

As Wade turned the scribbled pages of his father's journal, he couldn't stop imagining what was happening back in Berlin. His eyes glazed over. *Dad in a cell? Or worse.*

"Wade?" Becca said, leaning over.

"Right. Sorry." He focused, searched the pages, then stopped when he read one particular notation. "Quantum physics? They didn't know about any quantum physics in the sixteenth century."

"What are you saying—" Darrell started.

Wade held up his hand for quiet. He turned one more page, checked the diary again, then finally shrugged. "The formula, or one quite like it, is actually in Dad's journal. But I don't see how it's possible for it to be in the diary."

"What do you mean? It's right there," said Lily.

"Copernicus couldn't have thought of these numbers," Wade went on. "It's an equation from modern physics."

"He said he met a man," Darrell said. "Besides, Copernicus was modern in the way he thought. He revolutionized science, didn't he?"

Wade suddenly figured out something that made his brain do an uncomfortable twist. He tried to iron it flat, but it wouldn't go. "It's just that . . . I don't get how Copernicus is writing this in 1514."

"What does the equation even mean?" asked Lily. "Or signify? Or whatever you mathy people say?"

"According to Dad's notes, Uncle Henry was lecturing about exotic matter and wormholes, and these numbers," he said, trying not to sound like his father, "are one equation for the existence of a wormhole. And not just any wormhole, a traversable wormhole, in fact."

"Traversable?" said Darrell.

"Right. Traversable, as in being able to travel through it. A wormhole you can use to travel in time. Dad writes that these kinds of formulas come from astrophysicists like Kip Thorne. Dad *knows* Kip Thorne. I've heard him talk to him on the phone. This," he said, tapping the antique diary, "is not Copernicus. This is Thorne."

"Could I see the diary?" Darrell said. Wade passed it back to him.

"Hans Novak says Copernicus discovered it," Becca said, sounding suddenly a bit angry. "He based it on their weird journey. So, how did he come up with it? Answer that, Wade."

"Yeah, *Wade*," said Lily.

"I don't know. Maybe the diary is, you know,

doctored somehow. Or even . . . fake."

"Fake!" Lily snapped. "People have been—"

"I know!" he said. "People have been killed. Uncle Henry was murdered . . ."

"Excuse me," Darrell said. "My mom—Sara to the rest of you—deals with old stuff like this all the time. Just looking at the ink and the paper and the condition, I think when she's back, she'd tell us that the diary's real. Genuine, she'd call it."

"Then I can't explain it," Wade said, handing the diary back to Becca. "But if Dad copied this formula from Uncle Henry's lecture, and if Uncle Henry was killed for a diary which has the same formula in it, *he* must have thought it was real."

"Genuine, he'd call it," Lily said quietly.

It was hard for him to admit, but he nodded. "Maybe."

Their driver suddenly took a bizarre series of tight turns, then bounced off the highway onto local roads.

"Where are we going, anyway?" Lily asked. "Carlo told us an address, but I guess I didn't hear his voice when he was talking. Does anyone remember—"

"*Five, Via Rasagnole!*" everyone shouted at her.

"Oh. Right." Lily shrugged. "I leave memorizing stuff to other people. Or I used to. Without my computer I guess I have to start."

"Every once in a while," Becca said, elbowing Lily gently, who then elbowed Darrell just for fun.

All of which lightened the mood, until the Maserati squealed suddenly into a lower gear. The road ahead was blocked. Flashing lights from several police vans whirled brightly, making the night air glow like a carnival.

"Roadblock," Darrell whispered. "They're with the Order. They must be. I knew it. We're doomed."

"If they're not with the Order," said Becca, "we can at least assume that they're after the dumb kids who crossed the border illegally, are concealing a deadly weapon and—now—a priceless sixteenth-century diary. We should turn around. And I mean, like, now—"

"No, no," the driver growled. Following the gestures of a policeman dressed in riot gear and wearing a helmet, she downshifted again and pulled up to the roadblock.

"Maybe the police who arrested Dad told them about us," Darrell whispered. "We're wanted criminals. Or worse."

"What's worse than being a wanted criminal?" said Lily. "Being *un*wanted?"

Three policemen joined the first and surrounded the car. Their expressions were grim. They rattled off a string of words so fast that Wade wondered if even Becca could follow. The driver looked slowly at each of the children then back to the policemen.

"Sì, va tutto bene," she said.

Wade glanced out the side window. It was maybe ten feet to the edge of the road. There was a fence. Not too high. So, they could dash to the fence. Clamber over the top. Run across the field on the other side. Maybe there was a river. A boat. They could motor down the river. The police couldn't follow their scent. Follow their *scent*? Now he was thinking like Darrell. Besides, they had guns and ugly expressions, so he guessed that he and his friends would be picked off in seconds.

The driver pointed across him to the glove compartment near his knees. *"Apra, per favore."*

He lifted a delicate silver latch and the small door dropped open. Inside was the thick brown envelope Carlo had given the driver in the garage. *I should have known. A bribe! We're giving the police a bribe. We'll be sentenced to Italian jail for a hundred years for bribing law enforcement officials.*

"Open, *sì*?" said the driver, smiling at him.

Wade opened the envelope. There was no cash. No money. There were, however, five red booklets. Before he realized what they were, the policeman on his side of the car snatched them from his hands. He ran a flashlight over each one, then in the car at their faces, matching them up.

"Passports?" Lily said. "For us? But how—"

"Shh," whispered the driver.

The policeman returned the documents to Wade. On some kind of autopilot, he reinserted them in the brown envelope and tucked it back into the glove compartment, closing it with a click. He hadn't breathed for the last two minutes. The police backed away from the Maserati, calling to their counterparts. One of the vans pulled off the road and out of the way. Shifting smoothly into gear, the driver laughed and roared on into the night.

"How did we just get past those guys?" Lily asked.

Becca translated Lily's question to the driver, who, naturally, exploded in laughter.

"I documenti per viaggio di scuola. Le fotografie sono state prese dalle telecamere nei passaggi. Siamo a Roma in un'ora!"

"School travel documents, like passports for school trips," Becca said. "Our photos are from the cameras in the passages. I knew those cameras were taking our pictures!"

"And that last part, Becca?" said Darrell.

"We'll be in Rome in an hour!"

CHAPTER THIRTY-SEVEN

Somosierra, Spain
March 12th
8:09 p.m.

Sixty-eight-year-old Diego Vargas, a gray-whiskered grandfather with a comb-over he was beginning to think was no longer worth the effort, pushed the gas pedal to the floor of the school bus. The rattletrap barely seemed to notice.

Climbing the foothills of the Somosierra mountains day in and day out was getting the better of the ancient vehicle. When he calculated whether the bus was older than he was, he realized it was.

By three years.

The children Diego was hauling couldn't care less. They were screaming and shouting, tossing rolled-up paper balls over their exhausted teachers' heads. It had been a very long day, far longer than the teachers expected, but that wasn't Diego's fault. The noisy children—*los niños ruidosos*—were having the time of their lives, and because it was the last outing of the school term, they were going out with a bang.

Still, Diego had to admit that, running late or not, the field trip to Madrid, some sixty miles south, had been all right. In the time between ferrying the monsters from the museum to the park, he'd managed to visit his son and daughter-in-law and his grandson, Emilio. Good people, all of them. The future of Spain.

"Cut it out!" "That's mine!" "Make me!" "I'll stomp your foot!" "You're lying!"

You'd think these *niños* would be tired at the end of such a long day. Ha! Now that they were nearing home they grew more rambunctious than ever!

Diego—and his bus—were getting far too old for this.

He jammed the shift lever, and the bus growled into a higher gear as they reached a level stretch of road. A few minutes later, he spied the opening to the mountain tunnel.

A car idled by the side of the road, lights flashing. Its door swung open and a uniformed guard waved him down with his walkie-talkie. It was Alejo. He knew Alejo and had seen him that morning.

Diego slowed the bus to a stop. "Long day for you, too, eh? Any problems?"

The guard grinned. "No, no. Just that power is out in the tunnel. No lights. Rockslides earlier this afternoon on the other side. Repairs are nearly over now, but be careful when you come through. Workers on the road. Okay?" He waved his walkie-talkie. "I'll call Nacio, tell him to expect you. And remember, slow-slow-slow!"

Diego laughed. "*Sí, sí*, Alejo. Slow is this bus's specialty! We'll be on the lookout."

As the guard barked into his walkie-talkie, Diego wrenched the bus painfully into gear again and sputtered slowly into the tunnel. Like every time before, the children erupted in screams of delight as they entered the tunnel, louder now that the only light was from the headlights.

"Hush, hush!" Diego shouted over his shoulder. Like every time before, the children paid no attention at all.

On the far side of the tunnel, the night had cooled rapidly, as it always did north of the Guadarrama Mountains.

Wondering when he could go home and get out of his uniform, the tunnel guard Nacio paced back and forth, observing a handful of transportation workers shovel debris from the road. Another group was scrambling around the rocks above the tunnel entrance, securing a heavy wire net across the base of the hill. Nacio glanced at his watch.

Seven o'clock. And not a minute longer. I swear, my replacement had better be here. He paused as half the workers stowed their shovels on a truck and switched to push brooms. One of the policemen called to him.

"Where is that bus, eh?"

Nacio shrugged. It had been nearly twenty minutes since Alejo's call. "He said it was coming. Even a slow bus . . ." He drifted off. Even a slow bus—even *walking*—wouldn't take more than ten minutes. The tunnel was less than a mile long.

The police officer switched on his high-power flashlight. "Maybe it broke down, got stuck."

"Or attacked by werewolves!"

"Yeah. And the ghost of Napoleon," the policeman laughed. "Come on."

"After this, I go home!" Nacio grumbled. "Replacement or no."

The two men walked into the dark tunnel, their

flashlights combing the two lanes ahead. The tunnel had been cut through the mountain at a slight arc, so it was impossible to see through to the other end until they got to the middle.

It wasn't a long tunnel, after all, but as they neared the turn and still saw no trace of the bus, Nacio felt his heart pound faster. What would they see? Had the bus had an accident? A breakdown? Had its headlights failed, causing it to crash in the dark? But, really, if any of those things had happened, wouldn't the driver and the children have called out? Indeed, wouldn't he and the policeman have heard their echoing voices the moment they entered the tunnel? And wouldn't one of the teachers have come through to ask for help? And if, for some reason, it was still on Alejo's side, wouldn't he simply have phoned?

The policeman slowed to match his pace. They were side by side.

The silence in the tunnel was broken only by the two sets of quiet footsteps. They were nearing the end of the turn when Nacio paused to collect himself. The policeman hung back, too. There was a quiet glance between them. They started forward again. Ten feet to the end of the turn. Five feet. Two more steps.

And there in the center of the tunnel stood the other guard, Alejo. His eyes were wide. His mouth open. His trembling hand holding a flashlight. "It's you!" he said.

"Of course it's us. Where is the bus?" asked Nacio.

Alejo's face paled. "Why didn't you call me when it came through? You're supposed to call me."

Nacio turned to the policeman, then back to Alejo. "Because it never came through. Did it turn back?"

"It went into the tunnel," said Alejo. "I told you when it did. Old man Vargas drove it into the tunnel. It didn't come out on your side?"

"Of course it didn't come out!" said the policeman gruffly. "Why do you think we're standing here?"

Nacio hushed them. "Alejo, what are you saying?"

Alejo shook his head slowly. "I'm saying that I saw the school bus enter the tunnel. If it didn't exit the tunnel, then . . ."

"Then what?" said the policeman testily.

"Then it has vanished."

CHAPTER THIRTY-EIGHT

The wispy-haired driver jammed the brake to the floor of the Maserati so suddenly that Wade's forehead nearly split open across the dashboard.

"Benvenuto!" she crowed, waving her hand at the view beyond the windshield. *"Ci siamo a Roma!"*

They were barely fifty yards from the Colosseum, the monstrous old four-story arena of concrete and stone looming over them. Several wide streets splayed out from it in different directions.

"Which one is Via Rasagnole?" Becca asked from the backseat.

The driver, keeping her smile, took a wad of euros from a small pocket and held it in Darrell's face. *"Da Carlo,"* she said. Then she reached over Wade and pulled the door handle, giving him a push. *"Arrivederci!"*

He nearly tumbled into the street. "Wait, no—"

Summoning her entire English vocabulary for the first time on their 200-mile trek, she managed to say, "All—you—out!"

"You can't just leave us here!" Lily shouted.

"Really, what about Via Rasagnole?" Darrell said, squeezing out from behind Wade's seat. "We have to go to Five, Via Rasagnole."

"Non ho mai sentito parlare della Via Rasagnole."

Becca squirmed out. "What do you mean you never heard of it? It's Via Rasagnole! Your boss told us to go there."

"Via Rasagnole! Via Rasagnole!" the driver mimicked. *"Ciao!"*

Gravel sprayed them like bullets as the Maserati fishtailed away and disappeared behind the Colosseum, which, no matter how cheerily it was lit up in the golden glow of spotlights, looked to Darrell like nothing but a great big monument of death.

"What just happened?" Wade said.

Becca growled. "We were dumped."

"At least we have Carlo's phone," said Lily.

Darrell turned. "For emergencies only. Plus he has a last name."

"Nuovenuto," said Becca. "I remember it because I think it's a short form of something like 'newcomer.'"

"Guys, we need to focus," Wade said, hitching his backpack over his shoulder. "I don't know what that lady's problem is, but what we need now is an old-fashioned street map."

"Because without a computer, we're in the stone age," said Lily.

Darrell leafed through the bills the driver had given him. "The Colosseum is a tourist trap. Somebody's got to be selling street maps."

"Good thinking," said Becca. "Let's do it."

As they pushed their way into the crowd, looking for vendors, Darrell also kept his eyes peeled for Teutonic Knights. No one really looked the part, *but that's exactly what they want you to think!*

Lily poked him with her elbow. "There."

Next to a group of young men and women sitting on a low wall was a sign. "Tourist Maps." No sooner had they started over than the whole group of them jumped up and trotted toward them, smiling animatedly. "You want a tour of old Roma, yes?" one guy said. "Nice

American tourists. We show you Colosseum. Beautiful at night. Wild animals. Gladiators. All here. Fifteen American dollars each. Yes?"

"Sorry," said Darrell. "We don't have that—"

"Ten dollars each!"

"No, actually—"

"Seven. Final offer. Okay, five. My absolute lowest offer. Three?"

Lily drew in a breath. "No. Really. We just want a map to find . . . what's the name of that street again—"

"*Five, Via Rasagnole!*" the others yelled.

The young people looked at one another. One unfolded a giant street map. They chattered to one another in some language Darrell couldn't identify, but Becca whispered that it was probably Romany, the language of Gypsies.

Cool, he thought. *Lost in Rome with a band of Gypsies.*

Except that's not true. We know where we are now, and a map will tell us where to go, plus I'm not sure "Gypsies" is politically correct, so never mind.

After a few minutes, one guy shook his head. He handed them the map. "Take it. Is free. But no *Via Rasagnole*. Look. Index. Look!"

They thanked the people and stepped away to search the map privately.

"They're right," Wade said, studying the streets and

the index. "There's no such street in Rome."

"Which makes no sense," said Darrell. "Why would the guy at the fencing school—"

"Carlo," said Lily.

"—tell us to go there if there's no there there?"

Wade snapped his fingers. "Hold on, hold on. I know it's late and my brain really wants to shut off, but maybe the address isn't real."

"He wanted us to get lost?" said Lily. "Why would Carlo do a thing like that?"

"No, look. He made us memorize the address and even spelled it for us, remember? Why would he spell it, if he didn't want us to know the exact letters? He even said the *Five* was a *V.* As if it's a word clue. Becca, it's what you said. Clues leading to clues. Maybe all the things we're getting are clues. Rebuses, codes, stuff like that. And we have to be smart to figure them out."

"Here we go again," said Lily.

"Actually, it makes sense," Darrell said. "That's why the Guardians have been able to keep Copernicus's secret all these years. The levels of clues go on and on, and you have to be willing to follow them."

"Carlo told us they've been doing it for centuries," Wade went on. "It's how they kept the Order away until now."

Becca nodded. "So, *V, Via Rasagnole* might be a word scramble?"

Drawing them farther away from the glaring lights of the Colosseum, Lily said, "You know, there are computer programs that work out codes and word scrambles. We can't do it on the phone because it would take too long. But I bet if we can find a real computer, like a public computer that can't be traced, we can find out what the address really means."

"Smart, Lil, really smart," said Becca. "A public computer that can't be traced. Until then, we have to assume that the Knights of the Teutonic Order are still out there. And by 'out there,' I mean lurking around every single corner."

Darrell checked his watch. It was after nine o'clock. After the day they'd had, he wanted to lie down on the nearest flat surface, but Becca was right. They shouldn't stay anywhere too long. And they should keep their eyes open and their ears alert.

He located the Colosseum on the map. "We're here," he said. "Let's walk until we find a public library or internet café. Then we go in or wait until morning when they open—"

"Oh!" Lily gasped, then held up the phone. "It's

vibrating. Someone's calling me!" She tapped it. "Hello? I said Hello?"

She turned to Becca. "They're all Italian and stuff . . ."

Becca took the phone. *"Pronto?"*

Everyone hushed while Becca listened. *"Sì? Sul serio?"* She looked at Wade and Darrell, her eyes growing moist instantly.

"Oh no," said Wade. "What is it?"

"Domani? Sì! Sì! Ciao!" Even before ending the call, she wrapped her arms around both boys. "Your dad's been released by the German authorities. He's coming here tomorrow—"

"Yes!" Wade practically collapsed on Darrell, who could barely hold himself up. "Dad is back. I can't believe it."

"I knew he'd escape," Darrell said. "He's Dad!"

"How did he get free?" asked Lily. "And who was that?"

Becca hung up. "Carlo's assistant. Carlo knows a lawyer who knows a lawyer, so they made the police release Dr. Kaplan—Roald—on a technicality. She said the Order will soon figure out we're here. We need to be careful. But this is so great. Your dad will meet us at noon at a place called the Castel Sant'Angelo, near the river."

Wade breathed in and out. "Holy cow, awesome, yes, yes!"

Darrell rubbed his eyes and scanned the map. "Okay, we just have to make sure we stay out of the wrong hands. Castel Sant'Angelo . . . I can't read this thing. Who wants to lead. I'm too . . ."

"I got it," Becca said, taking the map. "Everybody agreed?"

"Agreed," said Lily. "Let's do this."

"Yeah, awesome!" said Wade.

Darrell floated after them. They'd see Dad by lunchtime. And Carlo got him out. The Guardians were helping them. It was like a shadow had lifted, not only from him but from all of them. They were bubbling.

Becca traced her fingers over the map. With the Colosseum at her back, she looked toward another bunch of ruins. "It's a pretty straight shot from here through the Roman Forum to the Tiber River. Castel Sant'Angelo is on the far side of one of the bridges. *Segui la guida!*"

She locked arms with Lily, who held her phone light over the map, and they set off down a cobbled path. They strode away from the square that surrounded the Colosseum and into the outskirts of what she said was "once the center of Imperial Rome."

"The key word being *once*," Darrell said.

The shadows closed quickly around them the moment they passed under a giant arch. It was like the air had suddenly changed, he thought, like entering the deep dark past. The paths between the ruins were jammed with clusters of slow-moving tourists, but the Forum was free of motorized traffic, which, given the crazy drivers they'd seen so far, was a good thing. As Darrell expected, Becca began pointing things out.

"This big arch is called the Arch of Titus," she read from the map. "It's from the first century. Titus's brother built it to honor him. Emperors did that kind of stuff back then."

"I'd do that for you, bro," said Wade with a pretend-serious face. "As long as it meant that I was the alive brother."

"Ha, ha. Never mind building an arch. Just give me the cash."

"What we're walking on now is Via Sacra," Lily added, reading the map under the phone light.

"The sacred road. I get it," Darrell said.

"*Sacred* is an anagram for 'scared,'" said Wade.

Darrell gave him a look. "I love history, I really do," he said. "In fact, I love it so much I want to *make* it history. Let's keep moving."

The Forum may have been restored as a place for

tourists, he thought, but there was still a ton of rubble and heaps of stone and single columns where giant temples to some god or goddess once stood.

He thought the place needed serious work.

On their right they passed what Becca told them was the Basilica of Constantine. To him, its thick black arches stared down at them like the eye sockets of a massive skull.

"This reminds me that we're spending another night in another graveyard," Darrell said, keeping to the path. "Are we sure this is the quickest way to the Castel Sant'Angelo?"

Becca nodded. "It is, but if we weren't on the run for our lives, I could spend a few days here."

"The key word being *days*," Darrell said. "At night, this is serious ghost territory."

This part of Rome was an old, dead city, a collection of crumbled stone, half columns, shattered statues, and earthen streets, leading to and away from buildings that weren't there.

The hair on his neck rose as they passed the imposing bulk of the Temple of Romulus. A stubby tower of thick stone, with a cupola on top, it was dense and dark and forbidding. He didn't want to think about what used to go on behind its massive bronze doors. Sacrifices probably. They took kids from other countries and . . . never mind.

"Darrell?"

He turned to Wade. "Yeah?"

"Look up there."

Darrell looked beyond the temples and columns to the blue-black dome of the sky and all its silvery stars. "Yeah. You and Copernicus and stars."

"Right," said Wade. "He was a scientist, an astronomer like Dad. And let's assume he figured out some modern physics. Fine. But then the question is, *what* is he talking about? And I think it comes down to the device in the sketch."

"Yeah, the sketch. I love that. I've been thinking about it, too."

They passed a grassy area with a flat stone in the middle that Darrell was certain was where ancient people sacrificed kids. A policeman wove his way past them, and he remembered that they were still hiding from the cops.

"Whatever the thing was, it had twelve parts," Darrell murmured. "But then what? What was it supposed to do?"

"That I can't tell you."

They were now walking up to the Capitoline Hill,

which, according to Becca and Lily, was one of the seven hills that Rome was built on. It was less a hill than a big mound, but that was just fine.

They were climbing out of the land of the dead.

Becca stopped to study the map, while Lily slung her bag to the ground and plopped next to it.

"I am so tired," she said. "These hills may look like nothing, but my legs are screaming at me. I need to rest for two minutes. Five. Ten minutes, my final offer—"

Darrell laughed and sat next to her.

"I mean," said Wade, standing with Becca, "I ask myself, what would be so incredibly dangerous in the wrong hands? A weapon? What could make people commit murder for five centuries—"

"Oh my!" Becca cried, rattling the map. "Oh! Oh!"

A policeman appeared out of nowhere, shining his flashlight over them. *Va tutto bene?*

"*Sì,*" said Becca. "*Sì, sì. Grazie!*" The policeman nodded and walked away. "Guys, guess what I just found on the map the totally old-fashioned way?"

"With light from Carlo's phone?" Lily added.

"That we're lost?" said Darrell.

"Nope. A museum!"

Wade laughed. "Becca, this is Rome. The whole city's a museum."

She grinned from ear to ear. "But I found a museum called . . . wait for it . . . the Museo Astronomico e Copernicano."

"Seriously?" Darrell said, standing up.

"Uh-huh! And I'm pretty sure it's all about you know what and you know who!"

CHAPTER THIRTY-NINE

"Our luck just changed!" Lily squealed. "Becca, take us there this instant!"

"Follow me this instant!" Becca laughed, and she marched out of the Forum. "The museum is in the middle of a park a few miles from here. We can walk it."

A Copernicus museum?

Their luck was changing, all right. And now that his father was on his way, Wade was surprised at how incredibly beautiful Rome was turning out to be. The old city, its winding streets, the comfortable temperature, his awesome friends, the innumerable cars—little

Fiats and Alfas buzzing around like mice in a maze—everything was suddenly and astoundingly and unbelievably . . . *right.*

Becca's ponytail bounced and spun as she forged ahead, acting as tour guide, tracing her fingers animatedly on the map.

"Right here. Left. Now straight on."

For the next two hours, they made their way across the city. Streets twisted and crisscrossed one another in a careless manner. Nearly every corner they came to offered a view of some piazza or fountain or church or monument. Lily was chattering again. Darrell bounced on his heels, humming a riff from Gary Clark Jr.

Everything was good.

Even the killers don't know exactly where we are.

A slow hour after that they found themselves meandering up a series of inclined roads into a quiet, forested park that might have been what was left of one of Rome's ancient hills, or maybe not, it didn't matter. What mattered was perched at the top of the park and lit with floodlights—a large villa with three observatory domes on its roof.

"The Museo Astronomico e Copernicano," Becca said when they drew close to a high wrought-iron fence surrounding it. "We could climb over and peek in the windows. Or just wait for the place to open in the morning. Any ideas?"

"Yeah. No more climbing," Lily said. "My legs won't stand for it. Get it? *Stand*. Never mind. I'm done." She sat on a low wall bordering the road, kicked off her shoes, and rubbed her feet.

The park behind them was heavily treed, quiet, and sheltered, and the night air was still temperate.

"If we have to spend the next few hours outside, this isn't a bad place," Wade said. "One of us could stay awake. We can take shifts."

"It's pretty quiet up here, and warm," Darrell said. "It's after eleven. If we're lucky, the museum will open at nine. Ten hours? I could totally sleep that long."

"Fine," Wade said. "Let's find a quiet spot in the park and hang out until morning. Sleep. Whatever. We need to get in there, but I'm tired of breaking laws."

"Good call," said Becca. "We must have a rap sheet a mile long."

Lily tramped among the trees and staked out an area of trim grass beneath a low-hanging tree. She rested her head on her bag. "Good night."

Each of them picked a grassy patch—not too far from the others—and settled in. Wade's bones ached from the inside out, but his mind was racing. No way could he sleep. "I'll take first watch."

"Me, second," said Darrell.

They were suddenly quiet, which was fine with Wade.

For the first hour, he found his thoughts returning to the first pages Becca had translated. Nicolaus in his tower, looking at the sky with Hans.

Copernicus dealt with all the regular stuff people in his time had to deal with—lousy medicine, smelly houses, weird food, long travel, no plumbing—but he still needed to discover things.

That's what really got Wade. That one man had an idea, and it changed the world. It meant that anyone could have an idea that could change the world too. He remembered what his father had told him Einstein said:

Imagination is more important than knowledge. Knowledge is limited. Imagination encircles the world.

Right? Nobody told Copernicus to study the stars. No one made him discover a new theory about the sun, but he did. He used his imagination, and he discovered new things.

I must know more!

And then the legacy. What device had he invented?

What did the *A* of GAC mean? What were the relics? Even if everyone was convinced the diary was genuine, how could Copernicus ever have come up with the wormhole metric?

Over and over the same questions, over and over the same no answers. His thoughts were like waves crashing against rocks that refused to change their shape.

I, too, must know more.

By the time he finally gave up cogitating, Darrell was snoring like a bass woofer, and he couldn't bear to wake him. Lily, it turned out, talked in her sleep as much as she did when she was awake. Right now she was muttering a long story about an internet link that led to another and another and never stopped.

Becca didn't make a peep other than her slow, measured breathing, which was just shy of snoring, until sometime past two a.m, when she bolted straight up from what must have been a coma-like slumber and said, "It's time!" And then fell instantly back, falling into the same breathing rhythm as Darrell's.

It wasn't time yet. Not with the sky still sprinkled with stars. But Wade was forced to admit that if he couldn't sleep, at least he had his friends to listen to, and he may as well finish his stint as lookout.

"I'll sleep after Dad comes," he whispered to himself.

He watched the slow turning of the dome of stars and imagined Copernicus studying the same stars five hundred years ago. People and science and history. Wade loved the old stuff more than he had before they began this crazy adventure. He imagined the vague machine in the sketch, its giant frame, the odd notations. Did the device really have levers and gears, leather straps, hinges, wheels, pulleys? And seats? What about the *hole in the sky* . . . what was that . . . *a hole* . . .

It was only later when he felt someone nudge his arm over and over that he realized he had fallen asleep. He sat up to see Becca on her feet watching the road. There came the sound of an approaching car.

"Everybody wake up," she said. "The museum is open. It's time!"

CHAPTER FORTY

After tramping up the long driveway to the parking lot, they found the villa's doors—flanked by a pair of giant palms—already open.

A little white-haired man in a rumpled suit sat at a small desk inside. He looked them up and down, ran his fingers along his thin white mustache, and smiled.

What began then was a strange, slow conversation in English.

A kind of English.

"You are Mary Cans?" he asked, smiling, inscribing the number 4 on a sheet of paper at the desk.

Lily turned to the others. "No, sir. I'm Lily and this is—"

"Yes, Americans," said Darrell.

"As I say." The man stood and bowed. "You love stairs?"

"Stars," said Wade. "Yes, we love stars."

"But we don't have much money," Becca added.

He laughed a fluttery laugh. "No, no. The *museo* is freezing for children under seven ton!"

That took a while. It was finally Lily who broke the silence. "Seventeen!" she said. "No, we're all younger."

"As I say," he said, and gave them a printed guide. "Forgive his translation. I did it yourself. Congratulations to visit our smell *museo*. But even with the smellness of us, we are flooded with, how you say, *de-feces* . . . ?"

"Devices?" said Becca.

"*Sì*, thems. So, get out of here. Make your house inside. Enjoy myself!"

"Thank you very much," said Wade.

As they entered a high-ceilinged, paneled room, Darrell whispered, "I can no longer remember a time when that man wasn't talking."

"In my head, he still is," said Lily. "Now let's keep our eyes open for a public computer."

Arranged in display cases lining the walls were

297

a series of old globes and antique instruments. There were several simple machines made of brass—Wade remembered his father explaining that these were called sextants and were used by sailors to navigate their ships by the positions of the stars.

"Celestial maps," said Becca, nodding at the wall. "Like yours, Wade."

He glanced over a dozen variations of the Ptolemaic cosmos. Some were quite fine, but none were as beautiful as the one Uncle Henry had given him. He took a moment to check the sheath and his backpack again. The dagger and the map were both safe.

In the middle of the room stood a wooden sky globe on which were painted the forty-eight constellations cataloged by Ptolemy in the second century. Next to the globe were several small orbs. Some had interlocking and concentric ribbons of iron or brass, each band representing the orbital path of one of the planets. Becca translated the exhibition notes and told them the orbs were called "armillary spheres."

"Dad has a book about them," Wade said.

"They're beautiful," Lily said.

"But inaccurate," Wade added, "because the bands are circular instead of elliptical, which they didn't figure out until later."

"Thank you, Professor," said Lily.

It was the series of objects they saw next that stopped them cold.

On a raised platform the wall was arrayed in a variety of what were called astrolabes—ancient devices to detect the distance and movement of stars. All had sliding arcs of brass or iron, and levers marked with measurements, and some were as simple as two pieces of brass mounted to each other and sitting as flat as a dinner plate.

The larger ones, however, were complex machines—*machinas*—that combined both the concentric bands of the armillary spheres and a complicated arrangement of sliding levers and moving wheels connected to automatic or spring-wound clocks. They looked just this side of being motorized. These were the first items they had seen that could by any stretch of the imagination be thought of as advanced devices and reminded Wade of the Painter Hall telescope in Austin.

"This is steampunk before they had steam," Darrell said.

"The sketch . . . ," Becca whispered. She opened her bag and flipped the diary pages to the picture she had found earlier. "What if Copernicus reworked Ptolemy's device and invented one of these machines? But a big one. One you could sit inside? Some of the ones here have twelve parts, more than twelve parts. Gears and wheels and things."

She turned several pages. "Listen to this again."

> *Nicolaus makes a decision.*
> *From the machine's giant frame, its grand armature, he will withdraw its twelve constellated parts—without which the device is inoperable.*

Wade closed his eyes. "Constellated parts . . ."

"Except that the diary also talks about traveling and a voyage," Darrell said. "Astrolabes aren't vehicles. They don't *go* anywhere. They just sit there, and you make calculations from them."

"We might need to think out of the box," said Lily.

"I agree," said Becca "Let's keep looking for information."

They entered a fourth room, where a number of books and scrolls were exhibited in display cases.

"Computers," said Lily, heading for a bank of monitors at a long table. "I'm going to see what I can find out about Via Rice-A-Roni." She sat herself down at the computer table and began keying furiously.

Becca bent low over a display case and tapped the

glass. "One of these is said to be the first biography of Copernicus, written only twenty years after he died. I wish I could take a look at the whole book. Maybe it says something about the journey of 1514 . . ."

"We have a pepper bag," said the white-haired man, who was strolling through the rooms. "Please wet yourselves here." He spun quickly on his heels and was gone.

Wade laughed. "He wants us to wait, but what are we going to do with a pepper bag?" But as soon as he heard the words aloud, he realized. "Paperback."

"If I'm right," Becca whispered, "the biography might help me translate more of the diary."

The short man returned with a large paperback volume and offered it to Becca with a bow. As the museum was slowly filling with visitors, she settled at the computer table across from Lily and started to read the book and the diary side by side.

Wade sat next to her. "I'm really glad . . ." he started. She looked up. Those green eyes, still a little sleepy.

"Yes?" she said.

". . . that you can read this stuff. We'd be so lost. Without you and your brain."

Her eyes sparkled for a moment, then her face frowned to the text again. "Except it's really hard, and some stuff I think I'm translating right doesn't make any kind of sense to me. I wish your brain and my brain could read it together."

Seriously? "Me, too," he said lamely, aware that Lily had just flicked her eyes at him before returning to her screen.

Becca flipped pages back and forth in both books, her fingers acting as bookmarks in several places at once.

"Find anything?" asked Darrell, returning from the astrolabes in the other room.

"I don't know," Becca said. "I'm trying to match up dates and things, and in one part both the diary and the bio seem to talk about the same strange thing that happened when Copernicus and Hans returned from their voyage."

Darrell frowned. "Strange like what?"

Becca shifted the paperback in front of her. "This biography refers to '*l'incidente dei due dottori identici.*' The incident of the two identical doctors. Which doesn't make a whole lot of sense. In the diary, Hans goes into Italian and writes, '*il momento favoloso dei due Nicolaus,*' which is something like 'the magical moment of two Nicolauses.' Finally, Hans writes this."

> *In five days, the second Nicolaus was gone, and there was only one of him again.*

"What does *that* mean?" said Lily.

Wade's temples throbbed and he held his head as if it were going to explode. So this was it. The real problem. The thing he'd been dreading ever since he saw the modern formula in the old diary.

"Two at the same time . . . traversable wormhole . . . I think I know what they're trying to say, and it's not really possible," he said.

Darrell cocked his head to the side. "What's not possible? People trying to kill us?"

"No, but look," said Wade. "What we're guessing is that Copernicus discovered some kind of big amazing astrolabe that could travel. Look, maybe I got the whole wormhole thing wrong, but I don't think I did—" His brain pounded. "I mean, it all makes sense except that it doesn't make sense, and I'm a scientist, so . . ."

Which sounded lamer than lame.

Becca shook her head. "Copernicus was a scientist, too. So was Uncle Henry. So is your dad. And Kip Thorne, the wormhole guy."

Wade grumbled. "I know, but—"

"Look at this," Lily said from the computer. "It took me forever, and I tried a bunch of city maps, even old ones, but there was never a Via Rasagnole in Rome. So, okay, like I said, there's this anagram site. I type in the letters of

303

the whole address, using the Roman numeral, V."

Darrell smiled. "Rome being where they *invented* Roman numerals."

"So I type in all the letters," she said, "and—boom!— we get a bunch of different words, most of which aren't even real words. But that's English. So I switch to Italian. I couldn't make sense of anything there, either. Then I get this brilliant Becca-like idea that maybe I should switch to Latin, and the list is *so* much shorter—"

They all hovered over her shoulders.

"Wait!" said Wade, his brain tingling. "Go back up the list."

Lily scrolled up a few lines.

"Stop," he said. "*ARGO* . . . Argo . . ."

"The ship in Greek mythology," Becca said quietly. "Jason was the pilot. Lily, remember we learned the story in Mrs. Peterson's class?"

She glanced up. "Sure."

"There's also this movie. *Jason and the Argonauts*," Darrell said. "Jason fights the skeleton warriors. It's a classic. I'm just saying."

"Lily, take those letters out and see what's left," said Becca.

She did. "It leaves *V VI ASANLE*. Unscrambling those, we get . . ."

A smaller list of words came up.

Becca grumbled. "Maybe it's not Latin, after all."

Wade practically exploded when a second familiar word appeared on the screen. "NAVIS! That's it! Constellated parts! Holy cow—"

He scrambled in his backpack for the star chart.

"What's *navis*, the Latin for the plural of navy?" asked Darrell.

"No, no, it's on here, the constellation." Wade traced his fingers over Uncle Henry's map. "*Argo Navis* is the name of one of Ptolemy's original constellations! It represents the ship *Argo*. Here!"

He showed them a cluster of stars near the bottom of the map. They were vaguely in the shape of a sailing ship.

Darrell leaned over Lily's shoulder. "What letters are left?"

Only *V, A, L,* and *E* remained.

Even as Lily entered them into the unscrambler, Wade worked the four letters over in his head and felt them shift into position as the letters of *blau stern* had days before.

Shifting, shifting, *click*.

"Vela," he said, standing up straight. "Argo Navis Vela."

CHAPTER FORTY-ONE

Wade stood over his celestial map.

"Vela," he said slowly, "is this smaller cluster of stars in Argo Navis. It's kind of a triangle, kind of a rectangle. *Vela* is Latin for 'sail.' I remember Dad taught me the parts of the constellations. Vela is the sail of the ship Argo Navis. The address V, Via Rasagnole is code for this part of this constellation."

"So," said Becca, "out of the whole sky, we get down to one constellation."

Darrell breathed in a long breath. "Wade, you said you can only see some constellations from certain places. How about this one?"

He shook his head. "We can't see it so well from Texas. Or even from Rome. It's best seen south of the equator. The Southern Cross is another one only visible from the southern hemisphere. There are a bunch of them."

As everyone examined the map, the sunlight fell lazily across the floor, moving slowly, infinitesimally across the tiles.

Becca stood and stared past them at the astrolabes. "Guys, I'm going to make a leap here and say that if each relic is named after a constellation, maybe it's hidden where the constellation is best seen."

Darrell wagged his head from side to side. "Okay, but this is a huge world. I mean, look at the globes. Even *if* we say that the relic is somewhere where you can see the constellation of it, we're still talking millions of square miles, and a lot of it is water."

"Which is why we have to narrow it down," said Lily. "If we figure out *who* the Guardian is, maybe it'll be obvious. We need to learn about his or her life to find out where he or she might have hidden the relic."

"Good idea," Wade said. "So . . . back to the diary?"

Becca closed her eyes for a moment, then opened the diary to halfway, then beyond. "It's got to be after what I already read."

Minutes went by as she flipped over more pages, both forward and back. From the look on her face, Wade knew the words were giving her trouble.

"Okay," she said. "The diary says, '*la reliquia prima*,' the first relic, "*è stata presentata ad un* legal man.' It says that in English, 'legal man.'"

Wade bit his lip. "Legal man. Seriously. In English."

"Yeah," Becca said, still reading.

"I'm writing this down, too." Wade copied these new words into his father's notebook. He looked at the list of clues.

The first will circle to the last
The world known and unknown
A hole in the sky
—The first relic will be presented to a man above all
men who will raise it as if it were his own child

Darrell set his finger on the list. "Wade, one thing, if it's not too weird. You said *vela* means 'sail,' right? Well, don't you 'raise' a sail when you go *sailing*? The diary talks about a voyage. Maybe Copernicus's making a pun."

Becca looked up from the paperback. "I like that, Darrell. It fits, right? Puns, I mean. Plus, the early sixteenth century was the age of discovery, so there were lots of sailors. Vela's Guardian might be a sailor or a captain of a sailing ship."

Wade closed his eyes and rubbed them. "Out of the whole sky, one constellation. Out of one constellation, one part. If the first relic is Vela," he said, "and it's hidden in the southern hemisphere, which is mostly water, then Darrell, I think you've got something. 'A man above all men who will raise it as if it were his own child.' It really does point to a sailor."

"Then what about 'legal man'?" said Lily. "Why say that in English unless that means something? What does a lawyer have to do with raising sails on boats and oceans and water anyway?"

"Copernicus studied law," said Darrell. "Dad told us that. Maybe he hung out with lawyers who liked to sail boats, and he gave the relic to one of them."

Wade wandered away from the rest of them. It was that too-many-heads thing again. But something else, too. With every word he read, or thought of, or heard, he couldn't help but wonder what other words could be spelled with its letters, and even talking began to seem like code.

He stopped at a large, flat display case. Under the glass was a map of the world in Copernicus's time.

The world known and unknown, the diary had said.

Naturally, much of the map was wrong. The shapes of the continents were not the shapes they are now known to be.

It was that thing Wade loved. Looking at charts and maps and notebooks, you could almost see how people figured things out. What were maps but pictures sketched by people trying to understand the world around them? These days, all that understanding was hidden inside computer hard drives or in wireless radio waves. If you hit the right buttons and clicked the keyboard, it all came out for you, all done. You didn't have to do much at all.

But this stuff. It was human and it was science. It was discovery. It was history that you could touch. Sure, it was brilliance and genius and imagination, but it was people, too.

Nicolaus Copernicus. Hans Novak.

On the map before him, a slender gold line was drawn across the seas, looping from what he knew was Spain, across the Atlantic Ocean to a blobby-looking New World, down the coast of South America, around its tip, and up along the western coast to the Pacific Ocean.

Next to the line across the deep blue of the South

Seas were tiny letters handwritten in gold ink.

Magellan.

His brain sparked. Constellations, ships, voyages. Letters began to shift places, combining, separating, recombining . . . *click.*

He turned to the others and he spoke the name aloud. "Magellan."

Darrell narrowed his eyes. "Magellan? The explorer?"

Wade followed the line from Europe to the New World to the Pacific Islands and back to Europe again. "Magellan was the first to sail around the world. Lily, key in 'Magellan,' please?"

She clacked away at the keyboard. The results came up quickly. "First circumnavigation of the globe, left Spain in 1519, made it halfway, died in the Philippines in 1521."

"So he was around at the same time as Copernicus," Darrell said. "But what makes you think—"

"Lily, I meant type Magellan into the anagram site," Wade said. "For English language results."

She gave him a look, but typed in the name anyway. She scrolled slowly down the list of nonsense words, then gasped. "Wade, you are a total genius."

Becca leaned over the screen. "Oh man. You so are."

"Why's he so great?" said Darrell, trying to squeeze in.

Becca laughed softly. "'Magellan.' 'Legal man.' Same letters."

There was a hushed moment. Longer than a moment. The sun bathed the wide wooden floorboards of the museum gallery.

Then Darrell spoke. "If no one else is going to say it, I will. People, let me be the first to announce that Magellan was the first member of the GAC, the twelve Guardians of the Astrolabe of Copernicus!"

Lily sat back from the computer screen. "That's it," she said softly. "We've figured it out."

The sun was moving higher in the sky. It would soon be time to meet Dr. Kaplan at the Castel Sant'Angelo.

Wade so wanted to tell his father everything they had discovered, but he also found he didn't really want to leave the museum. Not yet.

Neither, it seemed, did the others. They had discovered so much there, just the four of them. They'd been lucky, but most of what they deduced was by using their own intelligence and imagination.

Unable to stop herself from continuing to dig into the encyclopedia site, Lily said, "Magellan died in the Philippines, attacked by natives, so he didn't finish his voyage. It's pretty well written about. Curious fact. After the attack, his body was never found."

"Wade, I need your dad's notebook," said Becca. "For the cipher."

Giving it to her, Wade stepped back from the computer, his mind still clicking and swirling with questions about the Guardians of the Astrolabe of Copernicus. "Magellan's body was never found? So the relic was lost?"

Lily traced the text farther down the page. "Ha! No! There's a legend that Magellan's servant, a native by the name of Enrique, spirited the body away."

"Enrique." Darrell frowned. "Where did he take it?"

Lily began jumping in her chair. "Oh my gosh, listen to this! Their previous stop? The island they visited just before Magellan was killed in the Philippines?"

"Yes? Where was it?" said Becca.

"Guam," said Lily.

Wade wasn't sure what that meant. "So . . . ?"

Lily was still jumping. "Guess what Magellan called Guam and its smaller islands? Guess! Never mind, I'll tell you. *Islas de las Velas Latinas.*' Islands of the Lateen *Sails*!"

They hushed once more. Wade's head went silent, too, then he had to say it. "Guys, Vela is the relic, and it's in Guam."

"So we need to go there," said Darrell. "Right?"

"Um . . ." Becca frowned over the diary. "Wade, I have one of your impossible things here. This passage seems to hint at what the device actually is, but it's in code like the email. It says 'Hytcdsy lahjiua.' I decoded it using the key on the star map, but this time it didn't decode into English words. They're in Latin."

She raised her face to them. *"Machina tempore."*

Lily wrinkled her nose. "Mechanical tempura?"

"No," said Wade, his knees shaking suddenly. *"Time machine."*

CHAPTER FORTY-TWO

The sound of footsteps on an iron stairway always bothered Ebner von Braun. They were loud and grating and sad. Either they were his footsteps, in which case everyone would know he was approaching, or they were someone else's and—since he trusted no one—they could mean he was about to die.

Why should he be terrified of footsteps on stairs? That was simple. For the last four years he—a physicist of great esteem even in the tiniest upper circle of the greatest theoretical astrophysicists in the world—had worked exclusively for Galina Krause.

Galina Krause, the mysterious young woman who had appeared on the doorstep of a castle in northern Poland, an urchin in the storm, an orphan to time, a dishrag that had been wrung out once too often, but a dishrag with hypnotic eyes.

And why had Ebner been at the castle that night four years ago? For the same reason that his father and father's father and great-grandfather's great-grandfather had been there. A secret meeting of the Knights of the Teutonic Order of ancient Prussia, the vast global society built on old royal power and great wealth.

Little did Ebner know then—little did any of them in that room know—how brilliant this ragged young woman was. How uncannily knowledgeable she was about the Order's deepest secrets. How thoroughly she understood the most intricate mathematics, temporal physics, and theoretical astronomy. Not to mention where the Order's legendary treasures lay buried, as if she'd possessed a direct link to its long-lost royal vaults.

And all at such a tender age! How old was she that stormy night four years ago, fifteen? Yet how she mesmerized them all with her brilliance! Later came the silent vote, and Ebner himself was chosen to accompany her to the dark wastes of Russia for her treatment.

In the secret years since that night, he had only bowed before her increasing knowledge, the scope and speed of her mind, the wisdom that seemed utterly impossible for one so young.

Impossible?

The Order had lost track of many of the Guardians by the eighteenth century. Yet after four short years, Galina Krause had brought the Knights back from the brink of extinction to within reach of the first relic. Galina was proving daily that the word *impossible* had lost its meaning.

Ebner reached the top of the stairs and paused, breathing a long, slow breath to steady his nerves. He glanced down at the small bronze casket he cradled in his hands. What would she say when she opened it?

"Will you mention that I have brought it personally?" a voice said at the bottom of the stairs below him.

Ebner half turned. "If the moment arrives. Stay outside the door. I will call for you. Perhaps." He straightened his bow tie in the reflection of the aluminum door and keyed in a seven-digit code.

A whisper of air, the door slid away, and he was standing on the threshold of a penthouse overlooking Milan, Italy, that had the feel of a mountain lair decorated by Versace. Galina was dressed in black, a svelte, catlike silhouette against the glittering window.

"Well," she said, not bothering to turn.

Ebner's knees trembled. Another breath. Another straightening of the tie. He stepped forward. "The *Le Monde* story has died. It seems the journalist pressing the murder angle has vanished." He paused. No reaction. He glanced around the room. No crossbow, either. "In other business, we are monitoring every airport and train depot on the continent. The children must have picked up a new cell phone, or been given one. It appears to be scrambled. Though not for long."

"They now have the help of the Guardians in Bologna," Galina breathed. "I do wonder if the children know what this means for them."

Ebner bowed slightly, apparently to himself. "The fencing school could not be taken in the first attack. By the time our reinforcements arrived, it had been abandoned. Its armory and library were empty."

"The Guardians will re-form elsewhere. The Protocol demands it . . ."

"The children will not escape our grasp—"

"As they did twice in Berlin?" Galina snapped. "At the Austrian border? And again in Rome?" Her words were icicle sharp.

"You have my word. The Crows have been mobilized once more," Ebner said, mustering as much calm as his trembling voice could manage.

"And the Spanish Experiment?" Galina asked, finally turning her head, but not far enough to see what he was holding.

The delicate trail of the scar on her neck was more visible than usual, he thought. Did her anger bring it out? He cleared his throat.

"Certain elements of the equation have proved . . . unstable," he said. "It was our most successful experiment to date. Only . . . not successful enough. In fact, it is still unfolding."

"There is no way to trace it to our laboratory?"

"Absolutely not. The Spanish authorities are baffled," Ebner said, adding, "But then, they are often baffled." He thought this was amusing. Galina's expression did not change. "What shall we do with the Italian professor? Mercanti?"

"She will be useful to us for a later relic," Galina said, walking slowly over to the window and looking south. *Toward Rome*, Ebner thought. *We'll be going there soon, perhaps.*

She turned abruptly. "Is there anything else?"

Ebner swallowed hard. "I have saved the best for

last, Miss Krause." Holding the bronze casket against his stomach, he unlatched it and slowly opened its lid.

With the measured steps of a jungle cat, Galina strode slowly toward him, her expression somewhere between ecstasy and rage. She stopped inches away, her eyes riveted on the inside of the box. It was lined with rich black velvet. Lying on the shimmering fabric, coiled around itself three times, was a leather strap. On the strap was a single ruby in the shape of a sea monster. A kraken.

Galina gently removed the strap from the box and stepped back. Ebner grinned. "It was retrieved on the plains of North Prussia, exactly where you said it would be. Professor Wolff brought it to me personally. Professor?"

The door slid aside once more, and a white-haired man in a leather overcoat stood waiting. He nodded slightly at Galina.

Ebner, wondering whether she saw Markus Wolff at all, stepped forward. "Miss Krause, if I may—"

"Leave me. Both of you." Galina held the strap to her cheek and kissed the ruby kraken over and over.

For a fraction of a second, Ebner wished he were an old red jewel. Still, her intensity was odd. It scared him. Like iron stairs.

Stepping backward to the door, Ebner caught sight of a glassy tear, sliding down Galina's exquisite cheek to her scar. It originated, he noted, from the damp lashes of her silvery gray eye.

CHAPTER FORTY-THREE

"A time machine."

Darrell's voice sounded somewhere between utter disbelief and drooling desire.

"Copernicus discovered an astrolabe that could travel in time?" he said. "That thing in the sketch? I don't think so. I mean, of course it would be cool, flying around the years, the sinking of the *Titanic*, Lincoln's assassination, chatting with MLK and Jeff Beck—well, Beck's still alive—or sitting in the dugout of game three of the 2005 World Series between the Astros and the White Sox, all five hours and forty-one minutes of it—"

"Except it's incredibly not possible," Wade said.

"You're kidding, right?" said Lily. "A time machine is *so* possible. I want one. I'm only amazed it took so long to invent one."

"No, look," Wade said. "If you don't believe me, there's something called the grandfather paradox. Say you go back in time and kill your grandfather. There would be no *you* in the future to go back in time in the first place. It's just logical."

"Maybe," Becca said. "But what if we only know the kind of logic that works in one direction, past to present to future."

Where was she going with this? "Uh . . . okay . . . and . . ."

"People only go forward in time, like boats going the same direction on a river," she said. "We've learned to think in only that one way. But, Wade, what if there is another kind of logic? One that controls moving in two directions, back and forth in time? Maybe only when you actually *do* travel back in time, do you discover how logical *that* is."

She stared at him as if he had the answer.

"It's . . . it's . . ." He didn't finish.

When he was young, Wade would have loved a time machine. To go back before his parents split up and, somehow, fix things between them. But time travel was a fantasy, unreal, a dream.

"It's *what*?" asked Becca. "You're the scientist."

The museum had begun to fill with more tourists, and he didn't like the look of some of them. He lowered his voice. "It's late. If Dad's been released, it can't be long before the Order knows we're in Rome. I say we hightail it to the Castel Sant'Angelo, find somewhere to hide, and wait for him. As for the time machine, we need to reread the diary."

"Actually, good ideas. Both of them," said Lily, erasing her computer searches. "Let's get moving." They packed up their stuff and headed through the rooms toward the entrance.

"Hello!" the white-haired man said, standing at his desk near the door. "I never hope you will leave us again very soon!"

"Lo stesso con noi," said Becca with a smile. "Us, too."

They wound their way quickly down the hill from the museum, out of the park, and onto Via Trionfale, which ran straight for a long while, then doglegged to Via Leone IV, toward the Tiber River and the Castel.

At the intersection of the two streets, they stopped at a café. Earlier, they had passed a McDonald's and several outdoor sandwich stands, but Becca convinced

324

them to eat a true Italian breakfast of fruit, coffee, juice, and stuffed pastries. It was their first real meal since the picnic basket in the car the day before.

"I feel pretty good that our luck is turning," Lily said, munching the remains of a pear as they started down Via Leone. "We found out so much there. Don't ask me to explain it all or how it's possible."

"Only Wade could do that," said Darrell, laughing. "Right, bro?"

Becca glanced at him.

"I'll leave that for Dad," he said.

Besides, Lily had put her finger on it. Something *was* changing for them, and it was much more than their luck. They had discovered things. If he was too logical to accept that a time-traveling astrolabe was strictly possible—he was too rational for that, wasn't he?—he *loved* the idea of a quest for relics, and they were getting closer.

The clues, codes, dagger, diary, all of it was exciting, smart, and even—discounting that killers were after them—fun, and what made the quest that way was simple: being with these three people.

By noon the crowded sidewalks on Via Stefano were hot, the traffic snarling, fast, and busy. When a blue motorbike whizzed between jammed cars, bounced up onto the sidewalk past them, and raced back into the street, Lily screamed, "We're going to get killed by accident!"

"The next street is just as good," Becca said. She led them down to Via Plauto into a series of smaller streets and alleys nearer the river.

A few minutes later, Wade spotted the same blue motorbike idling two blocks behind them. Its helmeted driver was on his cell phone.

"Guys, that Vespa . . ." His hand went instinctively to his side, the dagger under his shirt.

"The Order?" said Lily.

"Could be," Darrell said. "I say we don't take chances. I say we run."

They took off to the next corner and zigzagged down the next two side streets as they had done in Berlin. Lily jerked suddenly through a door on her left, a clothes shop, where they slammed into customers until they found a way out on the next street over. They crossed a busy intersection against the light, then hurried down a narrow cut-through into a small, deserted piazza.

The motorbike roared in seconds later.

With a quickness that surprised even himself, Wade unsheathed the dagger, went into a crouch, and growled, "Leave us alone—"

"Put that back!" Becca shouted. She tugged him toward an open door. It was a grocery. They stumbled through to the next street over, when Lily's phone started ringing.

"What? Becca, it's the lady driver. What's a *tuber*?"

"Tiber? The river. This way—"

They entered the park surrounding the Castel. The banks of the river were visible ahead. The motorbike bounced over the sidewalk toward them. Wade turned, the dagger still in his hand. It was a reflex now. Crouch and show your weapon. Even if he didn't know what he was going to do with it. The bike roared at them, the driver's hand went inside his jacket—

There came a sudden shriek of tires, and the motorbike flew up in the air and flattened into a low wall. The biker was hurtled over the wall, where he landed with an awful sound on pavement.

The vintage Maserati spun completely around the kids. A voice cried out.

"Kids, get in!"

CHAPTER FORTY-FOUR

Jamming themselves into the Maserati, the kids screamed, *"Daaaaaad!"* and *"Roaaaald!"* and fell all over him.

"I'm fine, I'm fine," he said, hugging them as much as possible while the driver settled into a swift spin along the ancient river. "Is everyone all right?"

"Yes!" Lily said breathlessly. "Tell us how you escaped!"

"Hardly an escape," he said. "The police arrested me at the train station. I was in a cell for a day on a charge of something ridiculous, breaking into a cemetery.

328

Luckily, your friend Carlo contacted a lawyer, suddenly there was bail, and I was out. We drove down here overnight." He glanced at the driver. "That's an adventure I'll tell you about sometime."

Darrell tried to catch his breath. "We have an adventure for you, too, Dad. Wait'll you hear."

"You can tell me on the plane. We're flying home before anything else happens."

Wade shared a look with the others. "Dad, we can't really go home, I mean, not yet. We discovered, we *think* we discovered, some amazing stuff. Incredible stuff. Unbelievable—"

"Uncle Roald, Copernicus had a *machina tempore*!" Lily blurted out. "Which is the Latin way of saying 'time machine.' We even have a picture of it. In his ancient diary. Which we also have!"

Dr. Kaplan's jaw dropped. "Copernicus wrote a diary? There's no record of that."

"It was in Carlo's fencing school in Bologna," said Darrell. "Copernicus discovered an ancient time machine, an astrolabe so big you can sit in it. The details are real sketchy, but Becca can show you."

Wade nodded. "Yeah, plus the Knights of the Teutonic Order, the ancient organization of evil villains—"

"—are still around," Darrell went on, "and working

with the evil Berlin police. They've always wanted the time machine—"

"And still do," said Becca. "But Copernicus—"

"Took the astrolabe apart," Darrell interrupted, "that's the time machine. And he gave twelve pieces of it to people called Guardians to hide wherever they wanted. That was sometime after 1514. A whole army of other Guardians have been hiding the pieces ever since. That's who Uncle Henry was. But even after five hundred years the Order still wants the pieces. They're the creeps after us."

"The motorbike guy was one of them," Lily said.

"And the lady with the hair," Darrell said breathlessly.

He knew the others wanted to tell it, but he couldn't seem to stop talking until he got it all out. He finally couldn't think of anything else to say, so he glanced around and said, "You guys take it from here."

"Thanks a lot," Wade grumbled. "It's just that the twelve relics in Uncle Henry's message are the pieces that supposedly made Copernicus's astrolabe work."

"And we think we've discovered what the first one is and where it's hidden," Lily added. "The island of Guam. It was taken there by Magellan on his voyage around the world!"

The car fell quiet as Roald took the diary, which Becca had opened to the page with the sketch of the *machina tempore*. "So . . . Uncle Henry died trying to keep the relics away from those men."

"He was a Guardian," Becca said.

Roald studied the picture—his brow furrowing, his head shaking, all the while murmuring to himself, "Heinrich . . ."—and Wade realized that whatever doubts he'd had about the diary were vanishing.

If his dad believed it, he did too.

"Copernicus somehow figured out the theory of the wormhole," Wade said after a few minutes. "Something like Kip Thorne's equations is in the diary, too."

His father nodded slowly. "I see it."

"Wade thought it was impossible," Lily said, "but there it is in black and white. Well, sort of brown and white."

Becca and Lily alternately filled him in on the attack in Bologna and their discovery of the Copernicus museum.

"Carlo from the fencing school called me as we were driving down here," Roald said. "He said Uncle Henry deliberately contacted me for help. The Order has never been this close. The relics have never been in such danger as now. He said the Guardians have begun—"

"The Frombork Protocol," Becca said. "Carlo told us."

"And you're saying you know what the first relic is?"

"Vela," Lily said. "We're not sure exactly *what* it is, except that Copernicus gave it to Magellan. We put about a thousand clues together to narrow it down, and we're pretty certain it's hidden in Guam."

"Dad," said Wade. "I know you said we're going home, and I get that, but . . ."

"We're not going home," Roald said. "Not yet. Take me through this, every step of the way. I have to understand it."

Darrell tapped the driver on the shoulder.

"Sì?"

"Museo Astronomico e Copericano, *per favore.*"

She laughed. *"Sì!"*

CHAPTER FORTY-FIVE

For the next two hours, the kids detailed what they had found out that morning, what piece of information led to what fact that then led to which guess. Roald consulted his student notebook constantly, arguing at first with the notion of a time machine, but not as strongly as Wade would have imagined. He couldn't explain the modern formula's appearance in a sixteenth-century diary, but set that aside as a question to be solved later. He rightly said that it didn't affect the fact that the Order was after the relics.

Beyond his own notes, Roald studied Wade's

additions carefully while the language-challenged museum docent opened the display cases for "Dottore Kaplani" (but really Becca) to consult the documents inside.

The evidence invariably produced the same result.

When Lily related that Magellan had called the Guam islands *las Velas Latinas*, Roald just stared into space for minutes, shushing them when they tried to tell him more. At last, he wandered away from the kids and dialed his phone.

Wade and Darrell tried both to listen and not listen, then heard, "Sara, I know you won't get this until the weekend, but we'll be traveling for a few more days . . ."

It was all they needed to hear.

Fifty-seven minutes later, their wispy-haired driver laughingly announced, *"Siamo qui!"* and slowed in front of a busy airline terminal. She revved the Maserati louder and louder until the kids and Dr. Kaplan got out. Then she fishtailed away exactly as she'd done so many times before.

"She's a wee bit strange," Lily said.

"She is," Roald said with a smile. "But Carlo told me she's part of the reason the Order isn't on our tails this exact moment."

Inside the terminal the mayhem was a hundred

times worse than the Berlin train station—oceans of passengers, families, security, airline personnel moving in every direction, while shrill announcements in Italian, French, and English overlapped in a storm of noise.

"Be careful with everything you do," Roald said, huddling them together. "We lay low, we do not separate. Two of us stand outside the bathroom while the others are in there. The Order will be on our tail before we know it. The Guam Air counter is over there. Come on."

As it turned out, there was only one flight from Rome to Guam. Dr. Kaplan negotiated with the airline representative, using a credit card drawn on a Bologna bank, which Wade guessed Carlo had given him.

"It's a twenty-five-hour flight," Roald said, handing boarding passes to each of them. "Two stops. We'll be in Guam the day after tomorrow."

"Maybe the Order doesn't even go there," said Darrell.

"We can't count on that," Wade said. "We should act as if they're right behind us."

"I'll bet the Order goes everywhere," Lily said as they hurried into security. "Your home in Austin, remember?"

Wade remembered. He couldn't forget.

After finding their gate, Roald paused. "I should tell you that something happened while you were on the run. A school bus vanished in the mountains of Spain."

"Really?" said Darrell. "Do you know how many times I wished my school bus would disappear?"

"It was filled with children," said Dr. Kaplan.

Darrell blushed. "Sorry."

"If Uncle Henry predicted it, it means the Teutonic Order is behind it," Wade said.

"Of course they are," Becca added. "They know we're getting close."

"Boarding Flight Thirty-Seven to Dubai, continuing to Narita and Guam."

"Time to fly," Lily said, hooking her arm through Becca's and heading to the Jetway.

As Roald nudged the boys after them, Darrell turned. "How do we know that the Order won't make our plane disappear?"

Wade felt suddenly queasy. "I guess we don't."

CHAPTER FORTY-SIX

Time is a crazy thing, Becca thought.

When you can't sleep—and naturally she couldn't sleep, no matter how exhausted she was—a twenty-five-hour flight halfway across the world lasts three months. Each second drags out to thirty, each minute becomes an hour, each hour a week. A jet is nothing but a big metal box of noise. Lights are always on. You're squashed upright in a teeny seat, your stomach is pinching and rolling, your temples are thudding, your eyes are on fire—and then they serve you plastic food!

It reminded her of nights at the hospital after her sister's surgery. There was always something happening, lights, sounds, machines thunking and whining, strange smells, voices chattering, whispering.

She hadn't slept a wink there, either.

And to lose a day of your life in the process! She hated to lose anything, but losing time—*time*—was one of the worst things you could do. Time was all you had, wasn't it?

On the other hand, Copernicus had discovered a time machine. And some kind of "traversable wormhole."

What would she do if she had a machine like that? Where—when—would she go? What would she change?

Could you change anything? *Should* you? Wasn't there something called the butterfly effect? Altering one tiny thing, like where or when or if a butterfly flaps its wings, can change the future in huge ways, like eventually producing a hurricane.

Opening *Moby-Dick* at random, she found herself reading, of all things, about the moment the crew of the *Pequod* spots a giant squid in the ocean. It was described as a monster with . . .

> *. . . innumerable long arms radiating from its centre, and curling and twisting like a nest of anacondas . . .*

She closed the book. The kraken was just such a monster, and those words only drew her back to Copernicus's diary.

As difficult as it was to decipher some pages, it was strangely comforting, and Hans Novak, the Magister's young assistant, seemed like one of their friends, a part of their team in a way, and riding on the journey with them.

She set the diary on the tray table and studied its cover carefully for the first time since Bologna. It was as beautiful as it was plain: dark red leather, tooled subtly around its edges with a design of intersecting geometric shapes—diamonds, triangles, circles linked with circles—that met at the brass guards in the four corners.

The daggers on the corner guards, she now noticed, converged at a single spot in the center of the cover. Her heart quickened.

They met in the center of the line that read, in German, *Seine geheimen Reisen auf Erde und im Himmel*—His Secret Voyages in Earth and Heaven—at the word *im*—in.

It was then she noticed that, while the whole title was imprinted in gold leaf, the gold of the word *im* was nearly flaked off.

As if it had been touched often.

She ran a finger over it. Surprisingly, the wooden board beneath the leather pushed in with the pressure, as if the board itself had a small circle cut into it just under that word.

She lifted the cover of the diary and watched the inside endpaper as she pressed the cover word again. The endpaper bulged slightly, and its upper left corner lifted slightly away from the board.

"Oh!"

No one woke up. They were dead to the world.

Setting the cover flat on the tray table, Becca shifted the book around so that the upper corner faced her. Pressing the cover a third time, she pried the endpaper up enough to see that a slip of parchment was hidden beneath. She dug in her bag and removed an emery board. Pressing it under the flap, she tugged out the parchment until it fell free of the book.

"Wade," she whispered, elbowing his arm gently. "Wade?"

In a dark, uneven, and unfamiliar hand, were several lines in German with the English title,

Legal Man

Becca jumped in her seat. "Wade! Look what I found."

He grumbled, lifting his head to her. "Are we there yet?"

"This wasn't written by Hans Novak. Look. A piece of parchment. And the handwriting is different. It's about Magellan. Listen."

The engines roared around them as she translated.

> *I bow as the great explorer strides across the dock.*
> *"Magister Nicolaus!" he says. "You travel so far alone."*
> *"My assistant is away." I lean close and explain my purpose.*
> *The captain responds, "Upon my life, I will!"*

"It's the moment Copernicus and Magellan meet," said Wade, blinking his eyes wide open.

> *I reveal the contents of my palm and unwrap the velvet cloth. The sail-shaped stone lies shining in the moonlight.*
> *"Aquamarine," the captain says. "How fitting for a mariner."*

"Holy cow, Wade. Vela is a stone! A blue stone, small enough to hold in your hand!"

> *From a leather pouch I withdraw one of Achille's daggers and present it to the Captain. "The first shall circle to the last," I tell him.*

With thanks, he goes with the morning tide.

Upon my life, I will. I shall never forget the words of the very first Guardian.

Becca looked over at Wade. His eyes were glistening, studying the handwriting. "Becca, you got it. This is the best clue so far! We have to tell them—"

"Wait." She paused. The engines roared, but she found herself whispering. "I just want to . . . I mean, you kind of weren't sure at first. About the time machine. Do you . . . I mean . . . now . . ."

He looked her in the eyes, and the cabin dimmed as more lights went off, almost shrouding them. "I guess I do. Maybe I'll never be able to wrap my head around time travel. Dad knows way more. All the contradictions, you know? But I look at Uncle Henry and how he died. And the Order. And Dad. The Guardians. All of it. So, I think so, yeah."

They didn't wake the others. There wasn't going to be any rest once they arrived in Guam, so they may as well sleep, she thought. She and Wade talked together for a while until she felt herself getting drowsy and closed her eyes and fell asleep.

Hours must have gone by before Lily rustled noisily

342

next to her. "The plane is descending to the first lay-over."

Darrell stretched his legs out. "Is the pilot controlling the descent?"

"We can only hope!"

"Guys, Uncle Roald," Becca said, rousing herself. "Guess what?"

"Read it to them," Wade said.

They all listened spellbound as she read what she'd discovered.

"Vela is a small blue stone in the shape of a sail," Roald said in a breath. "Becca, this is amazing."

"It's one more clue," she said.

"A giant one."

Darrell slapped Wade's shoulder. "We are getting so close. From the whole giant world to one little island. The first relic is half a day and two more hops away. Unbelievable!"

After a brief stay in Dubai, the flight to Japan seemed a new kind of interminable. The flight from Japan to the islands was more of the same. Becca read and reread the Magellan encounter until she memorized it, struck by the different handwriting and wobbly lettering, wishing she had a sample of Copernicus's handwriting to compare it against.

Finally, Lily reached across her to lift the window shade. The row of seats turned golden in the light. It was an hour before dawn, but the sky was already brightening over the great blue Pacific. It was like flying into the very first days of the world. Back to the creation. The start of everything.

And there it was again.

Time.

"Less than an hour and we land," Wade said.

His eyes blinked into the orange sunlight.

She took a breath. All right, then. A new day.

CHAPTER FORTY-SEVEN

Because it was one of the first flights of the morning, the jet was able to taxi to the gate without delay. Twenty minutes after touchdown, they were in the terminal, while Dr. Kaplan made a quick call.

"We'll be picked up by one of my contacts at the University of Guam," he told them. "They have great researchers to help us determine where Vela might be hidden—"

"They're here," said Wade.

A black van was parked on the tarmac near a small private jet. Several men waited in front of it. They stiffened as if suddenly called to attention. The young woman from Berlin stepped out of the jet, sliding a slim duffel bag over her bare, toned arms to her shoulder. She was down the stairs in a moment, and the men gathered around her like players around a quarterback. She spoke, and they each nodded once. One of the men slid his right hand into his open jacket and patted the area under his left armpit.

"They're armed," said Darrell. "Dad—"

"I'm on it," Dr. Kaplan said, his phone out. After a minute of low talking, he pulled them close. "Our ride will meet us outside the cargo area. Here comes our escort through customs now. Let's move."

Becca turned to go with the others when she touched Wade's arm.

The pale man with the bruise on his head emerged from the jet with a small computer in his hands. He spoke to the woman, and she whirled her head around to the terminal. "Go!" she yelled, and the van took off, while the woman herself entered the terminal at a sprint.

"That's how they know," Becca said. "They've already unscrambled Carlo's phone."

"Come—on!" Wade pulled her away from the window and they ran for customs. They were whisked through in no time and pulled into a small beat-up Honda driven by his father's contact from the university. The kids crouched on the floor of the backseat, while Dr. Kaplan did the same in the front. They were able to squeak out of the airport parking lot without stopping. As their car slid past the van, Wade and Becca peeked out to see the young woman staring motionless through the terminal door. She was startlingly beautiful up close, but the expression in her eyes was not really human. As if she were a species of rare animal. A dangerous one.

The driver, a short middle-aged man with thin brown hair and sunglasses, jammed his car into top gear before turning completely sideways to Dr. Kaplan. "Your reason for coming here, to learn about Magellan's time on the island . . . I must say, it's rather common knowledge. Can you explain your research a little?"

Dr. Kaplan cleared his throat. "Actually, I . . . it's complicated."

"Mysterious!" he said. "Well, you're in luck. We've arranged for a hotel, but first, we're heading to Janet Thompson's bungalow. Her grandmother was, of course, Laura Thompson."

The kids shared a look. *Of course?* Lily mouthed.

"I saw that!" the driver said, turning around.

"A truck!" Darrell yelled.

347

The driver spun the wheel almost completely around while branches on the roadside snapped against the car.

"Maybe drive now and talk later?" Dr. Kaplan asked.

The little man laughed as he swerved back onto the road. "I've been driving on the island for thirty years without a real accident."

Darrell nudged Wade, whispering, "Define *real*—"

"I heard that!" the driver laughed. "I mean no fatalities."

He sputtered onto a broad road that skirted the southeastern shore of the island. On one side was the vista of the Pacific Ocean in the morning, thousands of miles of nothing but bright blue water. Looking straight east toward home, Becca could almost see the gentle arc of the horizon. To the south of the island stood a handful of low mountains.

"We're getting close," Becca said. "I can feel it."

"Me, too." Darrell nudged Wade. "It won't be long now, bro."

"Do you think it's just the one van?" Wade asked. "Or will they have more?"

"If we're as close as we think we are," his father said, "we have to believe they'll have more. If we need to get into the jungle, we'll have help, right?" he asked the driver.

"A retired Navy SEAL is the most knowledgeable guide to the island. If you need to go deep, he's your man."

Becca stared inland at the vast sea of beautiful tangled green that seemed as giant as the ocean itself. The seashore was sprinkled with villas and hotels, but the island's interior melted into a dense world of thick vegetation that looked as forbidding as it must have back in Magellan's time. As if the jungle would swallow right up anyone who entered. The sun bore down, and a heavy mist coiled from the interior like smoke.

The island must have been all jungle at one time.

She leaned over to Wade. "If Vela's hidden in the jungle, our only hope of finding it is to trace every inch of the story from Magellan down to the present."

"Before the Order does," he whispered.

The driver turned his head nearly around to the backseat. "Sounds like a scavenger hunt! But you should know that what you're seeing here is not the most dense jungle on the island. The real business is up north, beyond the air base. Ritidian, they call it—"

"Another truck!" cried Darrell.

Laughing, the driver plunged off the shoulder as the truck barreled past. "Ten minutes, and we're there!"

"If we make it," Lily whispered.

* * *

They did make it, finally, jerking to a stop in front of a winding driveway. Perched at the top was a modest pink bungalow with a wide, open porch across the front.

"Call me when you need a ride," the driver said.

"Or maybe we'll call a cab," Darrell whispered.

The man laughed. "Still no fatalities!"

As he motored away, a slender, middle-aged woman with red hair strode down the path from the house, waving. "The university called and told me to expect you. I'm Janet Thompson."

Dr. Kaplan greeted her and introduced the kids. "We're interested in whatever you—or your grand-mother—might know about Magellan's stop on the island in 1521."

"I'm sorting through Grandma's papers right now," she said. "Come in."

They gathered in her open living room, a homey collection of wicker furniture and island art, where she listened as they explained their search, giving her as much information as possible, but bypassing the "relics" or "time machine" or "fall into the wrong hands" business.

"Something Magellan might have left here." Janet frowned, then spun around and went straight to the back room of the house. She was back in a few minutes with a pile of books and pamphlets.

"Antonio Pigafetta was an Italian writer, a member of Magellan's crew and his friend. He wrote an eyewitness history of Magellan's voyage from the moment they set sail from Spain. Chapter fifteen is where he describes the landing on Guam. He mentions the crew in several places, including Enrique, the captain's servant."

"We've read that Enrique may have brought Magellan's body here from the Philippines," Roald said.

She unrolled a map like the one in the Museo Copernicano, marking the stops on the voyage. "That's the legend. No grave has ever been found."

"If Enrique was a friend of Magellan's," Darrell said, "and Magellan died in an attack, I mean, wouldn't Enrique get his body out of there? I think he'd do everything he could to get it out of there. Wade, you'd get my body out of there if it was me, wouldn't you? Bro?"

Wade pretended to think about it. "I would, bro. But please don't ask me to do that."

Darrell grinned. "I probably won't. But it's good to know that you'd be there for me."

"Pigafetta's account is a bit sketchy," Janet said, "but it was always Grandma's belief that Magellan must have visited the Ritidian caves in the north. Let me get you my best island map."

She smiled and left the room, patting the head of a

small wooden native sculpture of a warrior.

While everyone pored over the books on the wicker table, Wade knelt over the map of Magellan's voyage.

"Thanks to Becca's discovery, we know for sure that Magellan was the first Guardian. I'm thinking it's like this. Magellan carries Vela all the way from Spain, looking for places all along the voyage. I mean, he doesn't have any idea where he's going to land."

"Plus remember," said Becca, "Hans says that there had to be clues to the relic's location in case they needed to reassemble the astrolabe."

"Right," said Wade. "This is where Pigafetta comes in. Magellan tells him to write about each of these hiding places, because those descriptions may be the Guardians' only clue to where the relic is eventually hidden. So they sail on, Magellan finding hiding spots here and there, and they land in Guam. It might be a good hiding place, but maybe there's a better one coming up. So fine, he casts off to the next islands, the Philippines. Then, tragedy. The first Guardian is killed."

"And Enrique takes his body and Vela to the last safe place they found a hiding spot. Here in Guam," said Darrell. "It makes sense."

Lily raised her eyes from the text. "Enrique disappears from the history a few days after Magellan is killed. Which is perfect, right? Pigafetta has to assume his history might be read by the Teutonic Order. So what does he do to keep the Knights from catching on? He drops Enrique from the history. In a single stroke, both Magellan and Enrique vanish from the story. Vela is hidden safely on Guam!"

Roald was pacing and reading now. "Uh-huh, uh-huh, good. The clue to its exact location must be in this chapter."

"Except that half the chapter is Pigafetta talking about the *velas Latinas* that the island people had on their boats," Darrell said. "He even has a really bad picture of it—"

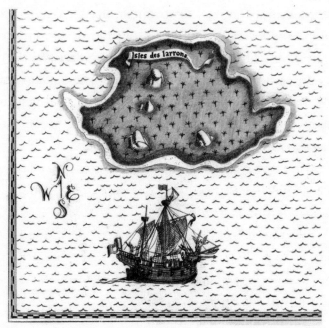

Roald studied the picture. He stood. "And that's it."

"Dad?" said Wade.

His father began to smile. "He doesn't tell the location. He shows it. Look at this drawing, page sixty-two of the paperback. It's labeled 'Isles des Larrons,' which is French for 'Island of Thieves.' This is what Pigafetta called the *velas Latinas* because the islanders stole from them.

"The island is lumpy and not the shape of Guam at all," Roald went on, "but that's not the point. The point is that he's drawn four rock formations, three in the south and central part of the island, and one in the north. They're not anywhere near geographically accurate, but they're not meant to be. He's giving the Guardians a clue to the relic's location. His mountains form a very distinct triangle, pointing directly north. It's the same shape as the lateen sail—*vela Latina*—and, as if that's not enough, the rigging of the boat depicted below the island is *also* a triangle, pointing to the same exact location—"

A loud gasp came from behind them. "You . . . ?"

CHAPTER FORTY-EIGHT

Lily nearly shrieked to see Janet Thompson standing in the doorway of the living room, trembling and pale as if she'd seen a ghost.

Roald stepped toward her. "Is everything okay?"

Janet stared at him. She was crying. "This is what she meant!"

Lily couldn't help herself. She went over to her. "What's the matter? Tell us . . ."

"Grandma told me there was something on the island. Something secret that I shouldn't touch, shouldn't lose, unless . . . unless . . . someone said a word . . . I heard you say it."

Roald tried to get her to sit. She wouldn't.

"There's the famous story of Shoichi Yokoi, a soldier who hid out in the Ritidian caves from the end of World War II until 1972. Twenty-eight years alone in the caves. Grandma met him once. She used the same word you did. She said Shoichi Yokoi was a . . . a guardian."

No one moved.

"Grandma told me that I should only open it if a 'guardian' approached me with a key. You said that word. Are *you* guardians? Do you have the key?"

Wade was shaking. "Dad?"

His father's eyes went back and forth between Janet and him, then he nodded. Wade removed the dagger from under his shirt. When she saw it, Janet put her hands to her face and her eyes filled with tears again.

"May I?"

Wade handed it to her. While she examined it, they told her everything as quickly as they could, sparing no detail of their journey, from the email in Austin to Berlin to Bologna, and all the rest.

Janet listened closely, then wiped her eyes with the back of her hand and wheeled around to the wooden statue of a warrior on the table by the door. She inserted the dagger carefully into the top of its head and turned it. It didn't budge.

"Counterclockwise," Wade said. "Three times."

Lily's heart was pounding hard enough to explode as she watched Janet turn the dagger three revolutions. A small compartment on the back of the statue flipped open and a small photograph fell out.

"Oh, Grandma," Janet said.

At the word *Grandma*, Lily shook inside. She understood that the mystery of the Copernicus Legacy was all about people, good and bad, over the centuries. Copernicus himself. Hans Novak. Magellan. Uncle Henry. Grandma Thompson. The Teutonic Knights. The creepy lady, too.

And now, finally, the legacy had brought their little group right here to Janet Thompson's cute pink house.

She handed them the photo.

It was a Polaroid snapshot of a rough stone outcropping near the blackness of a cave entrance. On the wall next to the opening, located about five feet above the ground, was the outline of a small, upside-down hand. It was blue.

"Grandma discovered many caves, many of them,

with native paintings," Janet said. "The paintings were always in black and red, the color coming from plants. Never blue."

Wade gasped. "So that's it, then. The cave with the blue hand is the one we want."

The room was getting more and more quiet, more hushed; then Lily turned the photograph over. And there they were.

"Numbers."

La 13.649323

Lo 144.866956

Roald sucked in a breath. "Coordinates."

Without delay, Janet keyed them into her computer, then turned back to them, her cheeks still wet. "In the jungle east of Ritidian Point . . ."

The room went quiet as the sun baked the bungalow, and the light between the blinds turned silver. Late-morning insects buzzed across the lawn and into the fringes of the jungle beyond.

"After her meeting with Shoichi," Janet said finally, "I remember stories about how Grandma went into the jungle alone one day. After that she never went back. Her final expedition, she called it. Grandma has been gone almost fifteen years now."

* * *

Becca's eyes closed for the longest time, then opened again. "Your grandmother understood that Shoichi must have seen the relic when he lived in the caves. She came back to Guam to make sure. And once she was sure, and the relic was safe, she let go."

"She never told me," Janet said.

Roald pressed her hand lightly. "I wonder if, in a way, your grandmother *did* tell you. You have all the pieces of the story. You wouldn't need to put them together unless . . . well, unless someone was coming for the relic."

"That's right," Lily added. "Carlo told us that some Guardians don't know they're Guardians until they need to."

Janet wiped a tear from her cheek. "So you're saying that Vela, this relic, whatever it does, is protected by the Guam National Trust. And the Trust is guarded by . . ."

Dr. Kaplan said, "You. You're a relic Guardian. The current Guardian of Vela."

As if the quiet weren't enough, the air itself seemed to sweep out of the room, and Janet slumped into a chair and covered her face with her hands. "Oh, Grandma! She always told me to protect the caves. I thought she meant for their beauty, but it was so much more . . ."

Becca realized then the real strength of the relic

Guardians. It was based on a kind of love. No matter how strong the Teutonic Order was, no matter how much money or jets or guns they had, this—what she was seeing right now—was something else entirely.

A bond that couldn't be broken by evil. She thought of her sister Maggie then and wanted to hold her as close as she had the day she left the hospital.

"Thank you, Janet," Roald said, rising to his feet. "This is . . . well, amazing. We never could have put this together without you."

"Nor me, without all of you," she said. "Good luck. Take the photo. I guess this means that . . . you're the Guardians now."

Wade placed the photo carefully into the notebook.

Becca barely held in her tears. "Thank you," she said, and they left.

CHAPTER FORTY-NINE

Now Becca wanted to scream.

No sooner had they checked into their hotel than the room phone rang. Lily dived for it. "Hello?" She passed it to Roald.

For the next several minutes they tried to read his face. His eyes narrowed, he sat, he stood, and finally he breathed out. "But she's all right? She's safe? Yes, thank you." He checked his watch. "And our guide to the caves? Thanks." He hung up.

"Is it Mom?" said Darrell. "What happened?"

"No, no. It was the university," he said. "Janet

Thompson's house was broken into. She got out, she's fine, but what they didn't steal, they burned."

"The Order knows," said Wade. "They followed us. They'll find the relic."

"Not without the coordinates they won't," said Becca.

It was deep afternoon when an olive Jeep Cherokee roared up to their hotel, an older man with graying hair in a military buzz cut at the wheel. "Sergeant Connor," he said, "but call me Connor." Then he went on to say that he used to be a Navy SEAL and knew the jungles backward and forward.

Becca had heard the term before. Navy SEALs were members of an elite combat group that handled only the most dangerous missions.

"I hear you have decimal coordinates," Connor said.

Roald gave him the numbers, and he plugged them into his GPS. "Ritidian Caves. It'll take us the better part of an hour to get to the general area. Another hour on foot to the caves. All aboard."

"Let's do this," Roald said.

Forty-five minutes later they were off the highway, bouncing over dirt roads and rutted paths into the northernmost section of the island.

Wade was keeping to himself, his face dark with worry.

The jungle surrounding them was immense, a sea of tangled green, wet and noisy and hot. Becca tried to keep the claustrophobia from getting to her.

Just focus on Vela, she told herself.

"We're entering an island preserve thousands of acres in size," Connor told them. "The northern jungle is home to tree snakes, giant pigs, wild boars. Also wasps. There was this one time a family like yours went in . . . well . . . never mind. The point is, be careful of wasps. They're big and numberless. Also, colonies of bats live in the caves."

It sounded as if he had good stories that probably wouldn't go over so well, so he didn't tell them. "Another three, four miles and we'll have to stop and go on foot. Two more miles from there to the cliffs. Two long miles. You can start gearing up."

Wade kept looking back over his shoulder at the road behind.

"It's old-school now," Darrell murmured. "A race to the caves."

Lily shifted in the seat next to Becca. "As long as we win. . . ."

"Can I ask what you're hoping to find in the caves?" Connor asked.

Roald said. "Well . . . it's . . ."

"Secret," Wade said.

Connor nodded. "Classified, huh? Understood."

The ride, as bumpy and uncomfortable as it was, was over too soon. The breeze stopped when the Jeep did, and a suffocating wet heat took its place. Connor transferred the coordinates to a topographical map and shut off the GPS. When they began the trek on foot, the talking stopped. Even at an angle, the sun was a furnace that burned all the words out of them. The air was silver and stifled breath. Becca's arms, legs, face, eyes—everything was sweating. A brief wind stole in over the water, and it was just as wet and hot. Then a bank of dark blue clouds moved in the western sky.

"Is it going to rain?" asked Lily.

Connor half turned his head. "The word *rain* doesn't cover what you'll see here, miss," he said, revealing a light Southern accent. "Those clouds there signify that a typhoon is approaching. The Chamorro word for rainstorm is *chata'an*. But even that doesn't cover the drenching we'll get. At most we'll have an hour before this here becomes a world of mud and snakes. Our best hope is to get you to the caves before it starts. After that, all bets are off."

Just keep moving.

A little farther on, Connor gestured to the path rising

ahead of them. "It gets rocky from here. The ground is exposed coral in some places, so watch you don't fall. I remember one time this kid . . ."

He drifted off.

Using only the map now, they came upon a narrow run of bare ground skirting the cliffs. "It's straight ahead, more or less," he said. But the path quickly disappeared into tall grass, prickly brambles, and densely growing vines and trees that Connor had to chop through with a machete.

Lily slowed, grabbing Becca's arm. "Shh . . . everyone . . ."

In the sudden quiet, they made out the sound of leaves whipping not too far behind them.

"They're out there," Wade said, pressing forward.

Time is running out.

The Order will find the cave.

The blue hand. The blue stone. Vela.

"Hoods up," Connor said.

The heat suffocated, the sky blackened by the minute, and after three abrupt turns through some new growth, Becca realized she no longer had any concept of direction. Her skin tingled and her ears buzzed with the unceasing roar of insects. The moisture in the air was already thick and heavy and was somehow getting

365

more so. It made walking seem like swimming and breathing nearly impossible.

"I don't like jungles," she gasped.

"You just decided that?" Lily said. "I feel like I'm underwater. Seriously, Bec. When we get home, we're going to Nordstrom. Not to shop. Just to get cool."

Becca wanted to laugh, but she couldn't bring herself to open her mouth for fear she would throw up. Everything hurt, her muscles felt sick, and her blood felt as thick and hot as engine oil. And the sight of fist-size beetles scuttling up and down on branches and across the ground, flying from tree to tree, made her more nauseous.

Keep walking, and don't stop until you find the blue hand.

The first drops of rain slapped through the upper branches.

Wind thundered in and seconds later the rain fell like bullets. They rushed ahead into an area of low growth and gnarly coral. There, hidden among the thick green, were black splotches, the entrances to the volcanic caves that the native people had discovered and occupied centuries ago.

Leaves shredded behind them.

Connor swung on his heels and went into a crouch. *Down!* he mouthed, waving his arm low. He handed

Roald the map. "I'll distract them. Keep going straight over this rise and down to the cliffs. There may be a few caves sharing the same aerial coordinates. I hope you know what you're looking for—" He scurried off, quietly at first, then making as much noise as he could.

The shooting began then—a quick series of dull, barking noises that whipped through the leaves, thudding into tree trunks in Connor's direction. The kids shared a frightened look. Lily's face was ghostlike.

The Order's hunting us like animals! They want us dead!

The passage from *Moby-Dick* came swimming back to Becca.

> *. . . that murderous monster against whom I and all the others had taken our oaths . . .*

"This way!" Dr. Kaplan whispered. The kids hustled after him down a rocky path to the cliff's face while Connor kept drawing fire.

A sudden thwack tore the leaves and Becca swore an arrow whizzed past her face. She fell flat on the ground. The others found shelter in a grove of thick-leaved bushes. She rose to her knees and peered over the growth. She was cut off. Her heart was thundering.

The ground pounded with footsteps hurrying toward her.

I have to run—

"Stay down."

Wade crouched ten feet away. Had he come for her? Had he been trapped too? *Stupid questions! He's here.*

"Your dad's far ahead," she said. "I didn't see where Lily went."

"She's with him. Darrell jumped away somewhere." He peeked over the high grass. "We can crawl to the bluffs. The cave's got to be close. We need to make our way down the cliffside."

She nodded. "You start."

He cracked a sudden smile.

What a smile! Probably the last one I'll ever—don't go there!

As they plunged into the growth, Becca tried to replace everything that usually swirled in her brain with only one thing. Vela.

The sail in the Argo Navis constellation was vaguely rectangular, but the *vela Latina* made a triangle a possibility, too. A triangle with a curve on one side. That kept her moving forward in the mud.

Blue hand. Vela.

Two muffled rifle shots burst through the leaves to

her left. She froze. Another shot. Wade was flat on the ground, his eyes wide in fear. A fourth shot echoed and a familiar voice cried out.

"Darrell?" Wade gasped. "Becca, they got Darrell!"

CHAPTER FIFTY

As he lay with his face in the mud, hoping no one heard him scream, Darrell wondered if he could take back the last seven days and start over. Reset to last Sunday morning, when he and Wade had goofed around in the Painter Hall observatory, wondering what to eat. Well, *he'd* been wondering what to eat, but then he almost always was. That was a situation he could wrap his head around.

But you can't really go back in time, can you?

Oh, wait. That's what this was all about.

Zipping around in time. *Machina tempore.*

For a brief moment, a large astrolabe whisked across his mind, its wheels turning slowly in different directions like gears. Was the old sketch what an ancient time machine might actually look like? He imagined a series of wide brass rings surrounding a comfy cushioned seat—his—and three smaller seats—theirs. Positioned around the innermost ring equidistant from one another were the famous twelve relics. Vela and . . . the other eleven.

The Copernicus Legacy.

A time-traveling astrolabe.

He would adjust his goggles, tug on his leather traveling gloves, push a big brass lever and—

Thud-thud-thud! The dull barking started up again and Darrell's astrolabe vanished into nothing.

Wishing he had goggles just then to keep the rain from stinging his eyes, he peeked through the dense growth. Black shapes moved like ghosts through the watery trees on his left. The jungle swished and bent on his right, where more black shapes moved. He couldn't tell how many there were, but clearly he was surrounded. It was a matter of seconds before he was discovered. He laid his head on the muddy ground. The coolness of the earth felt good. *Is a mud bath like this? Never mind that now! Hey, I wonder if I can distract the Order like they do in movies. Wade says I distract people all the time.*

Two, maybe three Knights fanned out, each one heading toward a different cave. The Order didn't know which one the relic was in. They didn't know about the blue hand.

Can I use this information? Can I . . . trick them?

Searching on the ground beside him, he found three rocks half the size of his fist. He could fling them in different directions, where they were sure to make noise crashing through the leaves. Put them off the scent. *This might actually work!* He rolled over onto his back and threw one of the rocks as hard as he could. It crashed through the trees far on his left.

"*Là-bas, vite!*" yelled a voice. "Go, go!" Two goons on his left swept away through the jungle.

Yes!

He did the same on his right, following one stone with another, and more goons veered off after them. He rose to his hands and knees. No one was moving. He had done it. He had cleared the way for his friends. He could run to them now—

Snap . . . crunch . . .

Someone was crawling stealthily through the jungle behind him. He stared into the ocean of green.

Movement. *Crunch* . . .

He flattened his face in the mud again. No more stones nearby. Hand to hand? *Crack . . . crunch . . .*

"Now I lay me down to sleep . . ."

CHAPTER FIFTY-ONE

"**A**nd if I die . . ."

. . . Wade slapped his hand over Darrell's mouth. "Quiet!"

"And come with us," whispered Becca, scanning the growth around them. "For some reason the Order has lost our trail."

Darrell wiggled out of Wade's grip. "For *some* reason? For *me* reason! Me and my pitching arm! I'm signing with the Astros if we ever make it out of here."

Wade knew they had seconds before the Order saw them. He tugged Darrell by his pitching arm and pulled him up. "Now!" They rushed through the tangled trees as quietly but as quickly as they could.

"If we find the right cave before the Order sees us, we can lose them. They won't be able to follow," Becca said. "Let's try them all."

They crawled under sagging tree limbs and jumped over fallen trunks. The fierce downburst was flooding the ground, making rushing little rivers every few feet. Vines whipped in the wind, crisscrossing wildly. Then, behind the green, a black space. The mouth of a cave. They hustled to it. On the wall beside the opening, a red hand.

"Keep going," Becca whispered, pushing on.

Another cave. No handprint at all. A third. A blotchy red hand. A fourth, papery wasp nests lining the mouth, clinging to the walls. They pushed on again. The Order was out there, but not on to them yet.

They scrambled up a jagged coral creek, and Becca made a sudden noise. Just inside the narrow opening into the rock was a faint handprint. It was upside down and terribly faded except for one finger.

The finger was blue.

"Wade—"

Holding his breath, he tugged the photo from his pocket. It was the same print. "We found it."

He shielded his eyes from the rain and studied the ancient pictogram. In what he knew was a rare flash of perfect insight he noticed how similar the shape of the outspread hand was to a sea star. Asterias. The fingers made their own kind of glowing star.

"The Order has doubled back and they're coming this way," said a small voice behind them. It was Lily. She and his father stumbled to the entrance to the cave.

"This is it, Dad," Darrell said. "We found Magellan's cave—"

Something traveling roughly half the speed of a bullet struck the cave wall with a loud ping.

It was an arrow.

Moments earlier—just as Ebner von Braun was about to say that particle physicists don't do jungles—Galina hissed over her shoulder.

"More arrows!"

Wrapped in custom form-fitting hunting gear that concealed a diving suit, the sleek creature pushed her way through the thick growth without caring for anyone tagging behind her.

Ebner followed her every move, the sodden jungle branches slapping his face with every step. If the burning of his fingers had subsided over the last few days, the bruise the old man had given his forehead with the paperweight stung and ached more than ever. It was now oozing some kind of yellow pus that even the bullet-like rain didn't wash away. His earpiece crackled.

"Galina, our divers have found the underwater entrance to the caves," he said, handing her a replacement quiver. "They are climbing up from below. We will join them and the relic will be yours within the hour!"

"If it is not . . ." She trailed off and reloaded her crossbow.

Ebner wasn't sure he liked it when Galina didn't finish her sentences. On the one hand, it might mean she believed he was smart enough to understand her. On the other, it might mean she couldn't waste her breath on him.

I will do something about that, he thought. *Galina will see my value to the Order—and to her, personally. If I survive.* He pawed his head with his burned hand. *There is no end to what a Teutonic Knight will do.*

As visions of ancient astrolabes swam about in his mind, Ebner glanced into that pair of miscolored eyes and wondered if Galina Krause, even in the midst of this stinking jungle, was pondering the astrolabe, too.

Galina Krause *was* pondering the astrolabe. In fact, her mind tingled with nothing else. Or *almost* nothing else. Her thoughts shuttled between the astrolabe, the jungle, and those strange days when her younger self was lost in the rooms of an ancient castle far away among the cold forests of Northern Europe.

The echoing laughter. The screaming.

In her mind, it all surrounded her.

Strange antique weapons ranged along a quivering wall of trees. Cold air spinning suddenly—light, dark, light, dark, then all dark. Portraits hung in opulent golden frames. The woman there. The man here. He in ermine, silk, and gold, the hilt of his saber, the ruby kraken of his crest. She, her pale dying face. The drenching rain flooding the marble floor. The coiling air.

The cold. The stone. The silence. The noise.

Galina's scar stung and the jungle blurred. Had something moved in the growth? Was it only the heat and rain? Or the centuries past? The mystery of time? Was it the closeness of the first relic?

"Arrows," she said softly, holding out her hand.

"Excuse me," said Ebner, pausing among the

strangled green growth. "You have already loaded the crossbow."

She turned her eyes down to the gleaming shaft with its triangular point. *Yes. Yes. I have loaded it.* Releasing the silencer—speed was more important than silence now—she lifted the bow to her shoulder.

How long it was before the trees twitched with movement, she couldn't say. The Grand Master's dark brow, his beard and mustache, his fiery eyes staring down from the cold, coiling air. The jungle moved again. What was this strange light-headedness? The astrolabe whirled in space. She squeezed the trigger.

Thhh—

CHAPTER FIFTY-TWO

W^{ack!} — *W*ack!

For a fraction of a second, Lily thought the arrow passed directly through the silver hoop dangling lightly from her left ear.

She doubled over, shrieking.

"Lily!" Becca scooped her up and dived into the cave entrance.

"Dad? Get in here!" Wade yelled.

Bullets ricocheted off the cave wall. Lily looked out; Roald was pinned down ten feet outside the entrance. "I'll be right behind you," he whispered. "I'm going to lead them to another cave. Get inside. Go!"

Roald scrambled around and hustled back into the dense trees toward the previous cave. Lily watched with horror as the Order changed direction and followed him. Her throat tightened.

This isn't supposed to happen. You can't use yourself as bait!

She felt a tug on her shoulder.

"Come on, Lil," Becca said. "We're out of time. Come on."

Jagged rocks hung at odd angles from the low ceiling, not a problem so much for her, but everybody else had to hunch over as they moved carefully forward into the cave. It was eerie how instantly the light of the day, even rainy light, vanished behind them. Five, six steps inside, and the darkness was complete.

"Hold up." Lily tugged Carlo's phone from her pocket. "There's no signal, but it has battery." *Carlo. Bologna. It feels like a previous life.*

And there was only *some* battery. The cave floor went dull blue-white under the app. It was clear from the first that they were going down. Rainwater poured in from the entrance and down from the ceiling and trickled past their feet in channels—more than trickled. Their feet were soaked anyway, but the downward incline made progress dangerous and slow-going. Darrell slid to his knees. "Whoa! Careful."

After some minutes, the meandering passage widened, but they still had to follow one another in single file. Outside were shouts and occasional muffled shots. Would Connor go back to his Jeep? Call his military buddies? *Chink, chink.* That horrible woman's arrows.

"Uh-oh . . ."

Wade stood over a ledge hanging some ten or twelve feet over . . . nothing. No, not nothing. The phone light reflected off a still surface of black water at the bottom of the drop.

"Do you think it's rainwater?" said Becca. "Or a deeper pool?"

"We've traveled down since the cave opening," Darrell huffed, leaning on the wall. "Water must collect during storms like this. Maybe the pools never really dry up. I hope the relic isn't underwater."

While they gazed down into the murky darkness, the last of the phone light faded. "Battery's gone," Lily said. "Now what do we do?"

"This can't be the end of the line," said Becca.

A burst of gunfire echoed in from the entrance. Wade and Darrell shared a dark look. Then came a shout. Not a scream. A shout.

Roald had to be okay. He just had to be . . .

* * *

Wade's stomach dropped to his feet when he heard the close gunfire. "Darrell—"

Then more shouting. A gunshot farther away.

"We have to believe he's okay," Darrell whispered, shaking his head from side to side like he didn't want to hear any argument. "Keeping those thugs from the cave. We're so close to finding it now."

Wade bit his lip. "Yeah. Right. Too close to stop."

Becca had said *the end of the line*. He knew what that felt like. He had sensed it at the cemetery in Berlin, and at the train station when his father was arrested. At times he'd felt hopeless wandering around Bologna, and again in Rome.

Yet each time something happened to get them out of the mess. And now a flooded cave? An underwater pool? No way. They'd gone too far to be stopped by a little water.

"Hey." Lily was staring into the black water that suddenly wasn't so black. Rippling through the water from the bottom was a vague brightness. "Where's the light coming from?"

"Somewhere under the surface," Darrell said.

"This is good," Wade said, his heart thundering. "The pool must connect with another cave that has an

383

opening to the outside. That's the only way there could be light. We can follow it."

Without thinking, he sat and tugged his sneakers off. "Who's going with me?"

"Wade, you're not going down there," Becca snapped.

"Yes, I am. This is the cave! You know it is. Shoichi knew it. Laura Thompson knew it. They all knew it. Vela is down there. I'm going in—"

Becca clutched his wrist tight. "You are not."

"Look, the Order will find Vela if we don't. Or kill us all. Or both. Either way, we have nothing to deal with if they find it first. I'm going down there!"

Becca tore off her sneakers and tossed them next to his. "Not alone, you're not."

Lily stared at Darrell. "Oh, I have a bad feeling about this. What if there's no outlet? You guys could drown trying to find your way back. This is super nuts."

"If there's no way out, then we'll come back up. Simple," said Becca.

So. She's thinking, too, Wade thought. *At least one of us is!*

"Keep watch," he said. Which he realized was dumb, but he couldn't think of anything else to say. He climbed down over the ledge to the rocks as far as he could, then dropped straight into the pool. The water was colder than he expected. He felt Becca splash next to him. He surfaced. She surfaced.

"Fresh water," he said. "Rainwater. You're right, Darrell."

"Omigod, if you don't come back, I'll kill you!" said Lily.

Wade gulped in a mouthful of air, plunged his head down, rolled over in the water, kicked his feet, and swam downward toward the source of the light. As he hoped, the passage opened into a brighter space. Turning his head to the dark water behind him, he couldn't see anything, felt only the cold. He hoped Becca was there, but he didn't know how long his lungs would hold out. He had to keep swimming forward. The passage was longer than he thought it would be. Deeper. The light dimmed suddenly. Had he taken a wrong turn? There was no opening. He kept swimming. Then his lungs began to tighten and burn. They screamed to take in air.

He pushed forward, swatting the water behind him, no breath left. Except now he wasn't sure he actually *was* going forward. It was like being in a coffin. His arms seemed like lead pipes. His lungs felt as if they were turning to water. *Where did the light go?* In his mind he screamed, *Becca, go back! We're trapped. I'll go on, but you go back! Save yourself! Save—*

The passage angled up. There was the light again.

With one final push of his leaden arms, he burst up inside a cavern that seemed as bright as the sun. Becca splashed up beside him, desperate for breath. They hung there in the water, their fingers clutching the rocks, gasping and coughing for minutes. They finally crawled up and flattened themselves on a stone floor, staring upward.

When he spied a small opening at the faraway top, Wade surprised himself by starting to laugh. The cavern's light was actually dim, but it seemed brilliant. They could feel raindrops falling in the opening, through the vault, and down over them, sprinkling their faces. It was as quiet in there as if they had surfaced on another planet, and he laughed and couldn't stop laughing.

"Wade . . ."

Becca pointed at the walls. They were carved and painted with hundreds of symbols. Stars. Constellations. A blue hand was printed on the wall in the midst of the stars, its fingers pointing down.

Becca slapped his arm gently. "We found it."

CHAPTER FIFTY-THREE

Wade stood, still breathing hard, his legs like rubber, boneless.

The cave walls formed an irregular cone of rock that had kind of the feeling of an ancient cathedral or temple, a holy place of stone.

The perfect place to hide a priceless artifact.

"If Shoichi knew this cave, he may have watched the stars through the hole in the ceiling," he said. "Maybe he added some of these drawings himself."

"Except . . ." Becca was up now, searching the walls, the floor, the high vault, everywhere for a sign. "I don't see a blue stone." She glanced back at the pool. "Could it be . . . hidden underwater? Did we pass it on our way here? I mean, maybe over the years since Magellan the passages filled up with water. Or maybe the cave collapsed, changed its shape."

Wade stepped over to the blue handprint. "But Laura Thompson must have seen the relic, right? Janet told us about her last trip here. That wasn't that long ago."

"I forgot that." She scanned the walls up and down. "Then I have no clue."

No clue. Except maybe there was a clue.

Studying the upside-down handprint, Wade realized that it not only vaguely bore the shape of a sea star, but that the palm and fingers formed a distinct geometric shape. "Bec, what does it remind you of?

She stood back. "An upside-down hand?"

Wade laughed again. *"And . . ."* He traced his finger in straight lines around the angles the hand made. "It's kind of a triangle, isn't it? With the wrist as the top point. The same triangle as in Pigafetta's drawing.

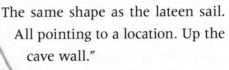

The same shape as the lateen sail. All pointing to a location. Up the cave wall."

They followed the point of the imaginary triangle up the wall. About ten feet from the floor was a narrow horizontal shelf of rock, an outcropping of volcanic limestone.

Becca looked at Wade. "You don't think . . ."

"I'll give you a boost."

"You'll . . ."

"Come on." Wade wove his fingers together, and she stepped in with her left foot, holding on to his shoulders. Wade lifted, and she set her right foot on his shoulder, then her left, bracing her hands against the cave wall. She steadied herself, reached up, and felt over the ledge.

"Anything?" he said.

Becca stiffened.

"What is it? What do you see?"

She drew her arm slowly away from the wall, gripping something in her hand. She made a choking sound. "Oh, Wade."

When he saw the wavy blade of the dagger, his knees nearly buckled. "Magellan's dagger! The one Copernicus gave to him with Vela! Is there anything else?"

Quickly slipping the dagger into her belt, she reached up again. "The dagger was stuck partway into the cave wall. Taking it out revealed an opening, a kind of compartment." Wade held her calves as she raised herself up on her tiptoes. One foot left his shoulder. Then her arm swung back and she lurched away from the wall. He twisted, catching her clumsily, and they fell to the floor together.

"Wade—" Becca opened her hand.

In her palm was a nearly perfect triangle of dazzlingly blue stone.

Roughly four inches long on two sides and two inches at the base, it was a smooth piece of lapis lazuli with a slight curve in one side. It was in a shape very similar to a lateen sail.

"Argo Navis Vela," Wade said in a whisper.

It instantly seemed as if all the air in the cavern, and all the light in the air, drew itself into the stone.

Vela pulsed with a kind of life, he thought, though he knew it wasn't possible. It seemed to him as if time and space combined and—he didn't even know what else—people, maybe, or family, or blood, or love, or something—were all joined inside the contours of the blue stone.

And it breathed.

It breathed and whispered secret after secret, but only to the two of them who were there.

This was before he even held the stone! Vela was luminescent, beautiful, and alive, and then Becca slipped it into his trembling hand, and he felt what he thought was the weight of history in his palm, as if the stone weighed a thousand pounds or was as weightless as light.

"Becca . . . ," he murmured, tearing his eyes away from it to look into hers for only seconds before the stone drew him back to it. He slumped on the floor of the cave, his brain clicking away with a kind of clarity he was certain he'd never known before.

"Becca . . . ," he said again, discovering something amazing, yet painful, about the stark syllables of her name. "More than all the craziness, the running, and the places and the arrows and the hiding and every-thing, through all the stuff we read and the sketches and equations and everything we found out, this blue stone proves there's a time machine. It's not like a math proof, but I . . ."

As he trailed off, Becca wiped a tear from her cheek, nodding.

"I guess what I'm saying is that holding it in my hand

makes Copernicus's astrolabe as real as if it's right here, and we're traveling back in time right now, you know?"

"I know."

"And no matter how impossible it is to do that, *this* is a part of a time machine, a relic of Copernicus's astrolabe, the astrolabe that could travel in time, the thing was a time machine, that actually existed, and this is a relic of it and we're holding it and it's real . . ."

Becca smiled. "You realize that's kind of a wormhole of a sentence."

"Yeah, I guess it is." Wade started laughing again, and the echo of his laughter coiled up the sides of the stone room, coming back down from the top and going back up again.

He didn't know how many minutes passed while they simply stared at the stone as if they were waiting for something to happen. It was like time itself had stopped, which is a thing only time machines can do.

Becca took it gently from his palm and turned the stone over.

On its back were a faint but perfectly engraved spiral and two small notches at the base of it that held minute traces of something dusty and red.

"Rust," Becca said. "Where the stone was in contact with metal."

Wade wanted to laugh again. He knew instantly where the rust marks had come from and began to feel the sketch of the device come whirring to life right there. "That's where Vela was attached to, what did he call it, the 'grand armature' of the astrolabe. Becca—"

The water bubbled suddenly, the silence broke, and Darrell and Lily splashed into the cave. "They're here! They're right behind us—"

The pool exploded. Four divers climbed out and stood on solid ground. Two men armed with underwater pistols. A pale man who lifted his scuba mask and dried his spectacles.

And the beautiful young woman with the wickedly ugly crossbow.

The Knights of the Teutonic Order.

CHAPTER FIFTY-FOUR

The young woman was impossibly beautiful. Otherworldly, Wade thought. Like a cross between a supermodel and a futuristic automaton. And her hair. Even dripping wet it was awesome.

He glanced over at Lily, Darrell, and Becca. They had to feel it, too. The woman wasn't much older than they were, but she had some kind of crazy kinetic energy running through her.

And that crossbow she held. What *was* that thing? An artifact from some ancient future? A weird robotic extension of her arms?

"You have witnessed the reach of the Teutonic Order," she said with a trace of accent he couldn't identify. It was almost hypnotic how her voice echoed up the walls of the cave. "You know our power. Let it not be the last thing you know. Give me the relic."

She took a step toward him, as did the three men, but Wade raised his hand. "I'll smash it!" he cried. "I will!"

She stopped. Everyone stopped.

Dangling around her neck, just visible in the opening of her form-fitting outfit, were two ruby stones, an identical pair of sea serpents with several arms. Krakens.

The hunched man beside her adjusted his thick-lensed spectacles. His suit was baggy in the chest, stretched in other places. He looked other than human in the opposite way. A misshapen little gnome.

"Since Berlin, you have taken us on quite a journey," the man said weakly. "It ends here. In this forsaken cave." His voice was halting, his words overenunciated.

"You killed Heinrich Vogel," Becca said, shifting to stand next to Wade. "And Bernard Dufort in Paris."

"Among others," said Galina, her eyes staring not at her but at Wade's hand, as if to burn it away and free the relic for herself.

"Countless others," the gnome added proudly.

"You're all horrible creeps," Lily said softly. Her eyes were pinched and fiery. "Every one of you."

"Why don't you give me the relic," Galina Krause said. It was not a question. Removing her left hand from the shaft of the crossbow, she held it out. The barrel barely moved. The weapon must either be lightweight, Wade thought, or she's very strong. It was still pointing steadily at his heart.

"The old man is your father?" she said. "Thanks to the Guardians, he escaped our grasp in Berlin. He will not come for you now. You are alone."

Wade felt his breath die. Had they shot him? "You . . ." was all he could say.

"He'd better not be hurt," said Darrell, shifting from one foot to the other, ready to spring into action.

Wade pulled himself from the thought of his father hurt. He tapped Darrell's left foot with his own, and he stopped moving.

Wait, Darrell, wait for it . . .

"Save yourselves a lonely death," the gnome said, stepping forward once more. "Give us—"

Wade backed up. "Not an inch!"

The thousand thoughts flashing through his mind balled up into a single one. Passing through that underwater tunnel, he and his friends had become different people.

How else to explain his own behavior with these killers, holding the relic high, ready to shatter it to dust on the cave floor?

The water had changed them. The light in the cave had changed them. The relic—the blue stone in his palm right then—had changed them, *was* changing them that very moment.

We've become Guardians, he thought. That's what it is. We're members of the secret society from Copernicus to Magellan to Enrique and Pigafetta and Shiochi and Laura Thompson and her granddaughter and all the countless others, on and on, through the centuries, with one goal—to protect the Copernicus Legacy.

The garbled sound of shouting echoed in from outside, and Galina Krause flashed her strange eyes at them. "You cannot stop time. We will have the relic. Will you make it easy?"

"No," Wade said, and Becca stepped back with him.

Galina exhaled a sigh of regret. "Wrong answer."

With no more than a flick of her wrist, the two armed divers holstered their pistols and leaped. Wade tapped his brother's foot, and Darrell sprang forward into one man's knees, screaming as he did. The second man lunged at Wade, who managed to toss the relic to Becca before he went down. She snatched it from the air, crouched, and rolled to the edge of the pool.

"Not in the water!" the pale man shrieked, as Becca slid into the pool, gulping in a big breath. Dropping his pistol, the gnome clamped his two thin hands on her free wrist and pulled.

"Don't you touch her—" Lily was on his back like a cat, clawing his face and yelling "Creep-creep-creep!"

The gnome must have been all bone and wire, because he shook Lily off and was still able to keep Becca from diving away. Dragging her back up, he wormed her fingers open. "I'm getting it, I'm getting it!"

"Back away to the wall!" Galina trained her crossbow on Wade and Lily as one man pinned Darrell to the floor, though he was squirming like an eel. The other goon helped the runtish German drag Becca roughly from the pool. Something flew down through the ceiling. It slapped on the floor near Lily's feet. A rope, dangling from the hole at the top.

A shout came from the surface. "Kids, get back!"

Connor was on the rope, edging down. Galina shot her crowsbow up at him—*thwack!* He stopped his descent.

While the first thug kept Darrell pinned to the wall,

Wade bashed at his knees, and he fell like a ton of bricks. There was a crack and a groan. "Go!" Wade gasped. Darrell and Lily both rushed to the rope. Connor was coming down again.

"Grab hold, and give me a clear shot!" He aimed a pistol at Galina.

While the second thug still had Becca, the gnome jumped at Wade, pushing him into the wall, but he twisted sideways. The gnome smashed his forehead into the stone, shrieking.

Wade spun around. "Becca—"

Galina was standing over her, the crossbow aimed at her throat. The thug had twisted Becca's arms behind her. A scream exploded in Wade's chest. He charged the woman. Her muscles were hard as stone. She barely moved, but her crossbow clanked to the floor.

When the goon dragged Becca away by her throat, Wade drew the dagger out and jerked it into the man's thigh. He cried out and released her. Gasping, she slunk to the floor.

Crack! A shot from above. Galina backed away. Wade tugged Becca to her feet. They grabbed the rope beneath Lily and Darrell.

"No—you—don't!" The pale man's face was smeared with blood. He snatched up the loaded crossbow and pulled the trigger. Galina knocked his arms, and the shot flew to the ceiling and clattered back down. "Fool! They will drop the relic. It will shatter!"

Becca began to slip. "I . . . can't . . . hold on . . ."

A slender thread of blood dripped down her arm.

"You're shot! That creep shot you!" Wade coiled his arm around her waist and half carried her as the rope rose higher.

"We will win this race!" the pale German squealed from below, swinging his fists in the air. "We will force you to give us the relic—"

Galina Krause slapped him across the face.

"But the first will tell them where—"

"Silence!" she cried. "Bring her to me. Only *she* can help us now!"

Near the top of the cave, the children felt the strong arms of Sgt. Connor pulling them through the opening and found that the storm had passed. When the hole was clear, he slid down the rope. Shots were fired, but a series of splashes followed. Looking down, they saw only Connor in an empty cave.

Galina Krause and her thugs were gone.

An engine sounded off shore. Seconds later, a motorboat roared out from the base of the cliffs. On its deck, the young woman, staring up at them.

400

"They escaped through the underwater passages," Lily said.

"Something tells me we'll see her again," said Wade. "Too soon."

"Kids! Kids! Are you all right?"

They whirled around. Roald Kaplan ran stumbling toward them, his face smeared with mud, but unhurt.

Wade hugged him tight. "Becca's wounded."

"Connor radioed the base," his father said, kneeling to her. "A helicopter is on its way."

Minutes later, the sharp thunder of rotor blades filled the air. Connor emerged from the cave, and the whole group was chopped to the naval base. On the way, a report came over the helicopter's radio. The motorboat was chased straight out to sea, but found bobbing empty in the water. No trace of Galina Krause. The Order had vanished.

CHAPTER FIFTY-FIVE

"Show your dad," Becca said, clutching her arm, but nodding to her pocket. After reaching his hand out instinctively, Wade decided to let Lily fish in her pocket and remove Vela.

Roald took it silently, traced his fingers over it.

"Uncle Henry didn't die in vain, Dad," Darrell said. "We found it. The first relic. We kept it from the Order."

Roald simply nodded, his eyes far away, then hugged them all again. At the base hospital, Becca was bandaged up by a navy nurse named Chris, receiving a tetanus shot to guard against infection from the crossbow's razor-sharp arrow.

Lily was as pale as she could be and still stay standing, which she did as close to Becca as she could. "I can't believe you actually got shot," she said, squeezing in closer. "Your mom's going to kill me!"

"Hey, it's what we Guardians do," Becca said, trying to smile.

When the nurse excused himself for a second, Wade said, "It's kind of incredible, isn't it? We found Vela, a piece of Copernicus's time-traveling astrolabe. Us. We kept it out of enemy hands."

"For now it's out of their hands," his father said. "We have to decide what to do with it and where it will be safe from the Order."

"Carlo will know," said Lily, not moving an inch from Becca's side. "The Frombork Protocol, and all that. Maybe in one of those underground bomb shelters in the Nevada desert."

"Or maybe the most secure place in the country," Darrell said. "The fortified bunker under the White House!"

Wade was glad that he and Becca had had those silent moments in the cave. The world had rushed back in quickly and noisily, and he knew he'd never be able

403

to fully explain the magical thing that happened inside that rocky space.

But that was fine. If he wanted to be mushy, he might say how he and Becca sort of bonded over the relic. They had shared something. Something *interesting*. She grimaced when the nurse returned and clipped up the bandages, and all that went away.

"You okay?"

"Fine," she said, forcing a smile. She hopped off the hospital bed next to Lily as if they were linked.

The emergency room doors slid open and they all went out. The rain had stopped, and the sun was burning off the humidity. What was left of the day was going to be scorching hot, and to Wade that was just fine. They could finally rest. No more jungle. No more Teutonic Order. No more danger. At least for now.

Roald opened his phone and flicked his thumb across the screen. "I promised Sara I'd call her when it was all over."

All over.

Was it? Really? Could they just go back home? Darrell to his band and his tennis, him to his star charts and astronomy books? Wade felt his heart sink at the idea of it being all over, though it was probably for the best. They had to go back to school at least. The fact that their home was known to the Order, well, maybe the police would help with that. Maybe. It would probably be more normal than he wanted it to be. Certainly more normal than the last week. He glanced at Becca.

"I won't tell Sara the whole story, of course," his father was saying. "Just enough so she'll know we're all safe."

"Dad, put it on speaker," Darrell said. "We all want to talk to her. She's going to flip when she hears what we've been doing."

There was a bright click as the call connected.

"Hello, Sara!" Dr. Kaplan said with a laugh. "We made it. We're all fine—"

"Hello? Who is this?" It was a man's voice.

Roald squinted at the screen. "I'm sorry. I was calling my wife. Sara Kaplan. I must have the wrong—"

"This is Sara Kaplan's phone," said the voice.

"I don't understand? Who's this? Where's my wife?"

"Dad," said Wade. "Dad . . ."

"I don't know," the man said. "Hold on . . . I'm terribly sorry. My name is Terence Ackroyd. I'm speaking from New York. Perhaps she told you. We—Sara and I—were supposed to meet this evening to talk about manuscripts she was bringing from my house in Bolivia for the archive in Austin. But she didn't show up for our meeting. Her luggage arrived at my hotel. Her cell phone, passport, everything was in it, but according to the airline, she was never on the flight—"

"Never on the flight?" Darrell said. "What happened to my mother?"

"I honestly don't know," the man said. "She never arrived in New York. It's only been a few hours, and communications with Bolivia are spotty, but I fear something is dreadfully wrong. I couldn't reach your cell and had to wait for you to call."

Darrell made his hands into fists. "This can't be happening! They have her!"

Wade felt as if he had been run over. "Dad—"

"Galina Krause said something!" Lily gasped. "She said only *she* will help us. *She.* Did the Order kidnap Sara to try to get Vela back?"

"Sorry? Did you say the *Order*?" said the man on the phone.

Roald waved his hand as if to brush the question away. "What do the police say? What are they doing to find her—"

"I haven't contacted them," said the man.

"You haven't contacted them? My God—"

"There's a reason," the man said.

Dr. Kaplan swayed, trying to keep his balance. He

couldn't, and slumped to the curb, wild-eyed. "We have to go to Bolivia. They have her. I can't believe it. They have Sara!"

"Dad!" cried Darrell, in tears now. "How did they take her? Where could she be—"

"Not Bolivia," said Terence Ackroyd. He lowered his voice. "Come to New York, please. I can't tell you over the phone, but there was something hidden in her luggage that you need to see. A message, I think, about her safety. It's why I haven't contacted the authorities. I'll be here until you arrive. The Gramercy Park Hotel. Tell no one you are coming to see me. I'll keep Sara's phone and call you with any news." He seemed to wait for a response, but when there was none, he said, "Until then," and hung up.

Wade stood over his father, his head spinning, his eyes brimming, while Lily took the phone to call the airport.

"Where can she be?" Darrell pleaded, fighting back tears, before letting go and burying his head in Wade's shoulder. "My mom, my mom—"

And that was it. Things *had* changed now. Were they already on the road that Carlo spoke about? The journey of sacrifice?

Becca wiped her face and paced the sidewalk. "That

creepy little man said the first relic will tell us where the second is. You heard him."

Lily was on hold with the airline. "Right. The first will circle to the last. But the second relic could be anything and anywhere. We don't even know what its constellation is—"

"Maybe not." Becca pulled Copernicus's diary from her bag and started turning page after page. "But I think he was saying that something about Vela will help us find the second relic. Galina Krause will definitely be there. When she said 'bring her to me,' we have to think Sara will be there, too."

Lily answered a voice on the phone, and Becca turned to the others. "Vela will lead us to the second relic and to Sara—"

"Wherever it is, we're going," said Darrell, still hanging on Wade's shoulder. "Dad, we're going to the ends of the world if we have to."

Lily hung up the phone. "A flight leaves Guam tonight. We can be in New York by tomorrow night."

Roald rose to his feet, his eyes dark, his face drawn. He wrapped his arms around both of his sons. "We'll find Sara, boys. We'll find her . . ."

Becca and Lily ran down the sidewalk, waving their arms and yelling, "Taxi!"

EPILOGUE

SPANISH SCHOOL BUS DISCOVERED IN MOUNTAIN PASS

MADRID—A bus carrying Spanish schoolchildren reported missing Wednesday evening in the mountains north of the city was located early Saturday. State police agencies responded to reports from witnesses who described seeing an out-of-control school bus "suddenly appearing in the center of the highway" north of the Somosierra Tunnel.

All the students except one, and their teachers, have been accounted for and were in good health despite suffering exposure and minor trauma. The driver of the bus, Diego Vargas, 68, was also reported missing. After their arrival at a local hospital, the students, aged 7 to 14, and teachers on the bus claimed that it entered the south side of the Somosierra Tunnel and was immediately struck by "a barrage of cannon fire and attacked by uniformed soldiers on horses, brandishing pistols and sabers."

The passengers' reports were at first dismissed by police but later confirmed by crime scene investigators when remains of musket shells and fragments of at least two nineteenth-century cannonballs were discovered lodged in the side panels of the bus.

A region-wide search is underway for the missing student and the driver, while all other passengers were treated and released.

The incident remains under investigation by local and federal crime units.

To be continued . . .

WWW.THECOPERNICUSLEGACY.COM

HarperCollins *Children's Books*

PSST! READER! YES, YOU.

Come join the quest. . . .

WIN A CHANCE TO PARTICIPATE IN THE COPERNICUS LEGACY RELIC HUNT!

Four winners will be chosen to win a trip for two

to New York City and a chance to

engage in a real-life relic hunt,

hosted by author Tony Abbott.

For official rules and to enter, visit

THECOPERNICUSLEGACY.COM

BECOME
PART
OF THE
ADVENTURE.

HarperCollins *Children's Book*.

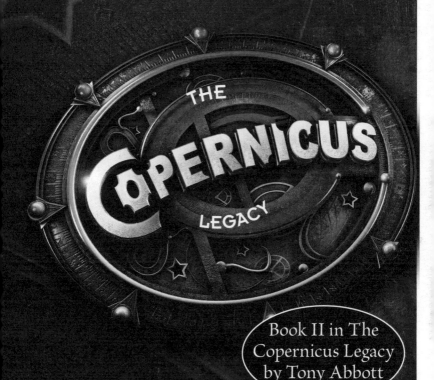

AUTHOR'S NOTE

The Forbidden Stone is undeniably a work of fiction; any real people who pass through its pages have been treated in a fictional manner. However, since all such books are built on a foundation of reality, I'd like to acknowledge a number of historical works I used in laying out the story.

The first volume to capture my interest about the "timid canon," his world-altering discovery, and his colorful times is *The Sleepwalkers* (1959) by Arthur Koestler, a volume I came upon during my college years. A novelist whose most famous book will find its way into the next volume of this series, Koestler instills in his chapters on Nicolaus Copernicus the excitement and living detail of his craft. This book remains the touchstone of my appreciation for the astronomer.

Jack Repcheck's *Copernicus' Secret: How the Scientific Revolution Began* (2007) is an illuminating biography, as is *A More Perfect Heaven: How Copernicus Revolutionized the Cosmos* (2011) by Dava Sobel. Both works combine scholarship with an engaging style and have the virtue of being recent and easily obtainable.

Desmond Seward's *The Monks of War: The Military Religious Orders* (1972) and Frederick Charles Woodhouse's *The Military Religious Orders of the Middle Ages: The Hospitallers, the Templars, the Teutonic Knights, and Others* (1879) have been and will continue to be helpful in fleshing out the murky days of the sixteenth century Order. I must also mention Kip S. Thorne's *Black Holes and Time Warps: Einstein's Outrageous Legacy* (1994), a brilliantly amusing and engaging text for humanities-heavy non-scientists like me.

Since I dislike spoilers and feel an obligation to keep secrets hidden until they are revealed at their proper time and place, this paragraph will seem vague until the reader completes the book. I am indebted to Laurence Bergreen's 2003 book about what he calls "the edge of the world," as well as Yale University Press's 1969 edition of Antonio Pigafetta's travel history. Thanks are due, also, to the Sterling Library at Yale and its Privileges and Reference staffs for locating and providing me space to examine Laura Maud Thompson's rare 1932 volume, *Archaeology of the* . . . Also helpful was Thompson's 1941 book about the people native to that area. Finally, *Private Yokoi's War* . . . by Omi Hatashin is a fascinating document made all the more so by containing Shoichi Yokoi's autobiography.

Any liberties and excursions from fact are, of course, completely my own.

ACKNOWLEDGMENTS

It's hard to separate these personal remarks from the Author's Note of the previous pages; all have combined to create what you're holding in your hands right now. Still, I want to express particular gratitude to the following constellation of stars.

My astonishingly smart, funny, beautiful, and talented wife, Dolores, has always been the rock upon which I've been blessed to conjure stories, from early disappointments to the glorious present. My equally amazing and lovely daughters, Jane and Lucy, you make each day a wonder of discovery. Together, you three are on every single page of this book.

My agent, George Nicholson, has been artfully building and shaping my career in stories since I began writing them. Yes, George, it was 1994 when we began our pleasant relationship (with Harper, I might add). Here's to the next twenty years!

I must thank Kip S. Thorne, astrophysicist extraordinaire, for collegially allowing me to use his name in a work of fiction. Kip, I am here offering you the use of mine.

To the entire team at Katherine Tegen Books, starting with Katherine herself, whose wry humor and excitement so sparked to the idea and nurtured that spark into a blaze. My editor, Claudia Gabel, delightfully present at the creation of *The Copernicus Legacy*, has always urged this epic story to ever-higher levels. Your creative intelligence and brainstorming are indelibly present in these pages, too. Also there at the beginning, Melissa Miller has been a shepherd, a microscopic reader, a sounding board, and a crutch; I happily depend on all of your talents. To the several copy editors and proofreaders whose native brilliance has offhandedly saved me from gaffes as numberless as the stars, I love you.

From the art department (oh, that awesome logo!) to the marketing, promotion, and sales forces—your support from the inception of this project has been a joy.

This is the beginning of the payback.